STARFOLK FALLING

ALSO BY MARTHA DUNLOP

The Starfolk Trilogy
The Starfolk Arcana
Starfolk Rising (out March 2024)

Wild Shadow

**Subscribe at www.marthadunlop.com
to hear about new releases first,
and receive a free copy of**

Starfolk Illusions
A Starfolk prequel.

STARFOLK FALLING

BOOK TWO OF THE STARFOLK TRILOGY

MARTHA DUNLOP

Copyright © 2021 Martha Dunlop
All rights reserved.

The right of Martha Dunlop to be identified as the author of this work has been asserted in accordance with the Copyright Designs and Patents Act, 1988.

No part of this publication may be reproduced, stored in a retrieval system or transmitted, in any form or by any means, electronic, mechanical, photocopying, recording, or otherwise, without prior permission from the publishers.

This novel is entirely a work of fiction. The names, characters and incidents portrayed in it are the work of the author's imagination. Any resemblance to actual persons, living or dead, events or localities is entirely coincidental.

This book is sold subject to the condition that it shall not, by the way of trade or otherwise, be lent, re-sold, hired out or otherwise circulated without the publisher's prior consent in any form of binding or cover other than that, in which it is published and without a similar condition including this condition being imposed on the subsequent purchaser.

Produced and published in September 2021 by TanLea Books, www.tanleabooks.com.

ISBN 978-1-913788-07-0 (paperback)
ISBN 978-1-913788-08-7 (ebook)

Cover design by Ravven, www.ravven.com
Edited by Kathryn Cottam,
Copy edited by Eleanor Leese, www.eleanorleese.com

www.marthadunlop.com

For Miriam,
Thank you for all your support.

PREVIOUSLY IN THE STARFOLK TRILOGY
CONTAINS SPOILERS FOR BOOK 1

The Fear began in a TV Studio in St Albans, England.

Event planner Beth Meyer was in the audience, after she received a birthday invite to a live chat show. The celebrity guest, Amelia, told a bizarre tale of paranormal attack by mysterious entities called the Soul Snatchers. And Beth met Jonan, the man with the violet eyes and the only other person who wasn't taken in by Amelia's stories.

Each of them was more than they seemed.

Beth had always hidden her psychic senses, but in Amelia's presence they were on full alert. And although she couldn't understand why people were drawn to the woman's fantasies, when Amelia locked her in an abandoned, haunted theatre, her stories took on a new and unexpected reality.

Jonan's life path was to wake Beth up to her destiny through their soul connection. But as Amelia inserted herself deeper into Beth's life, this became increasingly difficult. A long time ago, he had walked away from an affair with Amelia, but she didn't want to let him go.

Amelia came to Earth as a member of the Triad, one of three women with a destiny to rouse the world to its true potential. But she never recovered from being rejected by Jonan and was determined to get him back.

When Amelia hired Beth to arrange a high-profile launch event in a haunted hotel for her protection racket, Amelia's Haven, Beth, Jonan and Amelia were thrown together. Watching Beth and Jonan fall in love in front of her eyes, Amelia was determined to destroy their bond.

Beth befriended Bill, the old man who worked at the hotel, and when he went missing she confronted Amelia, believing her to be responsible. Amelia claimed to know nothing, but Beth searched the hotel and found Bill locked in the basement. After rescuing him, she left him with Jonan's aunt, Doriel, the second member of the Triad. But when Doriel and Bill went missing, Beth and Jonan were left to face up to Amelia with their suspicions.

Amelia had suspicions of her own to plant. Working with Jonan's estranged brother, Roland, she publicly claimed Doriel and Bill were kidnapped by Soul Snatchers. She accused Jonan of being their leader at a televised event and tried to have him arrested.

Only with the help of Jonan's mother Miranda, the final member of the Triad, were they able to interrupt Amelia's plans. But Amelia didn't fall far, she didn't give up, and Doriel and Bill were still missing.

Now Beth and Jonan must find Doriel and Bill, and stop Amelia's power-grab before she brings everyone into The Fear.

1

BETH

BETH PUT THE LAST CRYSTAL BACK INTO PLACE AND SPUN around, surveying her work. The shop looked even better than before. She had no more excuses to stay down here, away from the conversation between Jonan and his mother in the flat above. She was almost at the door to the stairs when a brick crashed through the window.

'Hey!' she yelled, running to the shop door and flinging it open. A man was running back up the path towards town. He looked over his shoulder for a moment, laughing.

'Damn.' She picked up the broom and started sweeping. There was glass all over the floor, but thankfully the brick hadn't hit any stock.

'Are you okay?' Jonan poked his head around the door.

She nodded. 'Just help me get this window boarded up. We'll need to call out the glazier again. We must be keeping him in business.'

'I'll email him now.' Jonan tapped on his phone, and then slid it into his pocket and helped her board up the window. 'Come on,' he said when she reached for the broom, 'The shop's closed so we can do this later. Mum's waiting for us.'

Upstairs, Jonan put three steaming mugs on the coffee table, and then sat on the sofa next to Beth, his shoulders slumped. Miranda, his mother, sat upright in the chair by the fire, her forehead furrowed in a deep frown.

'I still don't buy their story,' Beth said, unable to keep the sharpness out of her voice. 'Bill was weak. He could hardly walk. And I don't believe he had the strength to trash this place and cart Doriel out of here on his own. So what happened?'

Miranda pursed her lips. 'I've been trying to find Doriel on the astral, but there's no sign.'

Beth swallowed. 'Do you think she's dead?'

'Not at all.' Miranda fixed Beth with an unflinching look. 'If my sister were dead, I would have no problem finding her. If she's untraceable, she's alive and hidden.'

'Hidden?' Jonan murmured, and then looked up at his mother. 'Who would have the strength to hide her from you?'

'As far as I know, only Doriel or Amelia.'

'Neither Doriel nor Bill would have gone voluntarily,' Beth said.

Jonan pushed up from the sofa and paced. 'Amelia then. Where would she take them? Any ideas?' He looked at Miranda.

'Where they kept Bill before?' Beth said.

Jonan shrugged. 'We don't know where that was either.'

'Didn't you say there was a Polaroid of Bill when they had him last?' Miranda's voice didn't change, but she leaned forwards a little. 'Did you give it to the police, or do you still have it?'

'I kept it,' Jonan said, walking over to a chest of drawers, pulling open the top one and rifling through it. 'DC Ainsworth stank of Amelia's interference.'

Miranda took the photograph without a word. She looked at it, her face impassive, and then pulled out a crystal.

'What's that?' Beth asked.

'Watch and learn,' Miranda said with a smile. 'Do you have a local map?'

Jonan went over to the bookshelf. Previously, the shelf had been well ordered and neatly stacked. Now the books were piled everywhere, one on top of the other, some standing upright, some looking as though they were about to fall. Jonan pulled out a thin booklet and handed it to Miranda. She put it on the wooden coffee table but kept the Polaroid in her hand. Closing her eyes, she wrapped her thin, pale fingers around the crystal pendant and breathed deeply. A few moments later, she opened her eyes and placed the photograph on the table next to the booklet. Opening the map to the first page, she held the pendulum over the image. 'Are Doriel and Bill on this page?' she asked, her voice steady.

The pendulum hung still for a moment, and then circled to the left.

'What does that mean?' Beth asked.

'It means no,' Miranda said, not looking up. She turned the page and repeated the question. Once again, the pendulum circled to the left.

They were near the end of the booklet when the pendulum circled to the right. Jonan had been pacing behind Miranda. Now he stilled, and then sat on the arm of her chair, leaning forwards, his face bright with excitement.

'Is this the most detailed map you have?' Miranda said, looking up at her son.

'I'm afraid so, but if we use an online map we could zoom in and get more a specific location.' He stood up and went into his bedroom, returning a moment later with a tablet. Pulling up a map, he zoomed in on the area the pendulum had indicated, put it on the table and stepped back.

Miranda held the pendulum over the top left-hand corner of the map. It circled to the left. Slowly, she moved it in a straight line towards the right. It kept circling to the left. Moving down slightly, she went back across the screen to the far side. Bit by bit, she worked her way across the screen. It was over a large green space when it slowed and then circled to the right.

'Bingo,' Jonan said, and leaned forward to zoom in.

Now the map was bigger, Miranda repeated the process until the pendulum circled to the right. Once again, they zoomed in. There weren't many buildings. The pendulum was directing them to an area with fields and not a lot else. This time, the pendulum circled right over a single, isolated building.

Jonan zoomed in even further. There was no name, but there was a house with a cluster of buildings to one side.

'Any idea what that is?' Miranda said, touching the tips of her fingers to the screen.

Jonan shook his head. 'Do you get anything from it?'

'Nothing.'

Jonan touched it himself, closing his eyes. His lips compressed, going white at the edges. He shook his head, 'nothing.'

'I'll try,' Beth said, reaching out. She felt a buzzing in

Starfolk Falling

her head, and the echoes of something she couldn't hear. She shook her head, frustrated. 'Let me look at the map,' she said, reaching out and taking the booklet. She opened it on the page chosen by the pendulum and held her hand over it. This time, the buzzing retreated slightly. She reached her awareness out, looking for Doriel, but felt nothing. Instead, she focused on Bill. There was silence for a moment, and then she felt a barrier crumble. Her mind was flooded with screaming. She clapped her hands flat over her ears. Pain swamped her body, and she curled up into a ball, overwhelmed by sensation.

A large, pasty face with a heavy black beard filled her mind. She shuddered as she recognised the man who had broken into the shop and smashed the crystal wizard before Doriel and Bill's disappearance. She pulled back to get a wider view, and saw Bill lying in front of a small fire. The ground beneath his crumpled body was grey and featureless. It looked like concrete. There was a small square wooden table next to him, but when she tried to zoom out further, she met a blank wall of nothingness.

'What do you see?' Miranda said, her voice hypnotic.

'I see Bill and the man who broke into the shop, but then nothing. I think he has been moved outside the bounds of Amelia's shields. I can feel her energy all over the blankness. I get no sense of Doriel.'

'This is good,' Miranda said, getting up and putting on a pair of flat, black ballet pumps. Your connection to Bill is breaking through at least some of Amelia's fog. Keep that open.' She turned to Jonan. 'Do you have a car?'

'Yes,' Jonan said, 'and it's fully charged.' He didn't move. 'What do we do when we get there? We can't assume they are unguarded. If Amelia has gone to this much trouble to take them, she will make damn sure she keeps them. We need a plan.'

'Do you get any sense of how many people there are, Beth?' Miranda said in the same hypnotic tone.

'I only see the man who broke into the shop and smashed the crystals.'

Beth wanted to open her eyes, to see if Jonan was okay, but she held her focus and expanded her view. 'He's a big guy. I have no idea how we would get around him, but I don't see anyone else. Of course, I don't know if there's anyone with Doriel.'

'We're going to have to take that risk,' Miranda said, opening the door down to the shop. 'I'm not leaving my sister there a moment longer.'

'We risk leaving her there permanently if we don't get this right.' Jonan's voice cracked.

Tension prickled across Beth's skin and the image dissipated. She opened her eyes.

Jonan and Miranda stood facing each other, identical set looks on their faces.

'You need to do as I tell you, son.'

'I'm not a child.' Jonan's voice was soft, but energy crackled around him as he held his ground. 'You have been out of the world for a long time. You need to hear me. Doriel is relying on us to get this right.'

Neither of them moved. Their eyes shone purple, their ears stretched into shining, identical blue points. Jonan was surrounded by a shimmer of green and pink that made Beth's skin tingle. Miranda was surrounded by pure white light.

'I can't reach them when you are this activated,' Beth said.

Starfolk Falling

They didn't respond.

She slammed her palm down on the wooden coffee table. 'You are dominating the airwaves. Dial it down.'

'Of course.' Jonan nodded and stepped back.

Miranda looked at Jonan through narrowed eyes, and then nodded. 'You're right. You're not a child anymore, and you know Doriel better than I do now. What do you suggest?'

Jonan's shoulders relaxed and he sat back down. 'I remember the guard. He's frightened of us and it's hard to think clearly around him. We need to distract him so we can get to Doriel and Bill without his interference.'

'We're assuming Doriel *is* there,' Beth said, her voice quiet, 'but none of us can sense her.'

'Oh, she's there alright.' Miranda pursed her lips. I may not pick up my sister, but I recognise the energy signature. Only Amelia or Doriel could block me like that, and either way, that puts her at the scene.'

Beth nodded, trying to ignore the sinking feeling in her stomach.

'I will create a distraction,' Miranda said. 'You two go in and get Bill.'

'What will you do?' Beth asked.

'Leave that with me.' Miranda gave a smile that sent fingers of ice down Beth's spine. 'I will decide what to do when I can read the man's energy. There is more than one way to create a disturbance and not all distractions need to be physical. Something that plays with the mind and its fears can be the most effective.'

Jonan shuddered. 'You sound like Amelia.'

'I choose not to manipulate. That doesn't mean I can't.

Now, can we go?' Without waiting for an answer, Miranda opened the door and walked down the stairs.

'What are we going to do?' Beth said, as fear snaked through her.

'We will find Doriel and Bill and get them to the car. Trust Mum. She knows what she's doing and she's every bit as effective as Amelia.' He took Beth's hand and squeezed it. The warmth of his grip relaxed Beth a little, and she took a deep breath. She nodded. 'I don't think Bill is in good shape.'

'Well then we'd better get to him quickly,' Jonan said. 'We have no idea how much time we have left.'

2

DORIEL

THE DRIP, DRIP, DRIP OF WATER INTO THE PUDDLE IN THE middle of the room was driving Doriel crazy. Of all the nastiness that had surrounded her since her kidnapping, the cold, the damp, the hard floor that bruised her hips and shoulders when she tried to lie down, that incessant dripping took the deepest bite into her serenity and control.

She squeezed her eyes tightly shut, trying to block out her surroundings, trying to pretend that the irritating Brute on the other side of the bars was not watching her every movement. The thin dressing gown and silk pyjamas they had dragged her out in gave her no protection from the biting air, or the invasive damp. She clamped her teeth tightly together, refusing to let them chatter. She would not show him that she was cold. The appearance of strength was all she had left.

A groan from the other side of the cell jerked her into full consciousness. She sighed. Bill looked terrible. His skin was grey and his breath came out in shallow shudders.

'Please bring Bill closer to your fire. I'm the one Amelia wants to punish. He's just an innocent bystander.'

The Brute shrugged. 'He's staying right where he is.' He stretched out his trunk-like legs, the flimsy chair wobbling as he flexed his bulky muscles and rested one foot on top of the other. He scratched at his chin with one hand and then ran his fingers through the thick, black beard.

His side of the room was only mildly more comfortable than hers. He had a small camping oil lamp and had lit a fire on the stone floor on the other side of the bars, in an attempt to counteract the absence of electricity. His spindly wooden chair was pulled up close to the square table, which held an old-fashioned dimpled glass tankard, half full of beer. She could smell it from here, or was that stale drink on his breath? She wasn't sure which, but it turned her stomach.

'If I have to freeze my arse off in this nasty cell, so does he.' He took a swig of beer.

Doriel closed her eyes and took a deep breath, forcing herself to stay calm.

Drip, drip, drip. The sound ate into every attempt at serenity. Every time she tried to gather herself, to think clearly so she could be strategic, the dripping tapped away at the edges of her focus.

She shifted, trying to get her frozen limbs comfortable on the hard floor. Her legs were almost numb.

Doriel crawled over to Bill. His skin was hot and clammy. Moving back to the bars, she pulled herself up so she had some height over the Brute, who was still sitting at the table.

'What is your name?'

'Not a chance.'

'If you don't help Bill, he's going to die. He's really ill. Do you think Amelia will be blamed for his death? It'll be on your shoulders.'

'She'll take care of me.'

'I know Amelia well. She'll let you take the blame and you'll go to prison for the rest of your life,' Doriel said, leaning back on the wall. 'How would you feel if Bill were your father?'

He ignored her.

'Please, just move him closer to your fire. He's no threat to you. Look at him.'

The Brute glanced at Bill, then pressed his lips into a thin line. Muttering to himself, he pulled out a huge metal ring jangling with different-sized keys, slid one into the lock and turned. He yanked the door open, and then nodded his head at the back wall. 'You get back there. Don't. Try. Anything.'

Doriel raised her hands in front of her and inched backwards. 'What do you think I'm going to do? Surely you're not frightened of me? I'm half your size.'

As the Brute came through the door, she felt a rush of fear. She swayed, reaching out to steady herself on the stone wall, but her head swam and her stomach rolled. She closed her eyes for a moment but that only made it worse. She swallowed, watching as he picked Bill up and edged back out the door. Dumping Bill on the stone floor near the fire, he dragged the door shut, turned the key and threw the keyring onto the wooden table.

'There. Happy?' he said, sitting back down with an impact that nearly crushed the thin wooden chair.

Doriel nodded and swallowed again. The pressure had eased now he was gone, but her head still span. Well, that answered her question, at least: he was definitely frightened of her. She wondered what he thought she might do to him. No doubt Amelia had filled him with fears that she would steal his soul. She sank to the ground, her back against the rough brick wall. Noise clamoured at her mind, but she couldn't make out any words. There was just fear. Fear and an impending sense of doom.

But at least Bill might now have a chance.

3

BETH

It was pitch black outside and fog rose from the freezing tarmac as they sped silently along the unlit road. Jonan's headlamps provided the only light and threw eerie shadows as they swerved around an unexpectedly sharp bend.

Beth groaned as she was thrown against the seatbelt. The impact broke her trance, and her connection to Bill. A wave of nausea rolled through her.

'Sorry,' Jonan said, accelerating more slowly this time.

'I know we're in a rush, but there's an awful lot of interference between Bill and I already. This panic is only making it harder.' Beth snapped. 'I've lost them now.'

'I'll help,' Miranda said, reaching out and taking Beth's hand. The boost from Miranda's energy was immediate. Rather than watching from a distance, Beth was out of her body, speeding towards Bill. She didn't know where she was going but felt a magnetic pull as the countryside sped below her. She was alone but felt Miranda's palm on her own physical hand as a second awareness that supported her like a breeze underneath her astral wings.

A weight settled in her chest as she drifted to the ground. She looked around, trying to take in every feature of her surroundings. There was a large house with dark, smashed windows. Paint was peeling from the weathered woodwork and the front door swung in the wind. There was no sign of life in the house; it felt like a blank.

Beth lurched against her seatbelt as the car stopped. 'Where am I?' she croaked, gasping for air.

'Still in the car,' Jonan said. 'Are you okay?'

Beth peered out the window. 'This is it.' The road was a dead end, blocked by a heavy wooden gate that led into an abandoned farmyard.

Jonan climbed out of the car and peered at the gate by the light of the headlamps. There was a battered old sign warning of a dog, but the gate wasn't locked. He lifted the latch, swung it open and returned to the car.

'It's been freshly oiled, so this place can't be as abandoned as it looks.' He drove the car up the gravel lane and pulled in by the side of the farmhouse. The yard was ringed by tall, thick evergreens that completely blocked out the road and loomed, huge and imposing, over the derelict outbuildings. There were three structures, all in varying states of disrepair. One wooden barn was disintegrating so badly there were enormous holes in the walls. That one felt as dead as the house. The second had an energy to it, but it was deeply unfamiliar and Beth turned away instinctively. The third looked uninhabited but, still half in trance, she felt its pull. It drew her with a fizzing energy that sent off sparks of recognition. *Bill.* She wasn't sure whether she spoke the name or just felt it, but it seemed to tug at her, calling her closer.

Jonan swung into a circular clearing and parked next to the house.

Beth climbed out and looked around. Adrenaline surged through her as she stood and looked around at the clearing she had visited in the astral only moments before.

'Shall we go?' Jonan reached out a hand to Beth.

'Just wait.' Miranda's voice was flat. 'Give me a moment.'

They stood in silence watching Miranda. She didn't move but a crash in the woods behind them, followed by an eerie howl, made Beth widen her eyes.

There was silence, and then they heard heavy footsteps. The door to one of the outbuildings swung open and they melted back into the shadows from the house. Beth looked behind her to see that the black car was almost completely undetectable.

The man looked around and then strode off into the trees.

'Now, go,' Miranda said. 'But be careful. I will keep him out of the way for as long as possible, but I can't physically prevent him from coming back.'

Beth nodded. 'Thank you.' She turned and led the way towards the outbuilding.

The walk from the car to the wooden structure felt endless, but she could still feel the pull towards it. Her heart hammered in her chest in spite of Jonan's reassuring presence behind her.

She paused at the door, scanning the darkness. Then she grasped the handle and tugged. It stuck, creaked and then swung open. Beth slipped through and stepped out of the way to allow Jonan in. He closed the door behind them with a click.

4

DORIEL

The fire hadn't done much to improve Bill's colour. Rather than bringing pink to his cheeks, it served only to throw strange shadows onto his pallid skin. His breathing was shallow and there were long moments when he didn't seem to be pulling any air into his body at all.

Doriel felt her own breath becoming more and more raspy from the damp and the cold. 'Please,' she said, her voice cracking. 'I need to see a doctor.'

'It's not enough that I brought Bill to the fire, eh? Now *you* want something, too? You do know why you're here, right? Amelia wants to punish you. She said she wants to show you what it's like to be abandoned and alone when you're broken.' He grabbed a bottle from the stone floor. The label had been peeled off, leaving only a white, sticky residue, but it was full of amber liquid. He poured himself a huge shot and knocked it back in one.

Doriel swallowed. If that was what Amelia wanted, she was hitting the spot.

There was a huge crash from outside. The Brute stood

up, and then stumbled. He swayed for a moment, took a step towards the door and nearly fell over. Doriel frowned. She had seen him drink much more than this over the past few days with no reaction at all. He reached forwards, stretching to grab the door handle and hauled himself towards it, his muscles bunching as though he were dragging himself through water.

'Are you okay?' Doriel croaked. Her throat felt like it was filled with knives, but something weird was happening and she needed to understand. If Amelia was coming for her, she didn't want to be unprepared.

The Brute's fear beat at her in waves, sending her reeling. Strange shapes formed in the brickwork, sliding towards her across the concrete floor. Enormous spiders scampered towards her, circling her. Then a swarm of rats joined them, edging nearer, their pink noses sniffing at the dank air.

'No,' Doriel croaked, dragging herself backwards. 'Help me, please?' she called to the Brute, but he had gone. She swiped at a particularly adventurous rat, but her hand met thin air. She tried again. Again, nothing. She hit out at everything she could see, but her hands seemed to pass through them as they came ever closer. Were they real, or just in her head? They had her surrounded now. A moment ago there had been nothing. How was this possible? There was a shuddering in the air. She wasn't sure whether the ground shook, or whether it was her own body. All she could do was curl into a ball and wrap her arms around her head. With her eyes closed, she blocked it all out. Nothing touched her and the wall of her mind closed ever inwards, imprisoning her in her own imagination, and cutting her off from the world outside.

5

JONAN

'Doriel. Open your eyes. It's me, Jonan.' He wanted to shake her awake, but she looked so frail. What had they done to her in the past few days? His mind raged, but he pulled it back into line, for now at least. 'Doriel, we need to get you out. Now.'

Doriel's eyes flickered, and then bunched up, tightly closed. 'It's okay,' he whispered, pulling her shivering body to his chest and rocking backwards and forwards. Her skin burned even as her body shuddered with a cold that seeped up from the flagstones beneath his feet. 'Doriel, please. I can see you're awake. It's Jonan. I need you to come back.'

This time her eyes opened, slowly. She blinked a few times, squeezing her lids tightly shut each time. 'Jonan, is it *really* you? I'm not imagining you?'

'It's really me.' Jonan's voice cracked.

'Bill,' she croaked.

'We'll get him too. Beth is here with me, but we need to get you out of here. Mother drew out the man. He's distracted at the moment, but I don't know how long she'll be able to hold him for.'

'The Brute? Oh, she'll be able to distract him for ages,' Doriel said, rolling onto all fours and pushing herself up. 'He is riddled with fear. I could barely breathe when he crossed through the barrier into my cell.'

'What kind of barrier?' Jonan raised one eyebrow as he pulled her up and wrapped his arm around her waist, holding her firm against his body so she could not fall.

'The barrier Amelia set up. It was supposed to keep me imprisoned and keep me hidden. How did you find me?'

'We'll have time for that later,' Jonan said. 'Come on. Let's get you out of here. Beth?' He turned slowly, trying not to disturb Doriel.

She was hunched over Bill. 'I can't wake him up and I can't carry him alone.'

'Okay, help me get Doriel up to the car and we'll come back for Bill.'

Beth nodded and yanked the door open, held it wide and then ducked up the stairs ahead of Jonan. She stopped at the top and inched the door open a crack. It was pitch black outside.

'Now!' Miranda's voice pounded through her head. She threw the door open, stepped into the dark and waited for Jonan. Hooking Doriel's other arm over her shoulder, they ran towards the car together.

'Did you hear Miranda?'

'Hear what?' Doriel rasped.

'You didn't hear Mother?' Jonan's voice was impassive, but Beth felt alarm roll through him.

'Miranda is here?' Doriel lifted her head, her face brightening the tiniest bit.

'Yes, I told you that,' Jonan said. 'She's distracting that man.'

'The Brute,' Doriel's voice faltered as she spoke the words.

Jonan heard crashing in the bushes nearby and then a loud bellow. He heard nothing from Miranda but felt her energy and flinched at its force. He had no idea his own mother still carried that much fury.

'Time to go,' Miranda said. 'I'll meet you at the car.'

'We need more time.'

'I can't. He suspects something is up. He's heading back.'

'Come on, Beth. We need to get back to Bill before the guard does.'

They reached the car and Jonan flung the door open, helping Doriel to slide inside.

'Lie down and stay hidden. We're going to get Bill.'

Doriel nodded and slumped back against the seat. Her eyes flickered closed.

Jonan shut the door carefully with a soft click and locked it, wincing as the lights flicked on and off.

'This is worse than I thought,' Jonan said as they jogged back to the outbuilding. 'Doriel should be able to feel Mum's presence. They've never been this disconnected before. I thought it would be okay once we got her out of that cell, but the fog around her is impenetrable and that's not as easy to shift as Amelia's barriers.'

'We'll sort that out afterwards,' Beth whispered. 'Just stay focused.'

They flattened against the wall of the outbuilding and Beth inched the door open. She peered down the staircase, but there was no movement and no sound. Nodding at Jonan, she slipped through the door.

At the bottom, she lowered the door handle slowly and pushed it open.

The man stood in the room, jaw clenched, hands on his hips as he glared at Beth. 'You,' he said through gritted teeth. 'I knew you were trouble.'

A memory flashed through Beth's mind. Him, standing in the middle of Third Eye, smashing a huge amethyst wizard. What *was* he doing here? She looked over her shoulder at Jonan. He was glaring at the man as though trying to move him with his gaze alone.

Bill was lying on the floor behind the man. He was still unconscious.

'We've come for Bill,' Jonan said, stepping down to stand next to Beth.

'No,' the man said, flexing the muscles in his arms and pulling himself up taller. 'And you're gonna give Doriel back.'

'No,' Jonan said.

The man pressed his lips together and took a deep breath through his nose. 'You don't frighten me.'

'On the contrary,' Beth said, her voice soft. She stepped past Jonan, looking directly into the man's eyes. 'I think we scare you far more than you're willing to let on. After all, you can't use those muscles to fend off an astral attack.'

The man took a step back, looking from one to the other. His mouth settled into a growl, and he charged towards Jonan. At the last minute, he pulled up and clapped his hands over his ears, lurching into the flimsy table and sending the tankard flying. It smashed, spraying glass and beer across the room. 'No,' he moaned. 'What are you doing to me? Please, make it go away. I hate monkeys.' He hunched on the floor in front of Bill, shaking.

Get out now, Miranda's voice sounded in Beth's mind.

Closing the gap between them and Bill, Beth and Jonan hooked their arms under his and lifted him clean off the floor and over the top of the man, who collapsed onto the floor, shrieking.

'Go,' Jonan said. They skirted the man, heading for the door.

Beth screamed. Losing her footing, she landed hard on the stone floor, her shoulder cracking against the unyielding surface.

The guard's fingers were wrapped around her ankle. She rolled over, kicking at his hand.

'Salu,' Jonan yelled, his voice ricocheting around the hard, cold walls.

The freezing room was instantly warm and the scent of lavender filled the space.

Jonan stamped down, hard, on the guard's wrist. The man roared.

Beth jerked away and pulled herself up. 'I'm okay.'

Together they dragged Bill up the stairs and out into the dark of the night.

The car moved silently out of the shadows and stopped in front of them. Miranda was at the wheel. She reached over and opened the front door. 'Get in. Amelia is on her way.'

Jonan opened the back door, slid Bill onto the centre seat next to Doriel, and then climbed in after while Beth got into the front seat.

A loud bellow sounded from the outbuilding. Miranda reversed sharply and then drove down the gravel drive and into the road. They hadn't gone far when she swerved, driving across the lawn of the deserted house and pulling in behind some trees. A moment later a black SUV roared past.

They waited a few seconds in silence, and then Miranda drove silently back out onto the road.

6

AMELIA

'They got away?' Amelia's voice was shrill.

'I ... I just ... there was this noise.' The man put his hands over his ears and shut his eyes tight. 'And ... monkeys.'

'Get in the van,' she said, striding off towards the cellar. 'Come on, Rolo,' she called, without turning around.

She walked down the stairs, allowing the door to slam behind her, not caring whether Roland was in the way.

The room stank of beer. The door to the cage swung open on its hinges. Embers smouldered on the stone floor and there was broken glass everywhere.

'Damn!' she yelled at the top of her voice, slamming her hand down on the rickety wooden table. 'Damn, damn, damn, damn, DAMN!'

Roland stepped into the room and gasped. 'You kept people locked in here? You kept *Doriel* locked in here? What were you thinking?'

Amelia shrugged. 'She needed to learn her place. She's so full of her own importance, flaunting her skills as both oracle and mother while I have no place at all. If I can't have her love, I *will* have her fear.'

Roland gaped. 'You're serious, aren't you? This was all one big exercise in revenge. I thought you'd taken them to a nice hotel somewhere. For God's sake, Amelia, you told me Doriel was relaxing in a spa while Jonan was panicking. Are you taking me for a ride too? You know I would never have agreed to this.'

Amelia rolled her eyes. 'Dial it down, Rolo. The histrionics aren't helping my headache.'

'Histrionics? From me? After your little performance?'

'Darling, there was nothing little about my performance.'

'You're unbelievable. Are you at least going to check Doriel's okay?'

'And break the tension? Right now she's scared of me. What else was all this for?'

He gaped at her, and then turned on his heel and stomped up the stairs, slamming the door at the top behind him.

Amelia let out a shuddering breath. She had been performing. This had shaken her more than she would admit to Roland. She went into the cell, feeling the power of Doriel's energy signature. She hadn't given in easily, but something had broken her. What was it? She held her hand over the stone of the floor and felt the tingle of energy skating over the skin of her palm and up her arm. *Fear.*

She sat down on the spot, feeling Doriel's fear flow through her, feeding from it. She needed this. She hadn't been herself since the showdown at her event. Doubts had been creeping in and the energy at the inn had even been getting to her. If she was going to make Amelia's Haven the hit it deserved to be, she had to be on top form.

Doriel had escaped, but Amelia was in her head now and she would milk that for all it was worth. She would make sure Doriel was completely incapable of standing in her way.

7

BETH

BETH LEANED ON THE HEADREST AND CLOSED HER EYES. SHE was exhausted. Leaving Bill at the hospital had taken her last bit of strength. She could still see his pale face and the dark smudges under his eyes, and she wished they had allowed her to stay with him. Jonan tried to persuade Doriel to get checked out while they were there, but she huddled in the back of the car and refused to move. Miranda stood guard, refusing to let Jonan coerce her inside.

At home, Jonan parked in his usual spot and they helped Doriel out of the car, and down the road to the shop. It was dark and cold in the flat, and Jonan lit the fire while Beth went through to the kitchen to make hot chocolate.

When she put the mug on the table in front of Doriel, the older woman didn't move. She sat alone on the sofa and stared straight ahead, her gaze fixed on the leaping flames in the fireplace.

Jonan fussed around her, wrapping her in blankets and pumping her full of paracetamol. He didn't sit. He didn't

Starfolk Falling

say anything meaningful. He just murmured comforting words as though soothing a baby.

Miranda sat bolt upright on the single armchair, watching Doriel. Her eyes were clear, but focused. She didn't look away, didn't speak. She didn't engage with anybody.

Beth felt uneasy. Watching Doriel, she felt her own episode of The Fear seeping closer from the edges of her consciousness. Doriel and Jonan had helped Beth overcome her fears after Amelia triggered them. But if Amelia could derail someone as powerful as Doriel, was anyone immune to her manipulations?

Beth sat gently on the sofa next to Jonan's aunt. She rolled her shoulders, trying out her injured arm.

'Is it okay?' Jonan's voice was rough.

Beth nodded. 'Just bruised.' She reached out her good arm, placing her hand out, palm upwards, so Doriel could seek comfort if she chose. 'You're home.'

Doriel leaned her forehead on her knees, which were pulled up into her chest, her feet on the sofa. She said nothing.

Beth moved to put her hand on Doriel's back but Miranda shook her head and Beth pulled her hand away. She sighed and moved further down the sofa to give Doriel some space.

Jonan watched, the hot chocolate forgotten in his hand. His face was unreadable. He knelt in front of Doriel and took her hands in both of his. 'I'm so sorry,' he said. 'I put you in danger and I will never forgive myself. Please, tell me what they did to you. If that man hurt you, I will find him and …' He tailed off.

Doriel had shrunk into herself even further, squeezing her eyes tightly shut.

'Look,' Beth said. 'That's exactly what Amelia wants. She's trying to distract you because she can't scare you. We need to step past all of this and stop Amelia before she takes things even further.'

'Beth is right.' Miranda stood up and walked over to Jonan. 'We must not show weakness. She will exploit every chink in our energy to chip away at what we know to be true.'

'How can you say that right now?' Jonan stood and faced his mother. He was taller than her, his eyes filled with fury as he glared down at her impassive face. 'Do you have any idea what Amelia has done to Doriel? Or how? She uses our weakness against us. If we don't face up to our triggers, we hand her a weapon and show her how to use it. We need to stand firm, be real about who we are, where we are weak, and where we are strong. Last time we hit a crisis, you ran. That made Roland and I the men we are now. I stand by who I am, but I do not stand by your choice. And I will not make that choice now.'

'Please, Jonan,' Beth said, standing up and taking his hand. 'Now is not the time for revenge.'

Doriel shook her head but kept her gaze on the flames that jumped and spiked in the grate. 'We're not safe. She'll come for us again.'

Miranda pursed her lips and watched Doriel. 'Her energy is so muddled.'

Jonan's eyes unfocused. 'The energy is distorted. I don't think she can tell what's real right now.'

'Whatever happened to her,' Miranda said in a sharp voice, 'Doriel can't allow Amelia to affect her.'

Starfolk Falling

'Really?' Jonan spread his arms wide. 'You find it so easy to block out the emotions you don't want? Is that right? Is that what allowed you to walk out on your two teenage sons?'

'Oh for goodness sake,' Miranda rolled her eyes. 'You were acting pretty grown-up as far as I could see.'

'You think sleeping with my mum's best friend was a considered and adult move? It never occurred to you that my stupid behaviour was an indication I needed guidance?'

'And would you have listened to me?'

'I listened to Doriel then, and I'm listening to Doriel now. Shutting her up will only leave chasms of unresolved pain for Amelia to exploit. Positivity is not something you can turn on like a tap, Mother. Positivity has to be earned and sometimes that takes a trip through the depths. You weren't prepared to go through the depths with me, but I will be with Doriel every step of the way. Do you love your sister any more than you loved your sons, or are Doriel and I doing this alone?'

There was silence. The air was heavy with unshed tears and the weight of words that should have been spoken a long time ago.

Beth laced her fingers through Jonan's. 'You will never walk alone, my love,' she said, squeezing them gently.

Jonan drew in a shuddering breath. He turned his back on Miranda, facing Beth and locking her into his purple gaze. 'Whatever happens?'

She stood on her toes and kissed him gently. 'Whatever happens.' She felt a rush of energy through their hands as though her words had created something physical.

The air flushed with warmth and Beth smelled lavender. The tension in the room eased and she saw two faces in her mind. One was a man with long, blond hair, the other, a woman with dark ringlets.

You know what to do. The Triad has descended into chaos. Now is your time. The words reverberated through Beth's mind.

She let go of Jonan's hand and turned to face the room. 'Okay, enough now. Let's give Doriel some space. She'll talk to us when she's ready and we *will* hear her out whether we like what she says or not. For now, we need to look at what Amelia has told us and how we're going to respond.'

8

BETH

Jonan walked through to the kitchen and pulled a bottle of wine from the rack. 'Would you like a drink?' he asked as Miranda leaned against the work surface.

She shook her head. 'What exactly are you suggesting, Beth?'

Beth pulled the door shut behind them. 'We haven't even talked about Amelia's Haven yet. Amelia is bringing people together and making out that everyone outside her organisation is a threat. It's hard enough for *us* to counter her, and we understand energy work. How do you think other people will deal with her manipulations?'

'We need to bring people together ourselves,' Jonan murmured, his mouth spreading into a smile, as he sat down on the sofa. 'We need to create an alternative.'

'Exactly.' Beth nodded. 'You have a shop here, and a following. You sell crystals and other spiritual paraphernalia and you do tarot readings. But that's it, isn't it? There are other things we can do.'

'We?' Jonan said, a shadow of blue points playing around the tops of his ears.

'We, if you would like to have me.' Beth smiled. 'We can pull the Third Eye community together and expand it, teaching people how to handle themselves and keep clear of Amelia's interference. I can help you. After all, I need a new job!' she said with a laugh.

Miranda was staring at Beth, brows drawn in, eyes dark. 'You want to teach people what we are?'

'I want to teach them how to protect themselves and I want to group them together so they aren't easy targets. If we keep our focus solely on Amelia we're going to fail. I think she's *trying* to keep us centred on your history, so we miss what she's doing in the here and now. We need to stop dancing to her tune and start our own gig. Isn't that supposed to be what we're here for? Standing up to persecution when things go wrong?'

A ghost of a smile hovered around Miranda's lips and the scent of lavender spiked.

'Can't bring people in here,' Doriel murmured. They turned to see her standing in the doorway. 'Need to close the shop. Stop doing readings. Miranda is at risk. Amelia will target her. She is so angry. So angry. She hates Miranda for spoiling all her plans; for isolating her. She wants to punish Miranda, wants to punish me.' She turned around, wandered into the living room and sat on the sofa, huddling into the corner.

Beth frowned. 'You know Doriel far better than I ever will, but I've been in The Fear. I know where she is right now.'

'Go on,' Miranda said, crossing her arms across her chest.

Starfolk Falling

Beth nodded. 'We need to wake her out of this trance. The Fear becomes more potent and all-encompassing the less grounded you are. Doriel is an Oracle, right?' Miranda nodded. 'Imagine your gift turning against you,' Beth said. 'Imagine that you aren't seeing insights anymore, but instead a menu of potential disasters. Right now, I imagine Doriel is receiving a live stream from Amelia's personalised horror cabaret, but she doesn't know it's not real. We need to break her trance and wake her up. And we need to do it right now.'

Miranda pursed her lips, and then nodded. 'Excuse me,' she said, and followed Doriel out to the living room. Closing her eyes, she held her arms above her head and then brought them down in a snap. 'Wake up,' she ordered.

Nothing happened.

Miranda frowned.

Putting a hand on Doriel's forehead, she closed her eyes. She stood still for few moments and then swayed on her feet.

Beth reached Miranda in a few strides, and put out a hand to steady her. Dizziness overwhelmed her and she squeezed her eyes tightly shut for a moment. She was back in Doriel's prison cell. Doriel was lying on the ground in front of her, curled into a tight ball, surrounded by rats and spiders. One rat stepped onto Doriel's foot and Beth lurched forwards, hitting at it. But her hand passed right through. She crouched down, trying to ignore the creatures that swarmed around her, but didn't make contact. 'Doriel, Doriel, wake up.' The woman curled into a tighter ball, wrapping her arms around her head and whimpering, but she didn't open her eyes.

'Amelia has got to her more than I realised.' Miranda's

voice came from behind Beth. 'I'm surprised you got in here.'

Beth swallowed and stood up. 'I didn't mean to. You looked like you were going to fall over, so I ...'

'You touched me?' Miranda raised one eyebrow. 'Well, I'm glad you're here. This is a strong construct. You can help clear it.' She held out her hands.

Beth took them and felt a jolt as the energy connected.

'We will surround Doriel and create a circle with our arms,' Miranda said, and then started to sing. The sound sank into Beth's bones with a familiarity that took her breath away. It vibrated through her, and she found herself singing in harmony, without knowing where the recognition came from. As they sang, Doriel's body gradually relaxed and then started to fade.

Beth stumbled as she came back to full consciousness, but Miranda was already holding her steady.

'You'll be okay,' she said, her voice clipped. 'You did well. Your memories are close to the surface now.'

Doriel jerked upright. She blinked a few times, gazed at Miranda looking dazed, and then threw herself into her sister's arms. 'Miranda!' She held her impossibly tight for a moment, and then pulled back. 'Bill? What about Bill?'

Beth sank onto the sofa, her limbs still weighed down by the heaviness of trance. 'Bill is in hospital again.' Her voice caught. 'They don't know whether he'll make it.'

'No!' Doriel put her hands over her face. 'I tried so hard to keep him warm.'

'I know you did. Nobody blames you. I blame Amelia, and that man.' Beth said with a sigh. Then she paused. 'Wait a minute. What if we could help other people come out of The Fear?'

Miranda frowned. 'What do you mean?'

'We could develop the Third Eye as a place to help people who can't find a way out of Amelia's influence,' Beth said.

Doriel tilted her head to one side. 'Develop the Third Eye? You mean the shop?'

Beth nodded. 'We were just talking about turning the shop into more of a community hub, an antidote to Amelia's Haven, but don't worry. Jonan and I can handle it alone until you're ready.'

Doriel shook her head. 'I'm going to bed,' she said, pushing herself up off the chair and shuffling over to her bedroom door.

'Doriel,' Jonan said, getting up and following her. 'Are you okay?'

They disappeared into Doriel's room and the door closed behind them.

'This plan of yours, what made you think of it?' Miranda leaned forwards.

Beth shrugged. 'It's time to take a stand and the Third Eye is completely set up for this.'

Miranda nodded, the creases in her forehead deepening into a frown.

'Are you sizing me up?' Beth raised her eyebrows, trying to hold back a smile.

'Would you expect me not to?'

'If you have a better idea, I'd love to hear it.' Beth didn't move.

Doriel's door opened and Jonan came through, his hair ruffled, face pale. 'She seems peaceful for now, at least. Don't worry about her lack of interest, Beth, she would normally love your ideas.'

'I know.' Beth nodded. 'I'm not sure your mother agrees.'

Jonan looked from one woman to the other. 'Mother? What's going on?'

'I'm interested in Beth's plans.' Her mouth barely moved as she spoke. 'But I am concerned about how they might put us in the spotlight.'

'You want us to keep quiet? I thought you would be in favour of standing up to Amelia.'

'Dealing with Amelia *is* our job, but I don't think we should involve other people.'

'You would have us keep quiet while Amelia shouts her message to the world?' Beth took a deep breath, steadying herself. She could hear the anger in her own voice and Miranda's mouth was becoming increasingly pinched in response.

'Okay, have it your way.' Beth pulled on her coat and trainers. 'It's not my shop, and it really is none of my business how you run it. I'm going home. I'm exhausted.'

'Beth.' Jonan put a hand on her arm.

'No,' she said, stepping back. 'You incarnated together for a purpose. You tell me I'm a part of it, but you have to decide how involved you want me to be. Maybe this isn't my place after all.'

Beth picked up her bag, turned and went down the stairs.

Jonan followed her, closing the door behind them when they got into the shop. It was dark. The room was dimly lit by the street lamps outside, but Jonan didn't turn on the light. 'Please don't leave.' His voice was hoarse, and when he stepped out into the light from the street, his skin was pale.

Jonan bent his head down and touched his lips lightly to hers. She pulled him closer, breathing in the scent of him, leaning into the warmth of his body.

When he lifted his head, he held her gaze, his breathing ragged. He closed his eyes.

Beth put a hand on his chest and felt his heart beating fast. 'Don't let them get to you.'

'What about you? Should I let *you* get to me?'

'Oh yes.' Beth laughed. 'That kind of *getting to* is very different.' She reached up and cupped his cheek. 'You can accept my help or not, but you can't stop me taking on Amelia. She has already hurt my friends. I will stop her hurting anyone else, one way or another.'

'You'll go after her alone?'

'I will.'

'I'll talk to them, but I'll need time to make them understand. Doriel and Amelia have a tight bond. Your connection with Amelia was transitory. For Doriel, Amelia is family. They have connections none of us can impact.'

Beth gaped. 'There's nothing you can do to help her?'

'I hope there is, and I promise I will try my hardest. But I have no idea how this is going to play out for any of us.'

'But you'll try?'

'Of course.' He bent again and kissed her lightly on the lips.

Beth sighed, leaning into his warmth. 'Is this why you didn't turn on the lights?' she murmured into his chest.

Jonan chuckled. 'There are worse things than a bit of darkness.' He kissed her again.

9

AMELIA

'You let me down.' Amelia glared at the huge man standing in front of her, as he visibly shrank into himself.

'There was an animal shrieking outside. Some kind of monkey. I didn't want it getting into the building, so I went out. But then someone started chanting right into my head. I had to find them.'

'Interesting. The sheep going to look for the wolf. That was never going to end well. Did you find your monkey, Sheep?'

He shook his head, the flush of his pasty skin starting at his collar and then rising to the tips of his ears. He cradled one hand, the wrist blue and swollen. 'I tried. I tried so hard, but it was clever.'

'Did it ever occur to you that we don't have monkeys in this country?'

He flushed even redder. 'I know what a monkey sounds like.'

Amelia sighed and stood up.

The man flinched and edged backwards. 'By the time

Starfolk Falling

I got back down there, the woman had gone. I tried to stop them stealing the man, but they had some kind of magical power. They got into my head. The pain.' He swallowed, and then doubled over. 'I think I'm going to be sick.'

Amelia watched him struggle. Finally, he took a deep shuddering breath and straightened. She nodded. 'You say they stole him.' She suppressed a smile. 'Because he was yours to keep, of course.'

'No, Ma'am. He was always yours. Everything I did was for you. Please don't punish me.'

'Why ever not?' she asked, pushing him onto a hard, wooden chair and walking around him, trailing a finger over his shoulders. 'You failed me, Sheep. If you were truly a faithful follower you would have succeeded.'

'No, please.' He squeezed his eyes tightly shut. 'I *am* faithful. I tried so hard to succeed. I won't fail you again.'

'Open your eyes. You will not shut me out.'

'Yes, Amelia.' His eyelids flickered open. The whites were bloodshot. A tear slid from the corner of his right eye.

'Why should I believe you?'

'Set me another task so I can prove myself. Please?'

'And what if you don't?'

He flinched. 'Then I will ... have what's coming to me.' His face was so pale now he was almost blue.

Amelia looked at him for a moment, her head tilted to one side, and then she took out her phone and wrote an email.

Roland, If the Sheep fails me one more time, show no mercy. Amelia. She clicked send.

'There,' she said, and handed him her phone, the message was clear on the screen.

His hand shook as he took it and he flinched as he read her message.

'Wait for instruction. When you hear from me, obey as though your life depends on it. Go, Sheep.' She kicked off her high-heeled shoes and sank into the old-fashioned armchair in the corner of the small room. Picking up a champagne flute, she took a sip and then flicked her hand towards the door. 'And send Roland in on your way out.'

The man stood up, clasping his hands together in an attempt to hide their shaking.

'Did you hear me? Get out.' Amelia waved her hand at the door again.

He stumbled over his feet, but made it out before she had to repeat herself.

Roland walked in and slammed the door behind him. He leaned on the bureau and fixed Amelia with a hard glare. 'What was this email about?'

She shrugged. 'An incentive.'

Roland rolled his eyes. 'Was it really necessary to frighten him that much? I know it's your signature move, but if you turn every person on our side into a gibbering mess we won't have anyone capable of doing a half-decent job.

Amelia rolled her eyes. 'You can be so annoying, Rolo. Unfortunately, you may also be right in this case. The intruder that drew him up from the cellar has Miranda's energy signature all over it. Still, it'll make for a good story on social media: Soul Snatchers kidnap sick man in need of help.' She laughed and took another sip of champagne. 'Have you managed to track him down yet?'

'I've contacted all the local hospitals. No Bill Jones

anywhere. I don't like this. I can't believe you put a frail old man in that awful prison. What were you thinking?'

'Oh, lighten up, Rolo. Things really aren't that bad. We're making headway at last. We have the Triad on the run.'

'You are a part of the Triad.' Roland walked over to the small table and poured a huge shot of amber liquid into a lead crystal goblet. 'You're demonising them, but you're a third of the group you're trying to manipulate. You risk being pulled into this deception in ways you don't want.'

Amelia shrugged. 'That just adds to the fun, darling. Don't be such a worrier. Remember, I know Miranda and Doriel better than you.'

'Miranda is my mother.'

'And I've known her since we were children. I know every little chink in her armour.'

'You knew she would drop you like a hot potato when she found out about you and Jonan?'

'Well, no.' Amelia's jaw jutted outwards. 'I didn't know that, but she was being unreasonable.'

'Mother is often unreasonable. If you never expect that, you don't know her at all.'

Amelia threw her glass down on the coffee table and it shattered, spraying sharp fragments and Champagne everywhere.

Roland pressed his lips into a thin line. 'Was that really necessary?'

Amelia slid on a pair of slippers and walked towards Roland, glass crunching under her feet. 'It was. You need to remember who is in charge. You need to remember who the genius is. I am the one who picked you up off the floor when you were nothing. I was the one who took you in and gave you a home. I have done everything for you, Roland McLaney. Don't forget that.'

'As if you would ever give me the chance,' he said from between gritted teeth.

'Clean it up.' Amelia's voice was a mere whisper, but it held all the power of a slap around the face.

'No.' Roland set his jaw and glared at her.

'Clean it up.'

He closed his eyes for a moment, and then batted her hand away.

Amelia jerked back, her eyes widening. 'Roland?' she said, her whisper cracking, showing every ounce of vulnerability she didn't feel.

'Clean it up yourself.' Roland walked out, slamming the door behind him.

'Damn, damn, damn, damn!' Amelia shouted in increasing volume. Fury swamped her as she grabbed the small antique wooden table, enjoying the crash as the crystal decanter full of single malt whisky hit the door and smashed. She enjoyed every crack of ancient mahogany as she smashed the table to bits. Standing in the middle of the room, her chest heaved from exertion as she gazed around at the damage. 'I will not clear it up,' she muttered.

Walking out of the room and leaving the mess for Roland to find later was the only consolation in this whole, horrible mess.

10

JONAN

'Mother can handle herself,' Jonan said for the fifth time. 'Her mind is more focused and closed down than I would have believed possible if I hadn't seen it for myself. Amelia has no tools that can pierce that barrier. You're the one we need to focus on.' He took Doriel's hand in his and squeezed it. 'You and Beth. You're the ones she's targeted and that puts you at greater risk of being triggered.'

Doriel snorted. 'You act as though she's never targeted you.'

'Okay, you're right. I'm at risk too. But Miranda doesn't need your worry, and she doesn't want it either.'

'You have no real idea what Amelia is capable of.' Doriel put a matted bit of hair in her mouth and chewed. That lock of hair was getting shorter by the hour, but she didn't seem to have noticed. She pulled her legs up in front of her, wrapping her arms around the new loose, black trousers that swamped her legs. Her top was black too, hanging shapeless and unassuming. The bells and flowers were gone from her hair. Her henna was fading. Apart from a couple of chewed strands around her face, her hair was wrapped in a tightly packed bun at the base of her skull.

The fire was burning low in the grate and Jonan took the largest log from the basket, propping one end on the disintegrating wood to give it space to light. 'I have a lot of ideas about what she might be capable of. I'm hoping none of them are true, but I am sure of one thing: her route to controlling people is through fear. Miranda's mind is so fortressed I can't see her making any headway.'

'You're wrong.' Doriel shook her head. 'You're angry with Miranda and that gives you a blind spot. She is angry with you and Amelia and that gives *her* a huge blind spot. Amelia is probably the only person who could derail Miranda, and they both know it.'

Jonan frowned. He wanted to tell Doriel she was wrong, but her words had the uncomfortable ring of truth. 'Be that as it may, Mother will make her own decisions just as she has always done. She isn't a team player. We know that. We can't make decisions for the Third Eye based on what she wants.'

'Is this about Beth?' Doriel wrapped her arms around her middle.

'I agree with Beth. You would have too before Amelia got inside your head.'

'That doesn't mean I would have been right.'

'What did Beth come here for, Doriel?'

'To step in when the Triad began to disintegrate.'

'And what's happening now?'

'The Triad is shot to pieces. I get that. But it doesn't mean I have to agree with Beth's methods. We all make mistakes, no matter our purpose. We *have* all made mistakes, no matter our purpose. Why should I assume Beth is wise enough to avoid that?'

'I'm not asking you to assume anything.' Jonan sighed and leaned back on the soft cushions. He closed his eyes, feeling exhaustion weigh down his eyelids. 'Just think about her ideas without getting caught up in Amelia or Mother's agendas.'

'Okay,' she said, pulling herself up straight and planting her feet on the floor. 'I'm feeling pretty good right now. Tell me her ideas again.'

Jonan sighed. He got up, went through to the kitchen, and poured two cups of coffee. Handing one to Doriel, he sat next to her.

'We want to use Third Eye to counteract Amelia. We could treat people who are trapped in her Fear and offer psychic protection courses. We could even rebrand to attract a different kind of attention. We've had far too many bricks through our windows and I think the image we have at the moment plays into Amelia's games. We need to look like a safe space, even to someone in the grip of The Fear.

Doriel nodded. That does sound like a good idea. I particularly like the rebranding. I'm going for a new look myself. I've just ordered some new clothes.

'You've ordered them? Your favourite clothes shop is a couple of doors down.'

'I won't go out. I don't feel safe.'

'I understand that, but I'll come with you. I won't let anyone get to you.'

She shook her head. 'I want an alarm system. Maybe a camera?'

'Of course. I'll get something sorted tomorrow. And I won't leave you alone until you're ready. But we do need to talk about the shop. Beth is offering to help us, but we may lose her if we mess her around.' Jonan's voice cracked. He covered his eyes with his hands, searching for a composure he did not feel. 'She's our future. She's the one I came here for. I can't bear to see you and Miranda pushing her away.'

'Now, come on. You're overreacting. I didn't say anyone needed to mess Beth around or push her away.'

'If we don't work with her now, she will go after Amelia on her own. That scares me.'

'And you're planning to rebrand the shop so we're less obvious?'

Jonan rolled his eyes. 'That wasn't quite what I said. Remember when you saw Beth that morning? She'd been trapped in the theatre alone, subjected to Amelia's manipulation. Do you remember what you thought of her?'

'Okay, okay. I get it. Amelia's triggered me and I'm not myself. You and Beth can take over for a bit while I try to find myself again. But don't get any big ideas. I *am* coming back. I'm not handing the shop over to you forever.

'Of course not.' Jonan pulled her into a hug. 'We wouldn't let you off that easily.'

11

BETH

Beth shut the laptop, got up and walked through to the kitchen. She flipped on the kettle and took a pot of drinking chocolate out of the cupboard. Spooning in more chocolate than necessary, she leaned against the work surface and peered down at her fluffy socks. This was not where she had expected to be this morning. She had been so sure she would be working at Third Eye she hadn't considered any other options when she handed in her notice. She'd had a sense of destiny, of finality, as though she would be there for ever, arranging crystal workshops in her old age. But now here she was in her joggers, dressing gown and fluffy socks, making hot chocolate for one and trying to figure out how to go after Amelia alone.

The doorbell rang.

'Damn,' Beth muttered. She poured water on the chocolate, picked up the mug and ducked through to her bedroom, closing the door tightly behind her. She had no intention of dealing with Laura's crowd right now.

Beth heard Laura open the door, and then a familiar male voice.

She looked down at her joggers in horror.

'Beth?' Jonan's voice sounded oddly formal.

'Yes?' she said, not inviting him in. She threw her dressing gown on the bed, and opened her wardrobe door, looking for something she could change into in the seconds before the door opened.

'Can I speak to you?'

Beth sighed. Shutting the door to the cupboard, she straightened her top and pulled off her fluffy socks. 'Come in,' she said, wincing at the reluctance in her own voice.

Jonan pushed the door open a crack and peered through. 'Is everything okay? You sound strange.'

'If you'd told me you were coming, I would have changed.' She sat down on the bed.

Jonan smiled and the tension in his shoulders eased. 'You don't need to change for me. You look amazing in everything. And I have good news.' Jonan sat next to her, taking her hand in both of his. 'Doriel is giving you her share of the decision making for now. She's happy for us to develop Third Eye as we see fit. We're going to go for it, Beth. Will you still do this with me?'

Beth gaped. 'Are you serious? What about your mother?'

'It's not her shop. She doesn't make the decisions any more than Amelia does.'

'But she's just come back into your life. I don't want to get in the middle of that. You're angry enough with her already.'

'Beth, you have been in the middle of *everything* for my entire life. Have you not realised that yet?'

His eyes were an intense purple and his ears had the clearest points she had ever seen. Beth swallowed. She squeezed his hand. 'Is this real?'

Jonan smiled. 'It's real.'

'Will your mum and Doriel hate me for it?'

'Hate you for what?'

'Pushing you into this.'

Jonan frowned. 'I'm not agreeing to this because you suggested it. I will go ahead whether you do it with me or not, simply because it's the right thing for the business. But I will be a lot happier if you are the one walking beside me.'

'You'll do it anyway?'

Jonan nodded and handed her an envelope.

Beth took it, slit open the top and pulled out an A4 document. It was a job contract. She looked up at him. His eyebrows were pulled together, his skin pale. 'Are you nervous?'

'Of course. I know that's not the kind of money you could make elsewhere, but I'm offering you a share of the business. That means a percentage of profits too, and a long-term investment. We need you more than you need us.'

Beth shrugged. 'I don't know about that. I'm invested. I wasn't sure how to walk away.'

'Is that a yes?' Jonan raised his eyebrows.

'Yes!' She laughed.

His eyes turned a deeper purple.

Reaching up one hand, she traced the top of his ear. She had known it would feel normal, but she wished she could feel the points that rose clearly above the softness of his skin. 'I can't help feeling this is going to be an adventure with lots of unexpected turns.'

Jonan smiled. 'That sounds like a pretty good description of life.'

Beth let her hand drop. 'Before I sign your contract, you should know I'm not a branding expert. I may not be what you need.'

'You are what I need.' He leaned back on the wall behind the bed. 'And your events experience will be good too. But I thought we could hire someone specifically for branding.'

'Hire another person? Do we have the money for that?'

Jonan shrugged. 'I have a bit put away. It would be enough for a short-term contract to help us revamp. I think it will be worth it as long as we find the right person.'

Beth stood up and walked over to the window. 'Do you have a mailing list? I wonder if one of your customers has the right skills. At least we'd know they weren't planted by Amelia.'

'We have a good list. We could get something out today.'

'Let me get dressed.' Beth threw open the wardrobe and pulled out a pair of skinny jeans and an oversized jumper. 'Then we can head to the shop.'

'Can I get a drink?' Jonan said, opening the door a crack.

Beth nodded, relieved to have the space to change. So much had happened since their night together and she had no idea where they stood now, or how to move forward in any normal way. A joint destiny sounded so romantic in stories, but the reality was more than daunting. How did they deal with the normal relationship hurdles when they seemed to have lost any sense of choice?

Jonan was leaning on the work surface, an empty glass in his hand, when she went into the kitchen. 'Shall we go?'

Starfolk Falling

She smiled, trying to keep the atmosphere light. The past twenty-four hours had destabilised their new relationship and she felt unaccountably awkward.

'After you,' he said, straightening up.

It was bright and blustery outside. The chill wind was swirling the dirty-orange leaves in circles. A squirrel looked at them as they stepped out the door, and then raced across the lawn and ran up the tree.

'Are we really going to do this?' Beth zipped up her gilet and wrapped her arms around her middle. 'I don't want to get part way through and have the whole project cut because Doriel loses her nerve, or Miranda disapproves.'

'Did something happen with my mother? You seem very worried about what she might think.'

'She doesn't like my ideas.'

Jonan stopped walking and turned to face Beth. 'Of course she doesn't like your ideas. You want to push Third Eye out into the world, to bring in attention and openly counteract Amelia. Mother has spent the past ten or so years in seclusion. She's barely had private conversations. The concept of being visible terrifies her.'

'What does that mean for us?' Beth swallowed.

Jonan grinned. 'Absolutely nothing.

12

BETH

'BETH, THERE'S A WOMAN HERE TO SEE YOU,' MIRANDA called up the stairs.

'Wow, that was fast.' Beth stood up. 'I can't believe we invited her to interview half an hour ago.'

'I'm glad I kept those CVs,' Jonan said. 'I'd forgotten I even had this one. I had no idea I was going to need a brand specialist when she left it, but for some reason I couldn't bear to throw it away. Maybe this is why.'

'I wonder if she really is the woman from my vision?'

A thrill rushed through Beth as she saw the image again in her mind's eye. The woman had a fine-boned face, huge electric-blue eyes, and a bright pink bob which was tucked behind her ear on one side. She smiled as her face faded. Beth had been so sure this woman was the one, but now her prediction was being put to the test, she wasn't so sure.

'Use my reading room.' Doriel nodded towards the stairs. 'Put her in amongst all my stuff and see how she reacts. That'll give you a sense of how sympathetic she really is.'

'I thought you knew her from the shop?' Jonan frowned. 'Did she not seem supportive?'

'She did, and her daughter is a delight. I'll enjoy sorting crystals with her while you interview Layla. But I don't know them well. We can't be too careful.'

'Is this you talking, or The Fear?' Beth asked. 'It doesn't sound like the Doriel I know.'

'It's the Doriel you know now,' she said, enunciating over clearly.

Beth held up her hands. 'Of course, I'm sorry. And we will be very careful. Trust us.'

Doriel nodded and let out a breath, her body relaxing. 'Come on. I'm looking forward to sorting crystals with my little friend.'

At the bottom of the stairs, Beth stilled, forcing herself to breath normally despite the thumping of her heart. The woman standing behind the counter looked exactly like the one in her vision. Her smooth pink bob was startling, but captivating, and tucked behind her right ear. Her lipstick matched it, a shade lighter, but the rest of her make-up was subtle and understated. She wore a black pencil skirt, a tight black roll-neck jumper, and knee-high boots that tapered to points at the toes.

'You must be Layla,' Jonan said, stepping forwards with an easy smile. He reached out his hand and shook hers. 'This is Beth, and I believe you already know my aunt.'

Layla's eyes lit up as Doriel walked through the door, and then her smile faltered. 'Is everything okay?'

Doriel arranged her face into a semblance of brightness and shoved the chewed strands of hair behind her ears. 'Of course.' She walked round the desk. 'Hello, Abi darling. How are you? How are your crystals?'

Beth started. She hadn't looked beyond Layla, but behind her stood a little girl, leaning into her mother's arm. Her hair was a glossy dark brown and fell in impossible ringlets down her back. Her huge eyes were a bright blue. She was wearing a red, woollen dress with a layered skirt, and she fiddled with one of the layers, apparently unaware of the movement.

'My crystals are happy, Aunty Doriel,' she said, her big eyes mournful. 'I talk to them every day. I put them on the windowsill when it's full moon and they reward me by looking after me on the other days. Do you have any new ones for me to see?'

'Abi,' Layla whispered, flushing almost as pink as her hair. 'You can't call her aunty. You barely know her. She might not like it.'

'Do you not like it?' Abi asked, her eyes widening and her eyebrows arcing upwards. 'I didn't mean to make you sad. Is that's what's wrong with your colour?'

'My colour?' Doriel frowned, tilting her head to one side.

'The colour around you.'

'Abi,' Layla breathed. She looked up at Doriel. 'I'm *so* sorry.'

'No, no, please don't apologise,' Doriel said. 'Your daughter sees more than most adults. But no, Abi darling, you have not upset me and I would love you to call me Aunty Doriel. I need to sort that big bucket of crystals into types. Would you help me?'

'Ooh, yes please.' Abi clapped her hands then slid her palm into Doriel's and they settled into the corner of the shop.

'I assume you don't need me anymore?' Miranda raised one eyebrow.

'Actually, we are going upstairs to speak to Layla, and Doriel is with Abi. Please could you stay and mind the shop?' Jonan smiled, but didn't wait for an answer.

'I've never been up here before,' Layla said as they led her up to Doriel's reading room. 'It's beautiful. It's just so old.'

'It's certainly that,' Jonan said, swinging the door open wide and ushering her in.

'Ooh,' Layla's eyes widened as she gazed around the room. 'Can I touch?'

'Of course.' Jonan nodded, and then settled down in one of the chairs.

Layla walked slowly around the room, trailing a finger over the Buddha and holding a hand a centimetre above a huge crystal, her face lighting up. She paused at the bookcase. 'So many tarot cards,' she murmured, running her hand along the decks as though she needed to touch everything.

'You like this stuff?' Beth asked.

Layla shrugged. 'I live for it. I've wanted to work here ever since I first visited the shop.' She waved at the empty chair.

'Of course,' Beth said.

'I actually have another job waiting for me. I was just about to accept the offer when you got in touch.'

Beth let out her breath in a rush. She looked over at Jonan.

He held her gaze and nodded.

'Is that the only thing that makes you want this job?' Jonan smiled. 'Working around the crystals and tarot cards?'

'No. I can do this. I've worked in branding a long time and I have an insight into this industry that most people would lack. I know your audience. I am your audience. And I understand what our people are facing right now. I know what this kind of shop could be with the right direction. I can *feel* what this can be and I want the opportunity to manifest that.'

'I'm glad you understand what we're facing,' Beth said. 'Because Amelia is targeting us and things could get messy, maybe even dangerous. I know that could be a dealbreaker for you, with Abi to look after.'

'I'm not afraid of Amelia.' Layla tilted her chin up. 'I see what she's doing and I know she wants us to be scared. But she doesn't have teeth. There's nothing she can actually do to us.'

'Don't underestimate her.' Jonan frowned. 'She has already hurt people close to us.'

'I am a match for her and I know how to look after my daughter. I really want this job.'

'And the money?' Jonan tilted his head to one side. 'I expect you could make a lot more elsewhere.'

Layla sighed. 'I expect I could, but a high wage comes with big expectations. I'm hoping you might be sympathetic to my parenting responsibilities. I'm a single Mum. I need a job where I can bring my daughter into work sometimes, maybe work from home if she's ill or on holiday. She's the most wonderful child, but she's different. She doesn't fit expectations and that can be tough. But she's a good girl. She would never be disruptive in the shop. She loves it here as much as I do, and she absolutely adores Doriel.' Layla spoke in a rush and then paused, breathing heavily. 'Of course, I do understand you may want someone who's loyalties won't be split, someone fresher.'

'We have a very strong respect for family,' Jonan said, his voice firm. 'And your daughter is a dream. We would be happy to have her in the shop as often as needed. Does she always see auras? She read Doriel pretty well.'

Layla nodded. 'That's partly why she struggles to fit in at school. They don't like it when she talks about it.'

'I can imagine.' Beth nodded. 'I'm sorry, would you mind if we just took a minute?'

'Of course. I'll poke around a bit if that's okay?'

'Help yourself.' Jonan shoved his chair back, grabbed a box from one of the shelves and held the door open for Beth.

'What do you think?' she said, as soon as the door closed behind them.

Jonan put a hand on her elbow and led her to a small table away from the door. He put down the box, opened it, and drew out a tarot deck. It was *The Starfolk Tarot*. He shuffled through the deck and pulled out a card. 'I thought so.' He handed it to Beth. 'Your intuition was spot on.'

Beth gasped. The picture showed a woman standing with one foot in a lake, her hair cut into a pink bob as she poured pink water from a large jug. 'The Star. Layla is in the deck too. How can that be?'

Jonan shook his head. 'I have no idea, but it seems pretty clear that she's part of our picture one way or another.'

'So, we go for it?'

Jonan grinned. 'We go for it.'

Beth opened the door, smiling when she saw Layla admiring the large, amethyst cathedral in the corner.

Layla sighed. 'I could stay in here forever.'

'Well, maybe you can.' Beth grinned. 'If you'd still like the job, it's yours, subject to references, of course.'

'It is?' Layla grinned. 'I can start any time from tomorrow if you want me? If we're done, I'd better go and rescue Doriel from Abi. Goodness knows what she's saying to her now.' She grimaced.

Jonan laughed. 'Doriel looked pretty happy with her lot. I wouldn't worry.'

Downstairs, Doriel was sitting cross legged on the floor, her arms elbow deep in a huge basket of crystals. Many more stones were arranged around her in colourful piles. Her face was flushed and for the first time since the abduction, she looked something like herself.

Abi was arranging the piles on the floor into pretty patterns, her face lit with smiles, her hair curling around her face. Her eyes lit up when she saw Layla. 'Mummy!' she said, running over and wrapping her arms around her. 'Did you do well?' She looked up, her face shining.

Layla flushed.

'She did very well.' Jonan grinned. 'What about Doriel? How did she do?'

'Doriel is an excellent lady.' Abi said, her face earnest. 'She understands all the stuff most people don't see. I like being with Doriel. She makes me feel normal. Can I come here instead of school please, Mummy?'

Layla laughed. 'I wish I could say yes, pumpkin. But school is important. School teaches you all the things you need to know in order to live in the normal world. I can teach you the other things when you're home with me.'

'And Aunty Doriel? Can she teach me too?'

'Oh, darling.' Layla frowned, her cheeks colouring.

Starfolk Falling

'You try and stop me.' Doriel rose from the floor in a single fluid movement. You've done me more good today than the rest of them put together. You are welcome to come and see me anytime and I'll teach you about crystals and cards. But you need to earn that time by going to school and learning all the normal-world stuff. Can you do that for me, Poppet?'

'Of course, Aunty Doriel. Thank you.' Abi said, giving a little curtsey.

Layla laughed. 'Come on, Pumpkin, we've earned a treat. Shall we go for a hot chocolate?'

Abi clapped and jumped up and down on the spot.

'Thank you, Doriel,' Layla said, clasping the older woman's hands. You're a gem. Is there anything I can do for you in return?'

'Just bring your girl in more often.' Doriel smiled, but there was a tightness around her eyes. 'She helps me remember about innocence and possibilities.'

Layla nodded. 'We may be around here a lot more soon. Take care of yourself.'

Doriel reached out and pulled her into a hug. 'You too. Don't believe anything anyone tells you about that girl. Their inability to understand reflects on them, not her. With the right tribe she will make life glorious.'

Layla broke into a wide smile. 'I knew I liked you,' she said and kissed Doriel on the cheek. 'Come on, Abi.'

13

AMELIA

AMELIA WAS STILL FURIOUS.

The ballroom was empty. The mess from the party had long since been cleared away, but the energy had been ruined.

The monks had remained solidly upstairs, no matter how hard Amelia tried to lure them back down.

'That would-be Oracle has wrecked my room,' she muttered. 'She has the most nightmarish instinct for causing mayhem.'

'I guess that instinct must run in the group, eh?' Roland laughed, but there was no joy in the sound. 'You're peas in a pod, you two. Doriel is the one you should be focusing on. She's different. She's the one you've underestimated.'

'Huh, I think I know more about Doriel than you do.' She rolled her eyes, walked over to the bar and poured some extortionate whisky into a cut glass tumbler. Knocking it back, she peered around the room, eyes narrowed. 'We have to do something about this space. It's messing with my head, and my focus. I have to get your mother out of my house.'

Starfolk Falling

'My mother is not in your house.' Roland's voice was sharp. 'She's in your head and she will stay there until you sort yourself out. I know the setback at the ball was a blow. I know you're angry you didn't see it coming, but you still made huge strides forward. If you don't act on Amelia's Haven now, you will lose all that progress.'

'You're right.' She nodded, compressing her lips. 'I *will* focus.'

Roland let out a sigh.

'The thing is,' she continued, her eyes narrowed and distant, 'something has shifted with Doriel and Jonan. Beth too. Something major has changed. They're pleased with themselves, that much is leaking through their barriers, but I can't read more. It's maddening.'

'Stop trying to read them.' Roland slammed the pile of paper down on the bar. 'If you want to know what they're up to, go to the shop and find out. I'm sick of this. You're behaving like a stroppy child in the school playground. Where is the strong, independent woman I fell in love with? What have you become?'

'Oh, stop it.' Amelia glared at him, and then stalked forwards on silent feet. 'I can't keep them guessing if I pop in for a chat. You've thrown your weight around enough today. Quit your bitching and tell me how far *you're* getting with Amelia's Haven.'

Roland sighed, pulled a chair over and sat on it back to front. 'Look at this.' He picked up a large pile of paper from the side of the bar and flicked through the pages. 'You see all these names? These people have signed up to join Amelia's Haven. They have asked for your help and we have a duty to protect them from whatever these Soul Snatchers turn out to be. I have several drafts of a letter from you. Here.' He handed her several pieces of paper. 'They need to hear from you, Amelia. You are needed and you have so much to offer. We have so much to offer.'

'Great work.' Amelia's eyes sparkled as she took the drafts, sat down and flicked through them. 'No,' she said, crumpling one up into a ball and dropping it by her feet. Her forehead creased into a frown as she read the next one. 'Nope, not that one either. Who wrote this rubbish?'

Roland sighed. 'I did. But in the absence of any information about what you actually want to say, these are pure guesswork.'

'Not this one either.' Amelia screwed up the last bit of paper. 'You have no style, Rolo, that's your problem. You're all business. Your words are neither beautiful nor meaningful. You have no idea how to reach into people's hearts and squeeze. We need to show each person how much they need us. We need to show them there is more to any of this than they comprehend. We need to show them that Amelia's Haven is their only protection.'

'Well, you know what to do.' Roland shrugged and stood up. 'If you're so clever and eloquent, write the thing yourself. But do it tonight so we can send it out tomorrow. I won't work like this. This obsession with Miranda is pushing you into a vulnerable place and I'm not convinced you're ready to live there.'

Amelia got up, pulling herself to her full height. 'I am not vulnerable,' she hissed. 'Don't ever talk to me like that again.'

Roland shrugged. 'There's nothing wrong with being vulnerable. We've all been there. But launching Amelia's Haven would be a push with both of us at our strongest.

Unless you can convince me you're up to it, I'm out. There's just too much riding on it.'

'Oh, get out.' Amelia grabbed one high-heeled shoe from under the table and threw it at him.

Roland ducked. It flew over his head, right where his face had been the moment before.

He straightened up. His face was pale, but his jaw jutted out and his fists were clenched at his sides. His eyes were a bright purple, his ears elongated into sharp points. Roland shook his head, turned around and walked out of the room, slamming the door behind him.

14

DORIEL

Doriel looked in the mirror as she brushed her hair. It was like watching an entirely different person. The luscious red had faded to a washed-out brown, shot through with grey. How had that happened so fast? She should have had another week of life in it before she had to reapply the henna. Her hair had been leached of life along with her spirit. She ran her finger over the creases that had deepened around her eyes and mouth. She had always been proud to appear ageless. That spring seemed to have run dry.

She sighed and sat on the bed. Those moments with Abi had made her blood flow and the energy fizz through her fingertips. She had begun to wonder whether that would ever happen again. There was something about that girl, something that made her special. Layla too, but that was quite different.

Doriel lay on the bed, closing her eyes as her head sank into the pillow. She stretched her legs out, pointing her toes and feeling the muscles hit their limit and release. She had waited, not so patiently, to return to this space. Now she was here, the darkness pushed at the edges of her mind, clouding her ability to see and hear. She felt the flutter begin just below her ribs, and then it travelled down her legs, leaving them weak and ungrounded. She sighed. She had been hoping to avoid this after her time with Abi, but it seemed the benefit only held when they were together. What had Abi brought to her that she had lost? What was it that had been locked away when she was in that cell?

She allowed herself to sink into the silence, placing herself in the middle of a circle and turning slowly, watching the darkness approach. What was it? Was it from her childhood? No, that wasn't right. From Amelia's latest nonsense? No, that wasn't it either. It was the Triad. Awareness flared and the darkness turned into iridescent, black flames that snaked slowly towards her.

She had lost everything apart from Jonan when the Triad fell apart. Now Amelia was attacking the man she had claimed to love. Fury blazed in Doriel's chest, followed by a deep rendering. Her heart opened and grief poured out, dark and sludgy, surrounded by deep, sparkling flames. She had lost her sisters, lost those she incarnated with, and with them, she had lost her purpose and destiny.

The flames flared, engulfing her body in a fire that burned her anger, her grief and her sense of who she had become. Without that purpose, what was left? What was she now? By storming into seclusion Miranda had not only left her alone, she had taken her place as the Oracle. Doriel had adapted, flowed like water around the rocks and she had found a motherly love for Jonan she had never expected. That was a joy and a new side to her, but what did it make her?

Doriel is an excellent lady, the childish voice spoke into her mind with surprising resonance. *She understands all the stuff most people don't see. I like being with Doriel. She makes me feel normal.*

Was that her role? To help the next generation understand their gifts? She hadn't seen Layla or Abi's eyes or ears change, but she had no doubt she would. She recognised these women at her core and felt an odd possessiveness that made the flames burn brighter.

The image changed. Now Abi was growing older. She held something in her hand: a cup. No, not just a cup, she also had a sword, a wand and something small. Of course, it was a coin. The four suits of the Minor Arcana in Tarot. She threw them into the air, clapped her hands, and then drew her palms apart. Between them, was the most beautiful landscape, fields, flowers, a rainbow. *You have everything you need to manifest*, Doriel thought. *The Magician.*

Abi smiled and then faded away, leaving her landscape behind. The image grew until it engulfed Doriel. Now she was walking through the field towards the end of the rainbow. She came to a lake. A woman stood on the bank with one foot in the water, a large jug in the opposite hand. She poured water from the jug, and the liquid came out bright pink to match her vibrant hair. *The Star*, Doriel thought. *I knew I recognised her from somewhere.* The woman looked up at her, smiled and then was gone.

I will not let you dim their spark, Amelia. Doriel thought the words with purpose, and then cloaked them so Amelia would merely feel their discomfort, not their meaning. She watched herself wrap them in cotton wool, before sending them on light waves to the woman she had once called sister.

An image of Amelia flashed into her mind. She looked

pale, tortured and scruffy in a way Doriel had never seen her. Her hair was pulled out of its style as though she had been worrying at it. She saw a huge ballroom, old but newly refurbished. There was a pile of paper on the glossy wooden bar and the top sheet was lined with columns of names under the heading: 'Amelia's Haven'.

You cannot offer a Haven to anybody. She sent the words to swirl around Amelia like a breeze, making her shiver as she scribbled frantically in a notebook. *You have nothing but fear to offer and, unless you change path, nothing but fear to receive.*

Get out of my head you old hag. The words thundered through Doriel's body. *Your relevance is over. You allowed yourself to be broken and you will never mend.*

Doriel felt a pain in her chest as Amelia hit her trigger, felt the other woman laugh, and then jerked upright, trying to drag air into her lungs.

Even as she shook, a new resolve settled into her chest. No, she wouldn't mend. She would reform. She would bring up everything old and transform it into something so new Amelia would never see it coming. She would flow around the obstacles like water, reaching for the next level with every turn. She would transcend and, this time, her sisters would have no say in what she became.

15

JONAN

Jonan banged on Doriel's bedroom door. He tried to keep his voice calm, but he could feel her panic clawing at his throat, looking for a stranglehold. Her voice looped in his mind, listing worst case scenarios with increasing force. 'Doriel, what's going on?'

The door swung open. Doriel looked pale but serene. 'Nothing's going on. I don't know what you're talking about.'

'Cut it out,' Jonan snapped. Her fear was pounding through his blood, setting his nerves on edge and his mind racing. 'Tell me what happened.'

Doriel sighed. 'Maybe I can't hide it, but I'm figuring things out at the moment and I'm not going to go into it all with you right now. If you can't handle being around me, get some fresh air. Go out for dinner with Beth or something.'

Jonan sighed. 'Are you sure?'

'Positive. I haven't been on my own since the abduction. I need space. I will be fine.'

Jonan looked at her, eyes narrowed. Her aura was off, but she was looking better than she had for a while. Whatever she was doing was obviously working. 'Beth and I were thinking of going out but Mum's scarpered.'

Doriel shrugged. 'It'll give us a chance to try out that sparkling new security system you bought. Plus, we have neighbours and there are plenty of people on the street outside. We're in the middle of town. It's hardly isolated. Anyway, I wasn't alone when they took me. A fat lot of good company did me then.'

There were footsteps on the stairs. Beth opened the door, flushed and tousled by the wind. She smelled of fresh air. 'There's a band playing outside. Would you like to go and see?' She looked from one to the other of them, eyebrows raised, eyes bright.

'Off you go,' Doriel said, forcing her face into a smile. Her hands were shaking, but she clasped them tightly together.

Jonan frowned.

Doriel kicked her bedroom door shut. 'Go!' she shouted through the thick, wooden panel. 'Give me space.'

'Come on,' Beth said, taking Jonan's hand. 'This is the first time since the kidnapping that Doriel has asked for time alone. It's important to respond to that. And the security system means you're all but in the building. You'll get an alert if there's a problem, and you can check out the cameras any time.' She tugged at Jonan's hand. 'It's been a long day, but we've had one serious win in hiring Layla. Let's celebrate. All our problems will still be here in the morning.'

Jonan nodded and allowed Beth to pull him towards the

stairs. He grabbed his coat from the banister before shutting the door to the flat behind him.

On the other side of the path was a sandwich board advertising Amelia's Haven.

'She did that on purpose,' Jonan said from between gritted teeth. 'Why else would she put it right outside the shop other than to annoy me?'

'Probably.' Beth took his hands in hers. 'But that doesn't mean we have to let it get to us. We know what she's like, and somehow we have to try to have a life even when she's messing with it. Let's just ignore her.'

The air was icy but the sky was clear and stars blinked down at the bustling town. It was a Friday night and people were out in force, eating, drinking and celebrating with friends. A brass band played just outside the clock tower. Beth stopped to listen. Jonan wrapped an arm around her waist and pulled her close.

'They're good, aren't they?'

She smiled and looked up at him. 'This feels so normal, like a date anyone might go on.'

Jonan raised one eyebrow. 'Anyone? Are you suggesting I'm interchangeable?'

Beth laughed. 'No, but every time we've been out so far, something has happened to spoil it. Right now, in this moment, it feels like we're the kind of couple who might have a fun evening out with no drama.'

Jonan stroked her cheek. 'Long may that feeling last. I hope to have many uneventful dates with you, Ms Meyer. Shall we go inside?' He tilted his head in the direction of the pub next to them. 'We could even sign up for Amelia's Haven.' He rolled his eyes. There was another sandwich board, this time right outside the pub. It had a badge on the top right-hand corner with the words 'Sign up here!' in bold.

The place was heaving, and Jonan pushed through the crowds to reach the bar. He leaned on the damp wood, hoping to catch the barman's eye. Beth slipped in beside him. 'I haven't seen a pub this busy in a long time.'

Jonan frowned, trying to see through the crowd, which was focused in one corner, but spilled, noisily, across the entire pub. He could see a display stand protruding high above the sea of heads.

'I'll go and look while you order. Gin and tonic, please,' Beth said, and then disappeared into the crowd.

Jonan ordered fast, and then turned back to the room, trying to see Beth. For a moment, the crowds parted. There was a table in front of a large display stand covered with sheets of white paper and biros. Roland sat next to it in fitted dark-blue jeans and a black turtleneck looking up at Beth, who was talking furiously to him. 'Thanks,' Jonan muttered, waving his credit card in front of the contactless machine. Picking up the drinks, he threaded his way through the crowd. The space had filled up again now and several people bumped into his arms, spilling the drinks over his shoes.

He handed Beth the gin and tonic, and then turned to his brother. 'What are you doing here?'

'Inviting people to sign up for Amelia's Haven. You should join.' He stood up. They were eye to eye now, perfectly matched. 'We can give you protection against the Soul Snatchers and you would have access to our vetted and approved list of organisations as well as being able to sign up for courses and events. It's important to know who you're trusting, don't you think?'

'But then you'd have a Soul Snatcher in your midst,' Jonan murmured. 'Or at least, that's what Amelia would have everyone believe.'

Roland smirked. 'I walked past your shop earlier. I expected something more cutting-edge from you.'

Jonan wanted to punch him, but he forced himself to take a deep breath and smile. 'You should come in some time. Doriel would love to see you.'

'But you wouldn't?' Roland gave a hard laugh and held up one hand. I know why *I'm* angry with *you*, but I can't for the life of me figure out why *you're* angry with *me*.'

'Roland, I asked you to come with me.'

'Too little, too late. You left me and didn't come back for two whole weeks.'

'I left you? I was your big brother. I was always supposed to leave you. It's Mother who should have stayed.'

'Didn't I mention that I'm angry with her too?'

Jonan rolled his eyes. 'I was young and hurting when I left, and I made a mistake. But you are a grown man, and you are intentionally causing widespread panic in order to increase Amelia's power base. You are responsible for your actions, Roland, whatever childhood you may have had.'

'None of us has had it easy.' Beth put a hand on Roland's arm. 'But we still have to choose whether we're going to treat people with kindness, or create more fear.'

Roland grinned. 'You have Amelia pegged as quite the villain, don't you? What do you think she's going to do? Turn into a vampire and start sucking everyone dry? Or perhaps we're in a psychological thriller? Maybe she's a stalker who is going to start sneaking into your bedroom and leaving dead animals behind? Or she'll just abduct Beth, coax you out with ransom money, and then force you to marry her to stop me throwing Beth over a cliff? Have I missed any options?'

'You can joke as much as you like, Roland,' Jonan said. The fact is, Amelia has already had our home broken into twice, had two people abducted, intentionally locked Beth alone in an abandoned theatre, and tried to frame me by corrupting the police. And that's only the stuff I'm aware of.'

'Jonan, wait.' Roland sighed. 'I don't see what you see. Amelia is offering people protection and I have a duty to her and to the people we can help. You clearly think she's up to something sinister, but you don't see Amelia the way I do.'

Beth knocked her gin and tonic back, and then slid her hand into Jonan's. 'You keep telling yourself that. I'm ready. Let's go.'

'Have a good evening, brother,' Roland called after them, raising his glass.

16

BETH

THE PAVEMENTS WERE SLIPPERY AND SHONE IN THE GLOW OF the street lights, but the sky was black, clear and studded with stars. The brass ensemble had gone and a local band was setting up on the stage in front of the old clock tower.

'How can *your* brother be that infuriating?' Beth said, wandering over to the benches that faced the tower and sitting down. She wrapped her arms around her middle, trying to keep in as much warmth as possible, but it was nice to be outside in the fresh air.

'You only think that because he's working for the other side.' Jonan sat next to her.

One of the men on stage adjusted the microphone. 'I'm sorry, guys, we'll be up and running in a few moments.' He flashed a dazzling smile at the gathering crowd and a group of teenage girls to Beth's left giggled. Another man in shorts and a tank top with an enormous tiger tattooed on his bicep, crouched down in front of the PA, adjusting buttons and dials.

Beth's phone rang. She pulled it from her pocket and swiped her finger over the screen. 'Yes, this is Beth.'

'It's the hospital, Ms Meyer. I'm sorry to inform you that your friend isn't in a good way. If you want to say goodbye, I suggest you come now.'

'Oh God, no.' Beth's body turned to ice. The world retreated as she stood in the dark, damp street, listening to the woman on the other end of the phone breathe. She could hear her own heartbeat sounding in her head, branding her alive, alive while Bill was dying.

'Of course,' she croaked. 'I'll be there as soon as I can.' She hung up. 'We have to go to the hospital. Bill's not going to make it.'

Jonan froze for a moment. He took a deep breath and then nodded his head. 'I can't drive. I've been drinking. The taxi rank is this way.'

The journey went by in a blur. By the time they pulled into the hospital carpark, Beth's heart was racing and her mind was whirring. Had Amelia done something to Bill? Did she have plants at the hospital as well as the police station? Who could they trust?

The driver dropped them outside the building. Beth climbed out of the car and shivered.

Jonan slid his hand into hers. 'You can do this. You can make sure he doesn't die alone.'

Beth swallowed. 'I wanted to do so much more.'

They rang the bell to get into the ward, but nobody answered. They rang again. Beth peered through the window in the door, and saw two nurses behind the desk, but neither of them looked her way. Then they simultaneously rushed around the desk and into the ward.

Beth banged on the door. 'Let me in, please, I'm here for Bill,' she shouted through the door. Nothing.

Jonan put his arm around her waist. 'Beth, I think he's going. I can feel him reaching out to me.'

'No!' She pushed him away and started hammering on the door again. 'Bill!'

'Can I help you?' a voice said from behind her.

Beth turned. A woman in scrubs was watching her, face blank. 'Oh, thank God. I need to get in there. My friend is dying and I was called to say goodbye.'

'Let me through and I'll find out what's happening.'

The woman disappeared into the ward. A few moments later one of the nurses came out and led Beth and Jonan into a side room. She motioned for them to sit down.

'But I need to see Bill,' Beth said.

'I'm sorry.' The woman sat on one of the chairs and gestured again to the other two. Jonan sat down and took Beth's hand. She held his gaze for a moment. His eyes were a deep indigo and so full of sadness that she wanted to cry. She sat down.

'I'm afraid your friend just passed away.'

'No!' Beth clapped a hand over her mouth, trying to hold in the sob. 'I was here. You wouldn't let me in.'

'I'm sorry. We didn't know there was anyone outside. The bell must be malfunctioning.'

Beth leaned her elbows on her thighs and dropped her head into her hands. 'So he died alone.'

'I was with him. It was very peaceful and he was comfortable.'

'That's not the same,' she said, not looking up.

'I know. But I have become very fond of him over the past few days. I sat with him and held his hand at the end. He talked about you every day. You clearly meant a lot to him.'

'Do you know why he died? Was it natural, or could anyone have got to him?'

The nurse frowned. 'What makes you say that?'

'You know he was abducted? That's why he was in here.'

'I didn't see him have any visitors. I'm sorry.'

The woman's eyes were so full of pity Beth wanted to scream, but she forced her face into an approximation of a smile. 'Please? I need to find out what happened to him.'

'He was just too ill when you brought him in. I'm sorry. I wish there was more I could tell you. But whatever happened to him was too much for his body to cope with.'

Jonan took Beth's hand and squeezed gently.

'Of course,' she said, her voice hoarse. 'I'm sorry. I just thought that maybe there was more.'

'Take care of yourself and stay here for as long as you like.' She stood up and walked to the door. She looked over her shoulder for a moment, and then was gone.

Jonan put an arm around Beth's shoulders, lending warmth to her frozen body. She knew she was stiff and unyielding, but couldn't make herself soften, couldn't stop the ice that crept like fingers through her veins.

'I don't know what to do.' She squeezed her eyes tightly shut, feeling the tears creep from between her sodden lashes. 'I couldn't save him. I should have been able to save him.'

'You did save him.' Jonan wiped a tear from her cheek. 'He was alone before you walked into his hotel.'

Beth turned to look at him. She could feel her forehead crease, could see his face so open, his eyes a deep purple as he gazed at her.

Beth got up and walked out of the door and down the corridor. 'I *should* have been able to do more,' she said, not caring whether anyone heard. She could hear Jonan's footsteps behind her and spun around. 'Amelia killed him,' she yelled into the echoing space.

'Oh, Beth.' Jonan's voice was bleak.

Beth spun around. Jonan stood in the harsh light of the hospital corridor, his eyes dark purple, his ears tapering into points. She could feel his desolation. To his left was a cork noticeboard covered with a large, white poster. 'Amelia's Haven' was branded across the space in enormous lettering.

'Bill would have been alive if I hadn't dragged him into this whole sorry mess. She killed him, Jonan.' A tear slid down her cheek. She didn't bother to brush it away, but held her breath, trying to keep control of her body, to stop the shaking.

Jonan walked towards her and held out his arms. 'It's okay to grieve. You're safe with me.'

She went into his arms, allowing his warmth to thaw the ice, allowing him to hold her while the shuddering grief tore through her, leaving her broken and open. She would have fallen, but he held her up, took her weight while she gave her pain the toll it demanded.

'Let me get you home,' he said at last, cutting through her grief. He stroked damp hair from her face and smiled.

Beth nodded.

'Come on.' Jonan put his arm around her and tucked her into the warmth of his body. 'There's a taxi rank this way.'

'She killed him,' Beth said, climbing into the back of a black cab. She fastened her seatbelt, glad that the screen gave them a little privacy. She leaned closer to Jonan. 'Even if she didn't pull a trigger or poison him, even if she didn't go anywhere near him, it's still her fault. She had him locked up and denied him medical care until he was too ill to survive.'

'I agree. I don't think the police will see it that way though.'

'No,' Beth said from between gritted teeth. 'It's clear whose pocket they're in.'

'We need to focus on what *we* can do, not on what Amelia does,' Jonan said, as the car manoeuvred out of the carpark. 'If she keeps on like this, she'll paint herself into a corner. Remember, we have a plan. Layla will be with us soon, and we can really start to move things forward. Have you told your parents about any of this?'

Beth shifted in her seat. 'My parents? What do they have to do with anything? I don't really talk to them and when I do we stick to small talk.'

Jonan said nothing. He looked straight ahead, his large eyes purple, high cheekbones throwing shadows over his face that only increased his differentness.

She took a deep breath. 'My parents love me, but they don't understand. It's nothing special. I'm sure half the population would tell you the same story. I do my best to make myself more palatable to them. It's really not a big deal.'

'You told Roland that none of us has had it easy, and you said once before you'd always felt alone.'

'That's not unusual either.'

'I hoped life would treat you better.'

'You know, it's a little weird when you come over all parental like that.'

'Parental?' Jonan let out a burst of laughter. It was uninhibited and caught Beth by surprise. She gaped, and then felt laughter bubble up in her own chest.

'I have *never* felt parental towards you,' he said, his face serious now. 'I feel protective. You used to feel the same way about me.'

'I still do,' Beth said, feeling heat flood her face. 'Why do you think I would keep putting myself in Amelia's path when the woman clearly has a vendetta against me? I would be delighted if I never had to see Amelia again. Or Miranda for that matter. I know she's your mother, but she's cold.'

'She is an acquired taste. You'll get used to her. It's freeing when you realise you can say anything you want to her. She always takes it as your stuff, so she's never offended.'

Beth sighed. 'I can see the appeal of that. My mum is a social climber and thinks my weirdness is a comment on her ability to fit in. She would have loved to have been an old-world aristocrat.'

'I think your weirdness is perfect.' Jonan's voice was rough.

A shiver shot down Beth's spine as rain began to drum on the windscreen. She felt untethered from the Earth but deeply connected to Jonan. For a moment, she wasn't sure whether she was still in the car, or in the hall with the pillars.

'What is that?' Beth said, her voice quiet. 'When that happens, I feel as though anything is possible.'

Starfolk Falling

'You are potential, Beth. Possibility is the air you breathe.'

'And what is your air, Jonan?'

'You,' he said simply and the smile that lit his face dazzled her. 'You are my lessons, my goal and my shadow.'

Beth rolled her eyes. 'Come on. You can't say I'm potential and you are just about me. I don't believe that. I mean, I get what you've told me about our past. I sense what's between us, even if I don't understand it. But to tell me there is nothing else to you? That's rubbish.'

'Okay,' Jonan shrugged. 'You're right. There is more to me than that. I'm a healer and a teacher. I love showing people how powerful they really are.'

'Okay, that makes sense. Waking people up is your path, and right now I am the student.'

Jonan swallowed. 'You're far more than a student to me.'

They sat in silence, the fields rushing past the car. Beth leaned her cheek on the window, allowing the hard, cold surface to ground her. She felt untethered.

The flat was dark when they got back.

Jonan crossed the lounge and rapped softly on Doriel's door.

'I'm here,' she said, her voice thick with sleep. Please leave me alone.'

Jonan let out a breath. 'I'll tell her in the morning.' Crouching down, he lit a fire and then went through to the kitchen. He came back a few moments later with two glasses of red wine and handed one to Beth. 'Here, drink this.' He sat down on the sofa and watched her as she paced backwards and forwards in front of the fire.

Jonan put down his wine glass. 'You could contact him.'

'Contact who?'

'Bill. You contacted the girl at the Monk's Inn. This is no different.'

'Yes, it is. This is Bill. He *was* my friend. Plus, I knew that girl was in the room. I have no idea where Bill is.'

'That's the thing, it doesn't matter where he is. Time and space don't exist where he's gone. If you contact him with intention, he will hear. Plus, he may need a little help to cross. Why don't you have a look and find out.'

'Isn't this your arena?'

Jonan shrugged. 'Only because I say it is, and because I've put in the practise. You can do both of those things. I know you can do it.'

Beth let out a prolonged breath and closed her eyes. She focused on an image of Bill. *The only people here are dead.* She heard his voice in her mind. *They keep me company day-in day-out whether I want them to or not. Chances are I'll be one of them soon, stuck in this hell-hole for all eternity.*

Is that you, Bill? She sent out the thought and felt a smile in return.

Who else would it be?

You don't have to be stuck. We can help you.

You're a sweet girl, Beth, but this is my place, and it's been taken over by the woman who ended my life. I have unfinished business.

We will handle that for you, Beth thought back to him.

She felt Bill drift further away. *I'm not sure about that.*

'Jonan,' Beth whispered. 'I have him, but he's planning to haunt the inn. He doesn't want to cross.'

Jonan put a hand on her arm. 'He'll want something better soon. When he does, he knows how to find us.'

Beth nodded, her eyes still closed. *It's okay, Bill, you don't need to hide. I won't send you away.*

I'm going home. The words floated into Beth's mind as Bill faded.

She opened her eyes. 'I don't like this.'

Jonan nodded. 'You don't have to like it. Unless Bill is doing harm, we can let him make his choices. Let's give him a chance to deal with his unfinished business.'

'You heard him?'

Jonan nodded. 'Did he seem unhappy?'

Beth shook her head.

'Isn't that why you were contacting him? To make sure he is okay?'

Beth forced herself to smile. 'You're right.' Jonan was watching her and his face lit up in the warm glow of the fire. Her heart beat faster and she reached out, sliding her palm into his. He gave her hand a gentle squeeze.

'I can still hear the band from earlier,' Beth said, getting up and opening the window a crack. 'That's one of my favourite songs.'

'That fresh air is heavenly.' Jonan sighed and threw the window open wider. He stood behind her, sliding his arms around her waist.

She leaned back into him, relaxing into his warmth. 'How do we deal with Amelia now? I always knew she was dangerous, but to go this far …'

He turned her around and touched his lips to hers.

She shivered and wrapped her arms around him, pulling him closer. 'Amelia is trying to programme everyone to close off, to raise their walls. We need to let ours down. How do we do that now with all this threat?'

Jonan took her hand and led her to the sofa. There were

small flames dancing around the log in the fire, the embers glowing bright orange. 'We create our own safety. Amelia is annoying and dangerous. She's using her ridiculous stories to scare people into following her, and it works because she knows how to appear convincing. We can't afford to ignore her, but we have to try not to be frightened by her. That's what she wants and it gives her power. But we won't let her get between us again. Do you remember that past life you saw?'

'The one where I was burned at the stake?'

Jonan nodded. 'We allowed her to get between us that time and it cost us everything. She put fire between us. This time we will use the fire to burn away our fears and bring us back together.'

Beth smiled. 'You talk a good talk.'

'Does it feel real enough to you?'

'It feels real right now.' She pulled him to her and kissed him. The world swirled around her and she seemed to be in so many places at once. She was on the sofa in Jonan's lounge. She was in the hall with the pillars, that other Jonan in her arms. She stood in a small cottage kitchen, surrounded by herbs hanging to dry from the beams. Yet another Jonan pulled her close, and they clutched at each other, knowing separation was coming. Beth spun between those women and each time she pulled Jonan closer until there was no space left at all.

'You don't need to cry, my love.' Jonan wiped away the tear she hadn't even known she had shed. 'That time has passed.'

'Sometimes it feels so real.'

Jonan smiled. 'Let's create the one life we have never lived before.' He stood up and held out his hand.

Beth took it. In that moment, she saw it: the one, unwalked path amongst the many they had trodden. The others faded to grey as she placed one foot on the shining ground and walked. She smiled up at Jonan as she reached out and opened his bedroom door.

17

BETH

Beth stretched. She was warm and relaxed. Jonan was still asleep, facing away from her. She lay, propped on one elbow, watching his muscular shoulders rise and fall. Life had been so crazy and this one, quiet moment was a gift. She had assumed she would always be alone. Jonan was a surprise she wasn't used to yet.

She wondered how different life might have been if she had met Jonan sooner. School and university had been lonely. She had watched her friends socialising, having fun, as though she were a spectator at a show, glamoured by the scene but unable to step inside. 'I don't know why you can't get a boyfriend,' her mother had repeated year after year. 'Goodness knows you're pretty enough. What are you doing to drive them away?'

Beth had secretly wondered the same.

Jonan turned over and smiled. His blond hair fell over his shoulders as he leaned up on one elbow and kissed her. 'Did you sleep well?'

'Better than I have in a long time.' She smiled back. 'I

like it here. It feels safer than my flat. I couldn't tell you why, but my place feels off no matter how much I clear the energy.'

'That's Laura for you,' Jonan said, collapsing back onto the mattress. He took her hand and squeezed it. 'Would you like some breakfast?' He bounded out of bed and pulled on a pair of joggers. 'Help yourself to anything from my wardrobe if you need a jumper or something. I'll put the coffee on.'

When Jonan had gone, Beth climbed out of bed and pulled on the jeans and top she had been wearing the night before. It was cold and she shivered. She went over to Jonan's wardrobe and rifled through, curious. There was a whole section of jumpers made of fine wool. She pulled out one in dark blue and held it up to her face. It was soft and smelled of Jonan. She nearly put it on, and then imagined herself spilling her breakfast down the front and put it back. Instead, she found a charcoal grey hoodie and pushed her arms through the sleeves, zipping it up. She grabbed a pair of thick socks from a drawer and put them on, tucking the tops under her jeans.

There was cheerful whistling coming from the kitchen and Beth followed the sound. 'Doriel?'

'She's in her room.' He handed her a plate of scrambled eggs on toast, and a cup of hot coffee.

Beth's stomach growled as she smelled the food. She rolled her eyes. 'I wonder if Layla's references have come through.'

Jonan picked up his phone and scrolled. 'There's one here from her current employer. It's glowing, but a bit vague about why she's leaving. Did we ask her that?'

Beth shook her head. 'Only why she wanted this job. Does it sound like there's anything we should worry about?'

Jonan put his phone down. 'Nope. As I said, the reference is glowing. I think we're fine. Look, it's nearly nine. I need to open up.'

'I think I'll head home for a bit. I need to get changed. I can come back later if you need help in the shop?'

Jonan smiled. 'I'd like that. I doubt Mum will turn up. She's had more company in the last few days than she has since she went into seclusion. I think we can expect her to disappear for a good while.'

Beth tilted her head. 'It must be strange, your mum being so detached. I mean, I don't see mine often, but I always know I can.'

Jonan shrugged. 'Doriel has been more of a mother to me than Miranda has for a long time. I'm used to it.'

'Say hi to Doriel from me when she gets up.' Beth stood up and put her coat on. She pulled off the warm socks and slipped her feet into last night's shoes. 'Goodbye.' She leaned over to Jonan and kissed him, allowing herself, for a moment, to forget that she was leaving. She pulled back.

Jonan's pupils were dilated, his eyes a deep purple. 'Come back soon.'

18

BETH

The market was full of people laden with shopping bags. Beth called into a coffee shop and bought a couple of lattes and cupcakes. She hoped Laura would be home because she had some making up to do. She had been avoiding Laura for weeks and hadn't told her anything about Jonan.

'Hi,' she called as she pushed the front door open, holding up the coffee. 'I come bearing treats.'

The TV was on loud. Laura walked out of the living room and leaned on the door-frame, her face pale and hard. Her usual statement clothes were gone in favour of slouchy joggers that bagged at the knees and her hair was greasy, pulled back from her face. She glared at Beth.

Beth swallowed. 'I have coffee and cake. Let's grab a couple of plates and catch up.' She walked through to the kitchen, pretending to ignore Laura's frostiness.

'I don't think so.'

Beth turned.

Laura walked back into the lounge.

'Is everything okay? Has something happened?' Beth took the coffee and cake and followed her in. Laura was sitting on the sofa, the TV remote in her hand. Amelia was on the TV, her voice loud as she talked about the Soul Snatchers.

'You happened.' Laura's voice was soft, but brittle. 'You brought that man here, and you walked away from me. I know what you're up to. You may have organised Amelia's event, but that doesn't mean you support her. I know you are working against her, trying to silence her because she wants to protect us from people like you.' She pointed the remote at the TV and turned it up even louder.

Amelia's voice pounded through the room, eating into Beth's composure. She put the coffee down. 'Laura, we don't have to agree on this. I know you like Amelia. That's fine. We can still be friends.'

'Oh, we can, can we?' Laura turned to face her, eyes flashing. 'How very magnanimous of you. You should know, I have joined Amelia's Haven and promised to cut your kind from my life. We can't live together. Quite frankly, since you've been here so little recently, I thought it only fair that *you* move out.'

Beth's bedroom door opened. A tall woman with long dark hair and the letter A tattooed on her shoulder walked out, did a double take and looked Beth up and down. 'Is this your ex-flatmate?' she said, turning to Laura.

Laura smirked. 'Don't worry. She'll be out of our hair soon.'

The woman nodded and wandered through to the kitchen, whistling.

Beth gaped. 'You can't be serious?'

'Why not? We're flatmates, not friends. You've made that abundantly clear.

'Be careful, be vigilant. Don't trust anyone,' Amelia's voice blared from the TV. 'Don't let anyone suspicious into your space.'

Beth rubbed her temples, trying to focus. 'Hang on, I pay rent here. You can't just throw me out.'

'I can and I did. When I told the landlord that you are against Amelia, he was more than eager to help. Your stuff's in the shed by the carpark.'

Amelia's voice seemed to be getting louder, even though Laura hadn't touched the remote. 'Don't feel bad about pushing infected people from your life. If they have been infiltrated, there is no way back for them.'

Beth stared at Laura. She anchored her hands on the edge of the sofa to stop them shaking. 'Please turn the TV off. It's giving me a headache.'

Laura didn't move.

'Do your homework, make sure they have no recourse to stop you walking away.'

Beth took a deep breath and picked up the coffee and cake. 'I can see you've made your choice. Just don't believe everything Amelia tells you.

'Oh, get out.' Laura got up, strode out of the lounge and slammed the door behind her.

Beth turned off the TV, sat on the arm of the sofa and looked around. This had been her home for so long. How could this be real? Her eyes travelled over the room, noticing the lumpy patch of paintwork left by their DIY decorating, the red wine stain on the carpet that they always joked was blood. There were so many memories here. It felt as though Laura was locking her out of her past as well as their friendship.

Beth stood up, weary now. Her eyes misted with tears, but she couldn't bear to stay any longer. She walked out, pausing by the big tree in front of the building. Putting her hand on the bark, she breathed in deeply. Laura wasn't herself. Amelia had got to her just like she had got to Beth. She would not let that woman win.

By the time Beth got back to the Third Eye, the place was heaving, but Jonan sat behind the counter, writing in a hardback notebook. He looked up as the bells on the door rang and his face lit up.

Beth walked straight over and slammed her bag down on the counter. 'She's thrown me out.'

Someone coughed behind her. She turned, about to snap, but saw a lady with a crystal and a bunch of sage in her hands, a toddler clutching at her flowing skirt. 'I'm so sorry to interrupt, but I'm almost out of shopping time.' She gestured at the little boy, who was plunging his hands into the large basket of tumble stones by the desk. 'Can I just pay for these, and then I'll be out of your hair?'

'Of course,' Beth stepped back, gritting her teeth.

Jonan frowned, but served the woman and the two who followed behind her. By now the shop had quietened. Only one man browsed at the far side of the room. 'What happened?' Jonan said, turning to her.

'She's replaced me. The landlord is an Amelia fan too and was only too happy to help evict me. Although I'm not sure you can even call it eviction since they haven't followed any due process at all.'

'Do you want to fight it?'

Beth shrugged. 'She's already moved someone in. And

I'm not sure I can face living with her fury. I just have to find somewhere else fast.'

Jonan swallowed. 'Move in with me. I would love to live with you.'

'What?' Beth blinked. Did he really mean that? 'You don't have to do that. I don't need sympathy.'

'You don't have it.'

Beth let out a breath. 'If you really don't mind, maybe I could stay here for a few nights?'

'As long as you want. We can get your stuff later.'

A man shuffled up to the desk with a tarot deck, his eyes darting between Jonan and the door. 'Are you okay, sir?' Jonan said as he took the deck and rang it through the till. 'Did anyone bother you out there?'

The man mumbled something unintelligible, waved his card at the machine, grabbed the deck and bolted for the door.

Beth raised her eyebrows. 'Has something happened?'

Jonan shrugged. 'Not that I've seen.'

Beth settled onto a stool in the corner behind the desk. 'I've got enough here for now. You don't have room for all my things anyway.'

'We'll make room. I want you to feel at home. I want you to feel able to stay.'

'Thank you, but for now I just want to take some time out and get my head around what happened. What with this and Bill's death, my head is spinning.'

Jonan nodded. 'The good news is that I've asked Layla to start on Monday and she's agreed.'

Beth let out a long breath. 'That's great news.'

The bells rang on the door, and Abi, Layla's daughter ran in. 'Hello, is Doriel here?'

Jonan looked at her with a smile, his head tilted. 'She's upstairs. Do you need her?'

'Yes, I need to talk to her now please. Mummy is on her way. Can I go upstairs?'

'Let me just see if she's awake. You look at the crystals. Beth, would you mind the shop?' Jonan went up the stairs, closing the door firmly behind him.

The bells rang again. 'Hi,' Layla flushed as she walked into the shop in ripped jeans, an oversized T-shirt and biker jacket. 'I hope you don't mind us coming in so soon, and so informally. We were planning a trip here before I was called to interview.'

'It's great to see you,' Beth said, smiling. 'I'm so pleased you'll be starting on Monday.'

'Can I come too, Mummy?' Abi clutched at Layla's hand.

'You have school, sweetie. You can come another day though, and you have today.'

Abi pouted and plunged her arms into the basket of tumble stones.

'I hear someone's looking for me?' Doriel poked her head around the door.

'Aunty Doriel,' Abi squealed and ran to her, wrapping her arms around Doriel's waist. Doriel closed her eyes. It was the most peaceful Beth had seen her since the abduction.

'Why don't you come upstairs and see my very own crystals?'

'Is that alright, Mummy?'

'That would be wonderful, thank you, but we only have a few minutes.' Layla beamed as the older woman and the little girl disappeared up the stairs. A few moments later,

Jonan came down and perched back on the stool behind the counter.

'Listen, I have to be quick before Abi comes back. She tells me you have an amethyst elephant, and a purple dream catcher with a barn owl. I'm hoping to get them for her birthday.

Jonan smiled and came out from behind the counter. 'You're in luck.' He wrapped up the gifts and rang them through the till. 'Do you mind if I ask why you left your last job? Your boss was so positive about you. I wondered why you wanted out.'

Layla grimaced. 'He was always positive because I gave so much. I changed myself to fit in with exactly what he wanted. Even then he always pushed harder. I couldn't carry on that way. It was changing me. Abi needs her mum, not some clone. He also had no patience with me working from home when she was ill, or taking time off for her school plays and concerts.' Layla shrugged. 'I couldn't do it anymore. That's why I was willing to work for less, so I could hold onto more of myself.'

Jonan nodded. 'So, there're no big surprises waiting for me?'

'Well,' Layla paused.

'Go on. Tell me now.'

'Abi isn't like most kids. The other kids at school, the teachers, they don't always get her. She needs me to be more on it, more present. And ...'

'Yes?' Jonan raised his eyebrows.

'I will *always* put her first.'

'That's it? That's the big secret? Or is there a punchline?'

'No.' She sighed. 'That's it.'

Jonan let out the breath he had been holding. 'Thank goodness for that. I thought you were going to tell me something awful for a moment.'

'You mean you don't mind?'

'Mind? Mind what? Mind that you put your kid first? I'd be surprised if you didn't. Mind that Abi is different?' He shrugged. 'We're all different here. That's the point. That's why we're doing this, to offer support to other people who are different. I've met Abi. I know she's like us. She seems to have a very strong kinship with Doriel. Abi is always welcome.'

A clattering on the stairs was followed by the door slamming open and Abi tumbled into the room, giggling.

She was followed by a second, lighter set of footsteps and the jingling of bells. Doriel stepped out in one of her old outfits. Her ankle-length purple skirt was skimmed with bells at the hem, her feet encased in sandals and toe rings. Her long hair fell down her back in waves, released at last from the tight bun.

'Doriel,' Jonan breathed. 'You're back.'

'It turns out I can't say no to your daughter.' She smiled at Layla.

'It looks as though she's done a good job.' Layla hugged the little girl. 'I'm done here. Let's head for home.' She opened the door and ushered Abi through. 'Thank you, Jonan.' She nodded, and then was gone.

Beth walked over to the counter and leaned on it. 'You said Abi was one of us. Did you mean that the way I think you did?'

'I think they both are.' Jonan was still staring out through the window after them, his forehead furrowed. 'I just haven't figured out how they fit into the picture. But look at what Abi is doing for Doriel, and your connection to Layla was so strong before you'd even met her. There's more going on here than we've figured out.'

The scent of lavender filled the room.

'Any time you want to pipe up and enlighten us, I'd be pleased to hear from you, Salu,' Jonan said to the room in general.

Beth heard laughing in her mind. 'I guess he agrees then?'

'Oh definitely. But I was hoping for something a bit more specific and Salu knows it.'

More laughing.

'Seriously, though, could we get more answers? From Salu, or from the others, whoever they are?'

'We can certainly try.'

19

BETH

The light of the enormous moon glinted off pearly pillars that stretched high above her.

'Are you sure you are ready?' The woman with dark ringlets and a shining white dress took her hands. Her skin was so pale it was almost translucent and her eyes were wide, a deep purple. 'I've been to Earth. It's not easy.'

Beth nodded, holding the woman's gaze and relishing this moment alone with her in the vast throne room. She felt safe. Who was this woman? She felt she ought to know, just as she knew deep down that this moment was rare and fleeting. Right now, it was just the two of them.

It wouldn't last.

Beth squeezed her hands, loving the feel of her soft skin, and the gentle grip of her fingers. It was hard to believe she had forgotten this face, the long, glossy ringlets that fell around her shoulders, the rich purple of her eyes, the blue star tattooed over her third eye and the way it stood out against her almost translucent skin. And yet, at the same time, she wished she knew who the woman was to her.

Earth amnesia. The words floated through her mind and she whispered them aloud.

'*That's right, my daughter. You will forget, but one day you will remember again.*'

A door slammed. Beth winced, feeling the moment of closeness evaporate.

The time had come.

She turned.

Jonan stood in the doorway.

The man she loved.

Long, blond hair hung down his back past the slender, pointed ears that matched her own. His eyebrows slanted upwards over eyes that shone a startlingly deep purple. As Beth met his gaze, he broke into a wide smile that lit his beautiful face from the inside.

Jonan walked slowly and silently across the room without taking his gaze from her. He stopped a breath away, his purple eyes gleaming as they took in every detail. She could feel his closeness like a prickle over her skin.

'Betalia,' he whispered. His voice surrounded her, drew her in until the room faded from her awareness.

Betalia. That was her name here. And the woman with ringlets was her mother and Queen. Betalia smiled at Jonan. 'Are you ready?'

He nodded. 'We must go.'

'Are you changing your mind, my love?' The Queen laced her fingers through Betalia's, drawing her close and anchoring her attention back in the room.

Betalia smiled. 'Never.' She turned, shoulders back, head held high.

The Triad stood in front of her. Three women: Doriel, Miranda and Amelia. They all wore long indigo robes that matched her own. Each woman was strikingly different, but they were unmistakably linked.

The Queen, Lunea, nodded at them. She stepped up onto the dais and sat, straight-backed, on her huge, crystal throne.

'You have each been tasked with bringing a different energy to Earth. I want to hear from each of you that you still accept your role.' Her voice was different. Gone was the motherly softness, instead the sound rang out with a pure clarity that filled every corner of the gigantic throne room.

'Amelia?' The first woman stepped forwards.

She had embellished her form, manifesting the way she had chosen to appear on Earth. A curtain of dark, shining hair hung over voluptuous curves. Her full smile was warm, but more detached than Betalia would have liked.

'Amelia, you embody potential, excitement and possibility. You bring the energy of youth, which you will nurture throughout your life, regardless of age. You know the risks you must face and the challenges you must overcome if you are to complete your task. Do you accept?'

'I do.' Amelia inclined her head.

Light was flooding in through the gaps in the curtains when Beth opened her eyes. The scent of lavender filled the room. 'Salu,' she whispered. 'Maybe I will see you too.'

If you choose it, sister.

20

AMELIA

Amelia looked at her watch. She had been keeping them waiting for twenty minutes. That ought to do it. She checked the concealed camera in the corner of the room and then clapped her hands twice. 'Rose?'

Amelia heard the clicking of rushed footsteps, and then Rose poked her head around the door, a fake smile plastered across her face. 'Yes, Amelia?' She was out of breath and flushed.

'See them in please.'

Rose nodded and disappeared. When the door opened again, Laura stood there, looking uncertain. She was dressed completely in black, her pixie cut straggly. That would have to change.

'Laura darling, come in. I'm so pleased you accepted the job. Have a seat.'

Laura flushed, her eyes lighting up as she walked into the room and perched on the edge of the seat Amelia indicated.

'Are you coming?' Amelia smiled and raised one eyebrow at the Sheep, who was lurking in the doorway.

He sidled into the room and stood with his back to the wall.

'Please, sit,' she said, pointing to the second chair and waiting. She could feel his discomfort; it buoyed her up as he swallowed, clenching his hands into fists at his sides and then releasing them, over and over again.

'Erm,' he grunted, and then shuffled forwards a few steps, turning to scan the area behind him.

She raised her eyebrow a notch higher and held in the laugh that threatened to bubble up from her throat. 'Come on, we can't start without you.'

He nodded, shuffled to the chair and lowered himself into it.

'Good.' Amelia clapped her hands again. Rose appeared at the door with a tray of glasses and a bottle of champagne. 'Pour,' Amelia said. Rose did, handing glasses to Amelia first, then Laura and the Sheep.

Then Rose held the bottle over a fourth glass.

'Not you,' Amelia said. 'Go.' Rose's face tightened, but she set down the champagne and clattered out of the room.

Laura sipped her drink. The Sheep was less keen. He held it as though it were a poisonous insect, his lips pressed together.

'Please, don't stand on ceremony. Drink!' Amelia said, enjoying his discomfort.

He took a sip and then let out his breath in a rush and settled further back into his chair.

'I would like you two to work together.'

Laura looked at Amelia, and then turned to the Sheep, her face open and questioning. He flushed to his roots and swallowed, but a grin spread slowly across his face. It was the first time Amelia had ever seen him smile.

Well well, it looked as though she had found the way to reach through the protective wall of blankness he had surrounded himself with.

'Laura, you are in charge of monitoring Soul Snatcher activity in this region. I would like you to pay particular attention to the Third Eye. I believe you have a personal connection with Beth Meyer, who works there. Is this right?'

Laura flushed. 'Yes, I used to live with Beth. I have cut off all contact now though, I promise.'

'Have you now?' Amelia tilted her head and watched Laura, using her psychic sight. The woman was tethered nicely to Amelia's web of cords, her energy was muddy and, closed off as she was to the world around her, she was beautifully open to Amelia. Amelia could feel her energy reaching out to her, tugging to be let in. She breathed in the sense of desperation, allowing it to flow through her veins, igniting her system. 'I understand why you thought it was best to disconnect from Beth, and I commend your instinct for self-preservation. But unfortunately I am going to have to ask you to make a personal sacrifice and recreate some of your links with her. I would like you to watch, to monitor her activity and report back to me if there is anything I should know about. Can you do that?'

'Yes, of course, Amelia. For you, anything.'

Amelia nodded. The trap was shaping up nicely. This second part would be harder. 'And you,' she said, turning to the Sheep. 'You are her muscle. Prove your loyalty to me by being loyal to Laura. You have failed in the past and, as you know, this is your last chance. Use it wisely.'

'Yes, Amelia.' The Sheep nodded.

'I am going to leave you to get to know one another. Laura, you are in charge and you report directly to me.'

Amelia shut the door behind her, creating the impression of privacy, and made her way down to the cellar. Rose was already there, sitting in front of the monitors, watching Laura and the Sheep as she drank champagne.

Amelia sat down on the chair next to her and took a sip of her drink. 'Well done, darling. What's happening?'

'The Sheep is talking,' Rose said, leaning forwards and turning up the volume.

'How long have you been working for Amelia?' Laura smiled and leaned towards the Sheep.

'Oh, ages now,' he said, sitting straighter than usual.

'She said this was your last chance. What happened?'

He shrugged. 'That friend of yours? She came along and messed everything up. Amelia didn't like that.'

Laura's face tightened. 'She's not my friend. Not anymore.'

She glanced over at him, put a hand on his thigh and smiled up at him. 'So, you know how to please Amelia? Will you help me? I don't want to let her down.'

The Sheep's eyes widened and he sat up straighter. 'Anything. I'll do anything you need.'

'You chose well.' Rose folded her arms across her chest. 'She's smitten with you, and it looks like she might soon be smitten with the Sheep as well. That should bring him under control and give him something to fight for.'

Amelia smirked. 'This has more potential than I'd believed possible.'

21

BETH

'I brought cakes.' Layla strode into the shop in tight black trousers and shirt, with knee high black boots and a bright pink coat that matched her hair. She walked over to the counter and put the box down. 'And I have a pile of ideas.' She dumped an art portfolio next to the cakes. 'Can you provide the coffee? And when do you have time to talk things through?'

'Welcome to the team.' Beth smiled and put down the box of crystals she was sorting. 'We can chat now if you like. Can you spare me, Jonan?'

'Go for it. Welcome, Layla, and thanks for the cake!' He grinned, and then carried on his conversation with a woman in full gym kit, pointing out different crystals as he walked her along the aisle.

Beth pulled the door open and stepped back to allow Layla through.

The bells on the front door jingled.

'Roland,' Beth said, 'this is a surprise.'

Roland pursed his lips then stilled. He swallowed, his gaze on Layla.

They stared at each other for a few long moments, and then Layla coughed and stepped forwards. 'Layla Pinkerton,' she said, with only the slightest hint of hoarseness in her voice. 'I'm new.'

'Don't worry, Layla,' Beth said, 'you don't need to explain yourself to him.'

'Explain myself?' Layla frowned and looked from Beth to Roland.

He raised one eyebrow. 'Prickly today, are we, Beth? It's nice to meet you, Layla. I am Jonan's brother.'

'You're brothers?' Layla's face lit into a smile. 'I can see the resemblance now.'

'Roland, we're busy,' Beth said from between gritted teeth. 'Is there something you need?'

'Look,' he said, rubbing his forehead. 'I know we got off to a bad start, but surely there's no need for this animosity?'

'After everything Amelia has done to Jonan? And to Doriel and me?' Beth's voice rose in pitch.

'Is there a problem?' Jonan's voice was sharp and his head inclined towards his customer, who was looking at them with a huge grin on her face.

'There's no problem.' Roland gave a strained smile. 'I'd like to see Doriel, if that's okay? Shall I go up?'

'Not a chance,' Beth cut in. 'Not after what you and Amelia did to her. You can wait here for Jonan.'

Roland nodded. 'Fine. No need to look after me. I'll just look round the shop while I'm waiting.'

Layla walked towards him and put out her hand. 'It was nice to meet you, Roland. I hope I'll see you again sometime?'

Roland's face lit up and for a moment he looked so like Jonan that Beth's heart raced.

Layla flushed, her eyes glinting in the overhead spotlights. She pulled her hand free and walked over to the door to the upstairs flat. Turning back, she smiled at Roland, and then walked up the stairs, letting the door bang behind her.

Beth looked from the door to Roland. He looked stunned and his face flushed. He cleared his throat. 'Right, thanks. I'll just wait for Jonan.' Turning away, he pulled a book about crystals from the shelf and leafed through it.

Upstairs, Layla was perched on the edge of one of the armchairs, staring into the empty fireplace, a large book hugged to her chest. Beth looked over to Doriel's door. At least, sitting here, she would know if Roland tried to get anywhere near the woman.

'That was interesting,' Beth said as Layla turned to look at her.

Layla shrugged. 'I don't know what you're talking about. You clearly don't like Jonan's brother though, what's the story?'

'He's involved with Amelia.'

'Involved?' Layla swallowed. 'What do you mean?'

Beth sighed. 'I mean just that. They're romantically involved. I'm sorry. You like him?'

'No.' Layla slammed the book on the coffee table with more force than was necessary. 'He just seemed like a nice guy.'

Beth sighed. 'He may be, at that. Honestly, I don't know him well enough to say. He may be as taken in by her as everyone else. Maybe he deserves my pity rather than my irritation.'

Layla opened her sketch book. Inside there was a

detailed picture of the shop, completely rearranged. It had armchairs and coffee tables with large picture books on them. There was a kitchenette in the corner and people milling around, chatting and looking at the crystals. The branding outside was completely different. The New Age look was gone. Instead, it was modern and sleek. *LUNA* was blazoned across the top in modern, purple and gold lettering.

'Wow, it looks really different.'

'Do you like it?'

'I love it, but do we really need to change the name?'

Layla sighed and leaned back in her chair. 'Just think about it, okay? You want something accessible, so people feel safe coming in here no matter who's watching. The name Third Eye flags you as New Age, whatever we do with decor. That shouldn't be a problem. It should be a good thing, in fact, because it tells everyone who you are. But if you want to be accessible to people who are frightened of Amelia's followers, you need something different. Luna still places you, it's just more subtle.'

'She's right,' Jonan said.

Beth looked up. He was leaning against the door-frame, arms crossed loosely over his chest. 'I'm happy to change the name, but not Luna. Let's call it Lunea.'

'Lunea?' Layla raised her eyebrows. 'Does it mean something?'

Jonan gave a distant smile. 'It's a memory; someone from my past.'

Beth leaned back on the sofa and tilted her head. She had never heard him speak of Lunea.

'I like the idea of a relaunch,' Jonan said, sitting on the sofa next to Beth.

'Perfect.' Layla beamed. 'We give you a new name, a new look, rework your space to create an events room, and then we launch with a party and a web presence so the right people can find you.'

He leaned over to look at the drawings on Beth's lap. 'I like them. It would be great to see them in more detail.'

'Of course. Now I know I'm on the right track I'll drill down. Where should I work?'

'For now, I've set you up a desk in the storeroom. I hope that's okay?'

'Perfect.' Layla grinned and gathered up her things. 'Where will I find it?'

'I'll show you.' Doriel stood in the doorway, her face pale, dark circles under her eyes. 'I'll make sure Layla has everything she needs.'

'Thanks, just don't go down to the shop. Roland was still looking around when I came up.'

'Thanks for the heads-up.' Doriel gave a tight smile. 'Come on, Layla.'

'Layla seems pleased to be here,' Jonan said, watching them head down the stairs.

'What did Roland want?' Beth crossed her arms over her chest.

Jonan sighed. 'He wanted to see Doriel, but I told him she was indisposed. It was nice chatting to him though. The more connection we can make, the better. He may be Amelia's most established victim.'

'Huh,' Beth grunted. 'He doesn't seem much like a victim to me.'

'Give the guy a break. I'm more to blame for all of this than he is.'

Beth frowned and her expression hardened. 'Why did

you get involved with Amelia? Was she really so different back then? You've said you always knew you were here to be with me, so why would you take such a big risk on a relationship that wasn't going anywhere?'

Jonan sighed and dropped onto the sofa beside Beth. 'Yes, she was very different. There was none of The Fear stuff back then. She was charismatic and positive, a real force for change. She was a trailblazer, far more exciting than Mum or Doriel. Pretty much everyone was in love with her, men and women. I certainly wasn't the only one to fall for her.'

Jealously shot through Beth. She clenched her teeth and folded her arms tightly across her chest. She would not let that woman get to her again.

Jonan took one of her hands, gently releasing her arms, and massaged her palm. 'This is ancient history, Beth. I knew you were my destiny, but I didn't know who you were. For a while, I thought maybe Amelia was the woman I was looking for. I was wrong and it didn't take me long to find out. I wish I hadn't gone there. Things could have been very different.'

Beth nodded. 'I get it, but that doesn't mean I like it.'

'You and the rest of us.' Jonan sighed and propped his legs up on the coffee table. 'I wish I could undo it all. I've spent years agonising over everything I got wrong. But one of my biggest mistakes was abandoning Roland. He was so vulnerable and I should have been there for him. All I can do now is move forward and try to make things better.'

'Did you manage to get anything out of Roland about Amelia's Haven?'

'Only that it's based at the Monk's Inn. They have all kinds of plans for it, apparently: conferences, events, support groups, that kind of thing. They have the space and, of course, they have the ghostly back-up to keep people feeling edgy.'

'How are we going to compete?' Beth dropped her head into her hands.

'We're not. We're going to do our own thing and offer something different. The people who follow Amelia will want nothing to do with us. We don't need to fight for their attention.'

Beth relaxed, resting her head on the back of the sofa. 'You're right. You know, I wonder sometimes whether I feel her thinking about me.'

Jonan turned to look at her, his forehead furrowed. 'Keep your protections strong. Amelia can absolutely get into your head from a distance.'

Beth heard laughter in her mind, and then visualised a door slamming shut. The laughter stopped. She shuddered. 'Can Miranda help us keep her out?'

Jonan grinned. 'We don't need her to. The Triad's role has changed. It's up to us now.'

22

DORIEL

Roland was queueing when Doriel slipped into the shop. She looked over her shoulder and then shut the door firmly behind her. She was pleased they were looking out for her, but their attention to her safety was becoming suffocating. She wasn't a child.

'Roland?' Doriel put a hand on his arm. 'Is it really you?'

He turned to her and his face lit up. 'Doriel, I was hoping to see you.'

'The crystals are on the house,' she said, tugging him out of the queue and pulling him into a tight hug. He was stiff at first, but then she felt him relax, leaning his head against her own.

'I'm surprised you want anything to do with me,' he said in a whisper close to her ear.

She pulled back, holding him by the shoulders. His eyes had deepened into a bluey green and his ears were capped with faint points. 'Sweetheart, none of this was ever your fault. You were the truest victim of all. Don't be chained to

Starfolk Falling

the past. You deserve happiness and I am here for you at any time. I hope you know that.'

He cleared his throat. His eyes were damp, his cheeks pale. He ran his hand through his neatly cut, dark hair. 'Actually, I didn't know that, so thank you. Are you alright after your ... erm.'

'After my abduction?' Doriel raised her eyebrows. 'You did know about that, then?'

Roland sighed. 'It was a crazy move. I tried to talk her out of it, but she's so angry with you and Mother. She told me she'd had you taken to a spa. I couldn't believe it when I saw that cell after you'd escaped. I had to come and make sure you were okay.'

'Was she trying to kill me?' Doriel's voice was small.

'God, no. I know it doesn't look like it, but she adores you. She wants your attention, but since she's not getting it she is punishing you for ignoring her.'

'But I picked up the pieces when she shattered the Triad. Doesn't she take any responsibility for what happened?'

He shook his head. 'She blames Mother for the Triad falling apart.'

Doriel rubbed a hand across her forehead. 'Is there any way forward from here?'

He shrugged. 'Maybe if Jonan and Beth stopped opposing her and called a truce? Amelia's Haven is really important to her, and she is only trying to help people.'

Doriel frowned. So he really believed in the story. She had wondered. Roland had always been a good kid. It was hard to imagine him deliberately misleading people. 'Roland, have you ever seen one of these Soul Snatchers?'

He shook his head. 'I've heard all about them from Amelia.'

'And you trust her completely?'

He froze. His eyes darkened. 'I have no reason to distrust her.'

'Even after she kidnapped me?'

He swallowed. 'I owe her, Doriel. I can't abandon her now, not after everything that's happened.'

She nodded and put a hand on his back. 'If you change your mind, you know where we are. And please, don't hand Amelia your moral compass. You're better than that.'

She turned and walked to the staircase, feeling his gaze boring into her back. At the last moment she turned. 'We're always here, Roland. Just think about what I said.'

She walked through the door and then shut it behind her and leaned against the wall of the staircase. Her heart was hammering. What was wrong with her? Shaking her head, she went back upstairs. Beth and Jonan were still poring over plans for the shop.

'Is Layla settled?' Jonan asked.

Doriel smiled and nodded. 'I'll be meditating. Please don't disturb me.'

She shut the door behind her, lit a candle and settled onto the bed.

She could feel Bill's energy pulling her and sent her awareness straight to the right bedroom. *So this is where you've chosen to hang out,* she thought to him. *I can't claim to understand why.*

A girl waited for me here every day, he sent the words snaking into her mind. *Jonan helped her cross, but until then she was my only friend.*

And would she want you trapped here too? Doriel raised her eyebrows. *I can help you cross. You can still work with us, but you won't be trapped anymore.*

Doriel felt the word *No* juddering through her whole body. *This is where she was and this is where I will stay.*

But she's not here now. Doriel sent out the words, putting a vibration around them that heightened their power.

No, but I can call on her strength. I am getting to Amelia already and the more I do, the harder it will be for her to manipulate people. As long as she is here, there is work I must do. I won't let her win.

Doriel nodded. *Stay in touch, Bill. We may be able to work together. And once we're done, I will help you cross.* She opened her eyes. It was done, for now.

23

JONAN

Jonan had never seen so much mess. The crystals had been packed into boxes and put upstairs while the showroom was refurbished. The sign was down from outside and the huge windows looked in on a dusty room filled with sheets and wet paint. Jonan picked his way through the mess, nodding and smiling at the various workmen before ducking up the stairs. It wasn't much better up there. The entire contents of the shop had been rehomed in the small spaces they usually lived in.

Beth and Layla were both working on laptops on the sofa, surrounded by boxes.

'How's it looking down there?' Layla looked up at Jonan.

'Very much the same as this morning.' He sighed. 'How long is this going to take? I thought it was going to be quick, but they've been working for two weeks now.'

Layla shrugged. 'I don't think they're far off finishing downstairs, and then they need to work on the event space. This stuff is never quick, but at least it seems to have distracted people from attacking the shop. It was getting pretty hairy with all those bricks being thrown through the windows. We haven't had one pane of glass shattered since the shop sign came down.'

'I reckon people think we've left,' Beth said, shutting her laptop. 'I just hope it doesn't all start up again when they realise we're still here.'

'I'm sure with you two working your magic, we'll be fine.' Jonan grinned.

'Roland came by an hour ago.' Beth got up, walked through to the kitchen and put the kettle on. 'The builders sent him up. He asked for you but didn't leave a message.'

'Are you sure I'm the one he was here to see?' Jonan raised one eyebrow at Layla.

She flushed and buried her face in her laptop. 'I don't know what you're talking about.'

Jonan grinned, but said nothing. Instead he followed Beth into the kitchen, filled a glass with water and leaned against the worktop. 'I might pop by the inn and speak to Roland,' he said, his voice low so Layla wouldn't hear. 'There has to be more to these visits than he's letting on. It might just be an interest in Layla, and I hope it is. But I won't have him using her to get to me.'

Beth swallowed. 'I'll come with you.'

'No, don't. Roland is more likely to talk if I'm on my own.'

'Amelia might be there.'

Jonan shrugged. 'So much the better. I haven't seen her in a while. It would be good to get a read on her. I'd like to know what she's up to.'

Beth sighed. 'I get that, but remember how she got to

you at the ball? How do you know she won't get into your head again?'

'I'll be on alert and I will be fine.' He shifted to stand in front of her, wrapping his arms around her waist to pull her close. He leaned down, touching his lips lightly to hers. 'You have nothing to fear. I am all yours.'

'That's not what she thinks.' Beth's voice was rough.

'It is. It's just not what she wants.'

Beth leaned her forehead on Jonan's chest. She could feel his heartbeat through the rough wool of his jumper. 'Can I stop you going?'

'No.' He kissed the top of her head, and then stepped away and pulled on his jacket. 'It's too crowded in here anyway. You should get out too. Get some fresh air and a drink. Take Layla with you. It would be a good opportunity to get to know her better.'

Beth nodded. 'I'll do that. Be careful.'

Jonan let out a long breath as he walked down the hill towards the Monk's Inn. He wished he felt as serene as he had acted. Amelia *had* got into his head before the ball, and had done it more successfully than ever before. He would do everything he could to avoid a repeat of that, but he had no idea how powerful she really was. It had been a long time since he had been able to read her.

The sun was shining and the birds were singing in spite of the freezing cold. The wind had an icy edge, but it freshened the air and Jonan drew it into his lungs gratefully. The birds fell silent as he came to the inn, and he felt its heavy energy as a weight on his chest. Pushing it back, he surrounded himself with light and formed it into a hard bubble. He wondered whether Amelia was protecting herself from the sludge of her energetic creation, or whether she was soaking in the negativity she nurtured.

The door was unlocked and he pushed it open, hearing a bell ring.

'Who is it?' Roland's voice came from the room behind the reception desk, and when Jonan didn't answer, he came out. 'Jonan.' He raised his eyebrows and ran a hand through his unusually messy hair, smoothing it out of its distracted spikes. 'This is a surprise. What are you doing here?'

'You came to see me and I don't have your phone number. Is everything okay?'

'Fine, thank you. I just wanted to—'

'Would you care if things weren't okay?' Amelia came through the door after Roland and leaned against the door-frame. Her eyes were red-rimmed and her skin was puffy. She was dressed in a cocktail dress, but the pale fabric was creased and stained. He wondered how long she'd been wearing it. 'Are you ill?' Jonan frowned.

Amelia cleared her throat. 'You'd like it if I was, wouldn't you?' she said, padding over to him in her bare feet, running a hand over his shoulders.

Jonan shuddered. 'Don't be ridiculous. Although after what you did to Bill, it's less than you deserve. Do you even know he died?'

She chuckled, but the sound was brittle. 'Oh, I know. Believe me, I know.'

Leave Jonan alone. A familiar voice wafted through the entrance hall. *Can't you see he doesn't want you?*

Bill? Jonan sent out the thought. *Is that you?*

'Stop interfering,' Amelia snapped. 'And get out of my house.'

Jonan wondered whether she was talking to him or to Bill.

'Knock it off, Amelia.' Roland's voice was sharp. 'Jonan came to see *me*, not to play games. Why don't you get on with the work you've been complaining about. I'd like to talk to Jonan alone.'

'Why?' Amelia's forehead creased as she glared at Roland. 'What secrets do you have that you can't discuss in front of me? Are you colluding with *them*?'

'Colluding?' Roland's jaw was clenched and a vein throbbed in his neck. 'Not everything is that dramatic. I just can't bear the way the two of you fight constantly. I'm getting a headache.'

'Fine.' Amelia pulled her shoes on and then walked past Jonan, bumping hard into his shoulder. When he didn't react, she huffed, and then stormed up the stairs.

Jonan swallowed. 'What was all that about?'

Roland waited until Amelia had turned the corner. Then he leaned against the reception desk and shoved his hands in his pockets. 'What can I do for you?'

Jonan raised one eyebrow. 'I do care, you know. I hate the way things turned out between us, and I'm sorry I took things out on you the night of the charity event. I was angry with Amelia, not you. I thought … I hoped, that when you came to the shop you wanted to make up. Maybe I misread the situation. Perhaps you were looking for someone else?'

Roland flushed. 'I don't know what you're talking about.' He walked over to the table, poured two shots of whisky and handed one to Jonan. 'I just thought I'd see how the shop was getting on. This place gets stifling. I needed to get out.'

Jonan knocked back his whisky and moved closer,

pitching his voice low in case Amelia was listening. 'I can believe that. The building is big, but the energy …'

'It's okay, I just needed to clear my mind.'

'Does Amelia ever clear her mind?'

Roland's jaw tightened. He swallowed. 'What are you implying?'

Jonan shrugged. 'I'm worried about you both.'

'Ha!' Roland let out a bark of laughter. 'Fat lot of truth in that statement. You're out to get us and I know it well. I thought that maybe, after all this time, I might be able to forge a bit of a relationship with my big brother without things getting competitive. It seems I was mistaken.'

'Competitive?' Jonan frowned. 'That's not it at all.'

'I think you should go.' Roland strode over to the front door and jerked it open, ignoring the creak of the old door.

'Look, Roland, don't be like this. I'm just looking out for my little brother.'

'You stopped being my family when you walked away and left me alone. The same goes for Mother.' He opened the door a bit wider.

'Can we ever move past this?'

'Will you ever move past what happened and forgive Amelia?'

Jonan strode over to Roland. 'Brother, I'm not angry with Amelia for what happened. I'm angry about what she's doing now. I'm angry that she made up a crime and tried to have me arrested for it. I'm angry that she locked the woman I love in an abandoned theatre and left her for dead. I'm angry that she had Doriel and Bill abducted and took so little care of them that Bill died and Doriel is traumatised. These are the things I hold against Amelia. What happened all those years ago is irrelevant.'

'Irrelevant?' Amelia's voice was shrill.

Jonan groaned. He took a deep breath, squared his shoulders and turned. Amelia stood on the stairs, her face flushed and her feet bare. Her hair was scraped back now, and her face was newly caked with too much make-up. Even so, it failed to hide the puffiness around her eyes that showed she had been crying.

'Your actions changed the course of my entire life and you're calling them irrelevant?'

Jonan sighed. 'We've been over this. I've taken responsibility for what I did as a kid. You need to take responsibility for what you did, and what you're still doing, as an adult.'

'I didn't kill him, you know.' She stuck her chin out defiantly, but her lip trembled.

'Not directly, no. But your actions led to Bill's death all the same. That might make a difference in law, but it's the same thing to me.'

'You're just angry because I almost had you arrested.' Amelia smirked and the expression brought back her usual swagger. She sauntered down the stairs, swaying her hips, as though she were dressed for the ball. She leered at him, looking him up and down, and then leaned into Roland. Roland gritted his teeth but put his arm around her waist.

'I *am* still angry about that, and about the rest too. But I didn't come here to argue with you. Goodbye, Amelia.'

'Don't trip over the step on your way out,' Amelia called, and her laugh followed him out the door.

24

BETH

'Welcome to *Deep and Dark*. I am delighted to announce that we have a very special guest this evening, the one and only Amelia Faustus. Welcome, Amelia.'

'Thank you, Katherine darling.' Amelia put a hand on Katherine Haversham's arm and smiled, her face displaying a warmth that didn't reach her eyes.

'She's not looking so scrappy now, is she?' Beth said, sighing as she leaned into Jonan. They were sitting on the sofa in the living room. A fire was roaring in the grate, trying its best to spread a warmth that was zapped by the conversation on the TV.

Doriel sighed. 'Knowing Amelia, I'm surprised she showed the cracks to Jonan at all. There was never any way she would display them on national television.' She took a sip from the mug that steamed in her hands.

Katherine leaned forwards, her eyes glinting. 'Last time you came on the show you told us about the intruder at your mother's house. This time you have more news for us. Is that right?'

'It is, Katherine.' Amelia beamed at the camera. 'Not long ago I told you about Amelia's Haven and all the protections it would offer against the Soul Snatchers. Now, I am delighted to announce that Amelia's Haven has opened its doors. I have a hotel in St Albans called the Monks' Inn. This is our new headquarters and we will be offering events and services to our members there.'

'Do tell us more.' Katherine leaned forwards in her seat.

'I'd love to, Katherine darling.' Amelia smoothed a strand of hair away from her face. 'We will have workshops that will teach people how to recognise a Soul Snatcher, or someone who has been infiltrated. We will have support for people who have had to turn in friends or family. We will teach people how to protect themselves and their homes, and, of course, we will test people for suitability. Everyone who applies to join the Haven will have to be tested by a local representative to ensure the safety of our members.'

'What does the test entail?'

'I'm glad you asked, Katherine dear. I would like to offer you a complimentary test yourself and we can show your audience how easy it is and allay any fears they might have.'

Katherine swallowed. 'You want to test me here? Now?' She pushed her chair back a little. 'I'm sorry, we don't have time for that.' She went silent and put one hand to her ear. Her face paled, but she nodded. 'I'm told we do have time for that. So tell me, Amelia, how is it done?'

'All you have to do, darling, is sit on your chair and close your eyes. I will do the rest.' Amelia stood up and walked around to stand behind Katherine. She stretched her arms out wide and then brought her palms in until they were either side of Katherine's ears. Starting to hum, softly, she closed her eyes.

Beth leaned forward, closer to the TV, aware that Jonan and Doriel were doing the same. Switching into her psychic sight, she gasped. Amelia was wrapping long strands of grey energy around Katherine's head and throat. She moved her hands to the outside of her shoulders, and the threads spread further down, growing like vines around the woman's body.

'What is she doing?' she whispered.

'She's trapping her,' Doriel said, her voice clipped.

Kathrine's face was draining of colour as Amelia worked. She was wringing her hands in her lap now, and her eyelid was twitching.

Amelia dropped her hands and stepped back. 'Congratulations, Katherine. You have passed the test. You are free of interference from the Soul Snatchers and I would be delighted to welcome you personally to Amelia's Haven.'

The room erupted into applause.

'Give me strength.' Beth dropped her head into her hands. 'So that's Katherine Haversham's year messed up. Can you get to her to offer help? Laura was my only route into that place.'

'Too high profile,' Doriel said. 'Amelia would notice if you interfered.'

'Probably.' Jonan shrugged. 'But I won't let that stop me. I still have a couple of friends at the studio. I'll put out some feelers.'

Amelia was back on the sofa now, and Katherine was straightening out her skirt, looking more flustered than Beth had ever seen her.

'So. How can people join?' she said with a forced smile.

'We have a lovely website, darling.' Amelia picked up a beautiful cream hardback notebook with gilt edges and a subtle gold pattern. She opened it up and showed it to the camera. At the top of each page was a web address. At the bottom was a mantra: *Amelia's Haven Keeps My Loved Ones Safe* was on one side, and *Only Trust Members of Amelia's Haven* on the other. 'If you visit my website you can find all the ways we can help you. We have events listed already: retreats, books, support lines, counsellors and these beautiful notebooks with matching pens.' She held up an elegant cream-and-gold pen. 'You can find out more about everything, as well as signing up to join. As you've all seen, the vetting process isn't onerous and once you're in you will know you are supported, safe and amongst friends. I would love to offer you complimentary membership, Katherine darling. You have been such a friend to us. And this is a gift for you.' She handed Katherine the notebook and pen.

'Well, thank you!' Katherine flushed.

Beth shook her head. 'She used to be so sceptical. I guess that's why Amelia wanted to get to her. She's basically eliminated her opposition. She still seems pretty switched-on to me, in spite of what you saw at the inn.'

Doriel rolled her eyes. 'We don't even know if the performance she showed you was real. She could have been putting that on to distract you. You never know with Amelia.'

Jonan's frown deepened. 'It is possible, but I don't believe it. Both Roland and Amelia were so … disordered. I haven't seen them like that before. I think I took them unawares and she didn't manage to get her mask into place.'

Starfolk Falling

Beth sat forward, leaning her elbows on her knees and narrowing her eyes at the picture of Amelia on the TV. 'Well, maybe we need to act faster while she's disordered. We talked before about suing her for defamation. I know a couple of lawyers. I could talk to them and see what options we have.'

Doriel gave a bland smile and picked up her knitting. The needles clicked together as the wool flew through her nimble fingers. 'You can do that, but I don't think it will work.'

'You don't know that.' Beth felt a wave of fury, but bit it back. Why was she so angry? She closed her eyes and took a deep breath. She heard Amelia laughing in her mind and brought down a wall, cutting the sound off.

Doriel shrugged. 'Do your thing. I'm not trying to stop you.'

Jonan looked from Doriel to Beth, and then nodded. 'Honestly, Doriel, it's impossible to tell what's intuition and what's The Fear with you right now. I think Beth is right. We should try.'

Doriel nodded, her face impassive. 'As you wish.' She folded up her knitting, got up and went through to her bedroom, shutting the door firmly behind her.

'I'm sorry, I didn't mean to upset her,' Beth said with a sigh.

'Can we move the launch up?' Jonan stood in front of the TV, hands on his hips. 'Amelia's head-start is going to be insurmountable soon.'

'I think the shop is nearly done and I have some ideas for a launch party. Do you think Doriel might do some readings?'

'No!' Doriel's voice was sharp on the other side of the door.

Jonan smiled. 'I can offer healing sessions and I might be able to persuade Mum to come. She can be pretty spectacular and she's had a lot of publicity at various points over the years. I think we could get some attention if we had her come and speak. Every time she reappears the world clamours for her.'

'Do you think she would do it?'

Jonan shrugged. 'She might. Honestly, I don't know. I'll go and see her tomorrow.'

'We're going to need a big draw. Amelia is so far ahead of us already and she has a huge following, but I have a few ideas. We just have to hope Amelia's reach doesn't grow too fast.'

'You're being too simplistic,' Doriel shouted through the door. 'You need to understand why you're doing this.'

Jonan raised one eyebrow. 'Oh?'

'The High Priestess,' she said, her voice close to the door this time.

'Is there something you know?' Beth stood up and went over to Doriel's bedroom door, putting her palms flat on the wooden surface. 'Tell us, Doriel, please.'

'I can't.' Her voice was a whisper now. 'The High Priestess.'

Beth sighed and walked back to the sofa. 'What does that mean?' she asked, leaning back and sinking into the deep cushions. 'What does she want me to do? I really should learn to use that tarot deck.'

'The High Priestess uses intuition to find the way forward,' Jonan said, narrowing his eyes at the door as though waiting for more instructions. None came.

'So, I need to what, meditate?'

'You could ask Salu for help. That worked well last time.'

Adrenaline shot through Beth and she couldn't stop the grin that spread across her face. 'The throne room.'

25

BETH

'MIRANDA?'

The second woman stepped forwards. Of all the women, Miranda was the most elusive. Her lithe form never fully solidified, instead shimmering with a willowy grace. Her long, straight hair was bound back, and her gaze always held more transcendence than warmth. 'Miranda, you have chosen to incarnate as the Mother. You will bring love and nurture your children throughout their journey. This is a new role for you. Do you accept the challenge?'

'I do.' Miranda's smile was typically distant.

Betalia frowned. She didn't understand why Miranda had been given this task. She was the least likely candidate, and Betalia hoped she would find a little affection for Jonan as he grew up in this strange world of Earth.

'Doriel?'

Doriel laughed as she stepped forwards, and the sound was like tinkling bells.

Miranda shot her a frown.

Doriel rolled her eyes. She shook her head to flick back her long, fiery hair, and reached up to fiddle with the beaded earrings that mirrored the delicate upper points of her ears. Her hair rippled down her back to her waist in glossy, red waves.

'Doriel, you incarnate as The Wise Woman. Do you accept this task?'

'Sister, I accept any task I am given.' A look of silent understanding passed between the two women and Betalia narrowed her eyes, trying to pick up the meaning from their energy. There was nothing.

'Jonan, do you also understand your task?'

'I do.' Jonan nodded. He reached out, threading his fingers through Betalia's. 'I come to awaken your daughter, to set events in motion should the Triad stray from their path.'

The Queen took a deep shuddering breath.

'We will look after her, Lunea.' Doriel stepped up onto the dais and walked over to Betalia's mother. Stroking her sister's dark curls, she raised one delicate eyebrow, tilted her head and suppressed a smile. 'We will awaken her whether she likes it or not.'

'You know that is not the way.' The Queen frowned. 'Earth is for free will. If she chooses not to awaken, there is nothing you can do.'

'There is persuasion.' Miranda's voice was flat and Betalia wondered with a stab of anxiety what she had in mind.

The air shimmered and Betalia's brother materialised. 'However you do it, you'd better make it work.' He swept an arm around Betalia's waist and pulled her tight.

'Salu!' She leaned into him and felt a heartbeat. She laughed. 'Are you trying to get me into the mood for Earth, brother? Is that what all the bulging muscles and flowing golden locks are for?'

He made no attempt to hide the grin on his chiselled face.

'What do you think, sister? Is this the look for me?'

'I don't think there is one look that will ever satisfy you for long, but this one certainly fits your love of the dramatic.'

Salu shrugged. 'What's the point in being able to take any form we want if we don't use it?'

'Some of us like to focus the use of our energy more carefully.' Miranda frowned. She lifted her chin in the air, looking pointedly away from Salu.

He rolled his eyes. 'I'm sorry your energy needs to be rationed, Miranda. I had no idea. I'm used to abundance.'

Betalia sighed. 'How will I recognise you when I'm on Earth if you can't decide what you look like?'

'Oh, you'll know my energy, sis, whether you remember what it means or not. What do looks matter? They're only pretend.'

'On Earth they matter a lot.' Miranda's third eye tattoo wrinkled and her lips pressed together. 'This is important, Salu. We need to focus on where we're going, not on how you paint yourself.'

'Too right you need to focus.' He drifted over to Miranda, his body dissolving into a cloud that surrounded her in a thick fog. 'I know I'm supposed to trust you to do right by Betalia,' his voice came from the mist, 'but I don't. I don't know why you've chosen the role of Mother when you are so unsuited to it. This mission is too important to be your playground.'

'I have chosen a new lesson. This is what incarnations are for.'

'Not this one.' He appeared again beside her. Now his huge muscles were clenched, his face dark with anger. 'This time you have a bigger mission and I expect you to put it first.'

'Miranda will not be the only one there, Salu.' Jonan stepped towards his friend and put a hand on his arm. 'And Miranda is to be my mother, not Betalia's. Betalia will be alone for many years. She is going to need your support, even if she doesn't realise she's getting it. Please try to look kindly on our mission.'

'I'll be watching you too, Jonan.' Salu narrowed his eyes at the smaller man and paced around him, hands clenched at his sides. 'I will be watching every minute of every day. Wake the people of Earth up to the joy and connection they're missing, and then bring Betalia home. Otherwise, we'll be locked into a karmic cycle neither of us want.'

Jonan tilted his head to one side and stepped closer to Betalia. He slid one arm around her waist. 'Do you think I love her any less than you? Do you feel I take my path lightly?'

Betalia felt the touch of his aura mirror their physical contact. Her heart expanded. She would not let Jonan incarnate without her, no matter how much her brother hated her choice.

Betalia stepped away from both men. 'You act as though you have a choice in what I do. This is my path. My decision. Neither of you are empowered to change it. Stop treating me as though I'm breakable.'

'We're not trying to change your mind, love,' the Queen said. She stood. Her energy flared, filling the room with light. 'I have complete faith in you. Salu and I will miss you, that is all.'

'That is not all.' Salu stamped one foot and the sound reverberated around the room, magnified by the cold, hard surfaces. 'You know how badly this could go.' He shot a pointed look at Amelia.

'You think I want to be the weak link?' Amelia stretched her arms wide. 'Who else will take on this role? Without potential we cannot complete the task, but I have no attachment to taking that place. I will gladly hand over my role and act as mother, or wise woman.'

Salu laughed. 'Wise woman? Do you think I haven't seen your energy? I know why you chose potential.'

'What is there other than learning?'

'There is holding a high vibration.' He spat the words, moving between Amelia and Betalia. 'I have seen that you will not do this. You will drag Betalia into your darkness.'

'Have more faith in me.' Betalia reached out, touched Salu's arm and felt him relax a little.

'Have more faith in all of us.' Doriel's voice still rang, but this time it was firm. 'The Triad brings more than potential. This is why we incarnate together.'

'So Amelia can fail and drag Betalia down?'

'So we can bring new energy to Earth.' Miranda stepped forwards.

'The human race is stuck in the wheels of its own creation. It is our job to trigger the future. Amelia will provide those triggers.'

'And if it goes wrong?'

'That is why Betalia incarnates with us,' Jonan said.

Betalia's heart raced as he traced her palm with his fingers. *'She will awaken when the triggers have been set. I will find her.'*

'And this is guaranteed?' Salu's voice was sharp.

Doriel sighed. *'Nothing is ever guaranteed. You know that.'* She sat down on the edge of the dais. *'Free will is unsurmountable. We must hold faith that our essence will persevere, even in human form.'*

'And we will remember.' Jonan squeezed her hands. *'Except Betalia, we will all remember enough. I will awaken her when the time comes.'*

'Are you sure I can't bring my memories with me?'

'I'm sorry, love.' The Queen reached out and took her hand. *'If the Triad fails, we need someone from the outside who can see things clearly. That is your path.'*

Betalia took a deep breath and nodded.

'Do not forget me entirely, little sister.' Salu's voice caught as he pulled her into a tight hug. *'I will be with you for each of your Earth days. Try to remember to look for me.'*

'I will feel you with me whether I know it consciously or not.' She kissed his hand. *'I cannot forget a part of my soul.'*

Salu glowed at the praise. He towered over Betalia, and his energy shimmered in the bright white light of the throne room. *'You know I only want what's best for you, little sis.'*

Betalia stepped onto the dais, so she could reach to kiss the deep blue star in the middle of his forehead. *'Brother, remember I can never truly die. One way or another I will come back to you. Please give me love as a parting gift, not fear.'*

'You have it. Always.' He squeezed her hands, and then was gone.

. . .

Starfolk Falling

BETH BLINKED. THE ROOM WAS THICK WITH SAGE SMOKE and the fire had burned down to embers. Jonan sat watching her, his eyes still glazed from the visions they had shared.

'Lunea,' Beth whispered. 'She's my mother in that other place. I've been meaning to ask you who you named the shop after.'

Jonan smiled. 'Were you jealous?'

'Maybe a little.'

Jonan laughed now and pulled her towards him, kissing her gently. 'It's always been you, Beth, every lifetime.'

She leaned into him. 'Amelia seemed so different there, as though she really wanted to get this right.'

Jonan swallowed. 'We all did, but we've all had our challenges. Even those who remember can take the wrong turn.'

Beth sat up and turned to face him. 'But how does this change things? I can feel sorry for her, but does that mean I have to let her get away with what she's doing?'

'You need to understand why *you're* doing this,' Doriel's voice floated through the room like a waft of smoke.

And to remember who is here to help you. Salu's voice spoke into her mind as the air filled with the scent of lavender.

26

BETH

Beth settled onto the sofa with her laptop and logged into all the social media sites she could think of. She typed Amelia Faustus into each search bar. Every one came up with an account. Each feed was full of memes and pictures, but there were few personal comments or interactions. Well, Beth could do better than that. She just had to figure out how to attract a following. At least she had a bit of time before the launch.

She sighed and started creating accounts. Looking through the pictures Jonan had sent her, she uploaded a profile image that was particularly brooding and model-like. His charisma certainly drew women into the shop, but she had no idea whether she could make it carry online.

She hit create and then fired off a few posts. Now to find followers. Within seconds she had a notification. She clicked it. A new follower. Amelia.

'How did she find me so fast?' Beth mused. Moments later, another notification. There was a picture of the new sign on the shop and a post directly from Amelia.

> Please know I am looking out for you every moment of every day. Right now, there is a new shop in the centre of St Albans that I want to warn you about. It is called Lunea and it is run by people I suspect to be Soul Snatchers. Please keep your wits about you and stay away from Lunea. These people are among us and they are almost impossible to spot.

Within moments Beth's follower count shot up, and then the notifications began. There were threats and dismissive comments. She was tagged in shares of Amelia's post and she received private messages asking for support. Amelia was right in there, commenting, posting and driving up the anger, but also spreading the shop's message further than Beth could have believed possible.

Ignoring the notifications, she posted some more, getting her own words out as fast as she could to counter Amelia's claims. The positive notifications increased.

'Is everything okay?' Jonan came in two hours later and sat on the sofa next to her. 'I thought you were coming down to the shop. I would have come up ages ago but the phone has been ringing constantly. I wasn't expecting so many people to know anything about the shop, but they all seem very anxious that we open quickly.'

Beth frowned. 'Have they all been keen or were there any unpleasant calls?'

'One or two, but nothing alarming. Were you expecting this to happen?' Jonan took an apple from the fruit bowl on the table and bit into it.

'Amelia picked up our new social media accounts within seconds and she's been posting about us ever since. We already have followers in the tens of thousands, but most of them aren't the people we want to reach. The trolls are out in force.'

'Have they been abusive?' Jonan peered over her shoulder.

'Yes, but I've blocked those. Don't worry, I know what I'm doing. I'm more concerned about the ones that might turn up at the door.' She put her laptop on the coffee table, stood up and wandered over to the window. There were a few people with placards, sitting around, leaning against the wall of the building opposite. When a woman approached the shop, they jumped to their feet and started waving the signs around.

Beth sighed. 'It's been worse. I really wasn't expecting things to take off this quickly though. Now I have to find enough content to keep everyone engaged between now and the launch, as well as rebutting her trolling.' Her phone beeped. She picked it up and swiped to open it. 'The media are following us too. You wouldn't have thought a shop rebranding could draw this much attention, even with Amelia talking publicly about us.'

'Is it good?'

'I might be. It depends what kind of attention we get, and whether Amelia makes up any more wild claims.

The phone was beeping continually now. Beth turned it off and shoved it to the opposite side of the table. 'I need a break. Amelia has an uncanny ability to push her energy through her posts. If I don't stop now, she'll get a hold of me again.' She reached for the remote control, pointed it at the television and clicked. Amelia's voice blared through the TV.

Jonan took the remote, turned it off and put it back on

the coffee table. 'We need to switch her off entirely. She'll get to us from every possible angle if we let her. She is trying to take over the air waves.'

'She's not just trying, she's doing an expert job of it. We have to raise our game or this is not going to end well.'

27

BETH

Beth was exhausted. She'd been to every solicitor's office in St Albans and not one of them was willing to help her put together a case against Amelia.

The coffee shop was full, but there was one spare seat at a table in the back right-hand corner, so she ordered a coffee and a piece of cake. 'Is this seat free?' She asked the woman on the other side, who was working on her laptop. The woman looked Beth up and down, and then nodded and turned back to her computer without a word.

Beth sat down, sinking into the chair and closing her eyes. Her body ached from the effort of holding herself together through the meetings and she longed to be on her own.

'Did you see that New Age shop has had a makeover?' a voice said from the table next to Beth. She sighed, not wanting to allow in the outside world, but knowing she needed to listen.

'I did,' a familiar voice answered and dread settled into the pit of Beth's stomach. She kept her eyes tightly closed, not sure how she would find the strength to face Laura today. 'But nobody's fooled. I met the owner of the last shop and he's just rebranding. I saw him putting the crystals back on the shelves today. Amelia's right. It's the same place, but in more normal packaging.'

'I reckon they're running scared from Amelia,' the other woman said, her voice painfully smug. 'They know they're in the wrong. Amelia said he was the leader of the Soul Snatchers. You should stay well away from that place.'

Beth opened her eyes. Laura sat at the table next to her with Beth's replacement. The woman wore a tank top in spite of the cold weather, the A on her shoulder standing out in stark contrast to her skin. Laura leaned forwards, her elbows on the wooden surface as she whispered to her friend.

'What are you looking at?' Beth's replacement said, turning to glare at her. 'Hang on,' she added, her eyes narrowed, fine lines crinkling around the corners. 'Isn't she your ex-flatmate, Laura? The one from Third Eye?'

'That's her,' Laura said through gritted teeth. 'What are you doing here, Beth?'

Beth sighed. 'I'm here for a drink and a cake after a tough day. Please, feel free to ignore me. I'm not here to chat.'

'I was there,' the woman said, her eyes narrowed. 'At the charity event in the Monk's Inn. I saw that performance with your boyfriend, the Soul Snatcher. You should be ashamed of yourself, being out and about in public when you're involved with people like that.'

'People like that?' Beth said, her voice full of acid. 'Do you know anything about these people you are insulting? Do you know anything about the woman you're following so blindly? Just because she's on TV and social media doesn't make her right or virtuous.'

'She's not just on TV,' Laura said, leaning towards Beth, her hands clenched into fists. 'She's standing up here, in our city, and offering us protection. That means a lot in my book. I've always known there were dark forces about. Amelia is just telling us what we already knew and offering us a solution. I'm glad she's put herself out there for our protection, and I'm not surprised you feel threatened.'

The woman at Beth's table slammed her laptop shut, stuffed it into her bag and strode out, leaving a steaming cup of coffee and half eaten slice of cake on the table.

Beth sighed. 'Please, remember Amelia might not be all she seems.'

'How about you remember *your boyfriend* might not be all *he* seems,' Beth's replacement said, grinning at Beth, a bit of cake stuck to one of her front teeth.

'No wonder my ears were burning.'

Beth felt a wave of relief at the familiar voice. She turned. Jonan was standing behind her, watching Laura and her friend with one eyebrow raised.

'We'd better go,' Laura said, flushing a deep red.

'No, please stay and chat.' Jonan pulled the chair out and sat down facing them, his forearms resting on his thighs. 'You seem to have misconceptions about me, and I would prefer you addressed them to me directly rather than going through Beth. We can only answer for our own behaviour, after all, not somebody else's.'

Laura leaned back and crossed her arms over her chest. 'Amelia said you are the leader of the Soul Snatchers.'

'I'm afraid I'm not Amelia's favourite person at the moment.' Jonan flashed a dazzling smile at the woman who brought his coffee and then turned back to Laura. 'Amelia and I were together a long time ago. I hadn't realised she still held a torch for me, but she was upset when I became involved with Beth. My presence at her event was just bad timing, I'm afraid. I have nothing to do with any Soul Snatchers and Amelia knows it. Why do you think the police officer didn't arrest me? There was nothing to arrest me for.'

Beth's replacement frowned. 'You weren't arrested?'

'No and there are no ongoing investigations,' Jonan said. 'Can I get you another drink?'

'No, thank you.' Laura held up her hand. 'And you're actually *friends* with Amelia?'

'Oh yes, we go way back. We've known each other long enough to forgive each other for these stupid outbursts.'

Laura cleared her throat. 'So, are you a member of Amelia's Haven?'

'No, but my brother runs the show.'

'Amelia runs it.' Laura narrowed her eyes.

'Oh, she certainly heads it all up, but you don't seriously expect her to deal with the admin and databases do you? Amelia is far too busy for that kind of work. My brother manages the project on her behalf. Are you joining?'

'We're already fully vetted members.' Laura straightened as she spoke, her shoulders going back and her face lighting up with pride.

'It looks as though you've found somewhere you're happy.' Jonan smiled and took a bite of cake. 'That's all any of us can hope for. Just remember, Amelia is only human. She can make mistakes too. Support her rather than following her every move and do your own research into whether the Soul Snatchers exist. I'm not personally aware of any other accounts of them.'

'You would say that.' Laura got up and put her coat on. 'You're the leader of the Soul Snatchers.'

'There are many scary people about, but I am not one of them. Don't let yourself be blinded by prejudice. You could miss the real warnings signs.'

Laura froze. Her face drained of colour and she swallowed. 'Is *that* a threat?'

'Not at all. As I said, I'm not the one you should be scared of. Enjoy your day.' Jonan turned his chair away from them to face Beth, effectively cutting off the conversation.

'Erm,' Laura said.

Jonan ignored her. 'How were your meetings?'

Beth raised her eyebrows at Laura. She flushed, and then both women picked up their bags and made their way towards the door, muttering loudly.

'My meetings were a washout,' Beth said, draining her coffee. 'Nobody will represent us. There's no point going any further down the legal path. We clearly don't have anywhere near enough of a case, and I think the lawyers are all afraid of Amelia. Doriel was right.'

Jonan nodded, reached out and took her hand. 'That's okay. It was a great idea but it's not the only one. Attacking is Amelia's signature. We can be more creative.'

Beth let out a long breath. 'You're right. It's too easy to be drawn into her drama. She took a sip of coffee. 'Laura and her friend have been vetted. Did you get a look at their energy?'

Jonan nodded. 'They're all wrapped up in those grey cords like Katherine Haversham. That must be part of her process. She tells people she's vetting them, but actually locks them in by tying them to her, and to their own fears.'

'But she said there would be vetting stations all over the country. How will she make that happen when other people are doing it?'

Jonan shrugged. 'She'll probably create some kind of ritual for them. It wouldn't be hard.'

Beth's phone beeped. She picked it up and swiped the screen. 'Urgh, Laura has posted about us already, saying you threatened her. Now Amelia's shared it. Nothing good is going to come from that.'

Jonan took her hand. 'She will spin everything in the worst way she can, but we still need to live. Take a break. Stop thinking about her.'

Beth let out a breath and felt her shoulders ease. 'Did you see your mum?'

Jonan grinned. 'I did and she's very happy to help. She has offered to speak at the shop launch, answer questions and do a group healing session. I will offer individual healing, so we can leave Doriel out of things unless she changes her mind at the last minute. Miranda McLaney is a big enough draw by herself.'

'Miranda McLaney?'

Beth looked up. A man stood behind Jonan, his thick eyebrows drawn tightly together, a phone clutched in his hand. He was dressed for the outdoors in brown corduroy trousers and a heavy coat. 'You shouldn't be bringing Miranda McLaney here. St Albans needs to become a safe zone. We need to keep people like her out.'

Jonan stood up. He was almost a head taller than the other man. 'That's my mother you're talking about and she is no threat to anyone. You, on the other hand ...' He allowed the implication to hang in the air.

'What do you mean?' The man did his best to bulk himself up as he glared at Jonan.

'If you want St Albans to be a safe zone, stop trying to intimidate strangers.' Jonan's voice was quiet, but icy cold. 'Come on, Beth, let's get out of here.'

Beth stood up and pulled on her coat, not taking her eyes off the silent confrontation between the two men. She took hold of Jonan's arm and tugged him towards the door. He held still for a moment, and then turned and followed her out.

28

AMELIA

Amelia wrapped a scarf around her head, put on her oversized sunglasses and walked through the revolving doors of the TV station out into the street. Sunlight streamed down as the clouds shifted. Amelia turned her face upwards seeking warmth but there wasn't any. She shivered as an icy breeze cut through the sunshine. The Sheep drove her black saloon up to the curb, climbed out and opened the back door of the car. She slid into the seat without a word, pulling her bag in close as the door slammed shut.

'Happy?' Roland put down the spreadsheet he had been looking at and turned to face her.

'Delighted.' Amelia took off her glasses and turned away from him to look out of the window. 'I've completely won Katherine Haversham over. I knew I could do it. She was a tough nut to crack; my best conquest so far.'

'You're going to come out with something like that in front of the wrong people if you don't watch your words.' Roland picked up the sheaf of paper from his lap and scanned the spreadsheet, tracking his gaze with the tip of his fountain pen.

'Honestly? I think I could say whatever I wanted in front of anyone right now and they couldn't touch me. People love me. If I say it's good, it's good. And if I say it's a danger, they will run from it in droves. Right now, I am everything.'

'Ugh.' Roland shook his head. 'You're not concerned about hubris then?'

'Don't be ridiculous. I know what I'm doing. None of this has happened by chance. I am offering people what they want and they are rewarding me handsomely for it. This is a good thing, and you are getting as much out of it as I am.'

'You think?' Roland held up the pile of papers. 'I don't see you doing much to help keep things going in a practical sense. Do you think I like going through all these spreadsheets?'

'I do. You just like to moan about it. Most people feel they have to pretend to be unhappy in order to be worthy of what's coming their way. It's lack mentality and it's restrictive.'

'Maybe I should give up on lack mentality and quit working on these spreadsheets?' Roland raised an eyebrow.

'God, you look so like your brother when you do that.' Amelia's voice was husky.

Roland gaped. 'I am the one who stuck around, and you're still holding a torch for him. You're not even trying to hide it anymore.'

'Don't be ridiculous.' She took out a mirror and reapplied lipstick. 'You know I love you best. You're my rock.'

'Cold and inanimate?' Roland glared at her. His

eyebrow did not lift and Amelia wished she hadn't said anything. Those moments of similarity were all she had of Jonan now.

'Roland, you're an absolute star. I don't know what I would do without you. Please, don't misunderstand my words.'

'I'll make sure to come to you next time I need a reference.'

Amelia winced. She knew what Roland wanted and wished she could give it to him, but sex just wasn't enough. He wanted her soul and she hadn't had that to give since Jonan walked out on her all those years ago. 'Roland, please.'

'Stop the car.'

The Sheep swerved over to the side of the road and pulled up in a lay-by. Roland dumped the spreadsheets on the seat next to Amelia and swung the door open, putting his foot out to stop it slamming back from the force.

'Don't go, Rolo.' Amelia softened her voice, trying to make it sound loving, maybe even a little desperate. She heard it in her tone whenever she spoke to Jonan and had been trying to recreate it for Roland, but she hadn't succeeded yet. She could see in his eyes that he knew she was faking.

'I need some air. I'll see you later.'

'But it's a long walk home.'

'No, it's not. I'll be in St Albans within the hour, but I have things to do. Don't wait up.'

Amelia frowned. 'It's only midday. How much can you possibly have to do?'

'Just don't wait up.' Roland all but leapt out of the car, slamming the door behind him.

Amelia stared after him, feeling her heart thud too fast in her chest. Her throat felt tight and her breath was noisy as she forced air into her lungs. She would not let him go. 'Wait,' she said as the Sheep fired up the ignition. 'Stay here.'

Swinging the door open, she half stumbled out of the car in her haste. Roland was already striding off down the street and she had to run to catch up with him. She let out a yelp of pain as she went over on one of her high heels, so she reached down and pulled the shoes off, not caring that the rough concrete would shred her fine tights.

'Roland, get back here,' she yelled into the wind. 'You can't walk out on me like that.'

Roland stopped but didn't turn around. She ran towards him, yelping again as a stone bruised the soft skin on the sole of her foot. She limped the last few steps, and then stood behind him, breathing heavily. 'Roland?'

He turned around, his face grey and lifeless. 'What do you want, Amelia?'

'Come on, Rolo, there's no need for us to argue like this. Come back to the car where it's warm. The weather is brutal out here.'

Roland's shoulders slumped and his face crumpled. 'I can't do this anymore, Amelia, I'm sorry.'

She gaped.

He stepped closer and took both of her hands in his. 'Amelia.' His voice cracked. 'I loved you for so long, but you have never felt the same.'

'Don't be ridiculous. You've been the only one in my bed for years.'

'And Jonan's been the only one in your heart. I know I

remind you of him, but being a memento isn't enough anymore.'

'What are you saying? You're leaving me?'

'In my heart, I left you a long time ago. It was just too painful to acknowledge the truth.'

Amelia's chest tightened even further. Her stomach churned and she reached out to grip the icy railing next to her. 'What's changed all of a sudden?'

'Nothing,' Roland said, stepping backwards and putting space between them. 'I'm just being more honest. I can't dedicate my life to someone who doesn't love me back. I will help you with Amelia's Haven. I owe you that much. And you can call on me for anything you need, but I will move into a different room at the inn from now on.'

'You're assuming you're still welcome at the inn.' Amelia reached down and pulled on her shoes, wanting the power of extra height. Her body was shivering with cold, but she held herself as still as she could, straightening her back and pushing back her shoulders. 'Why would I take you in?'

'Because whatever we may have failed to become, we have always been good friends.' Roland held her gaze, not backing down or looking away.

Amelia swallowed. 'Who is she?'

'I don't know what you mean,' Roland said, his jaw hardening.

'There's somebody else. You wouldn't leave me otherwise.'

Roland sighed. 'As of this moment I am single, Amelia, and if I choose to become involved with someone else that is my choice. But I have never cheated on you.'

Amelia held his gaze, trying to read his energy, to find out whether he was telling the truth. But she had taught him too well, nothing got through his shields. She sighed. 'They will humiliate me.'

Roland frowned. 'Who?'

Amelia froze. Why had she spoken? This was bound to make things worse.

'Jonan. You mean Jonan will humiliate you?' He took a deep breath, shook his head and walked away.

'Please don't go.' Amelia chased after him, not caring who saw now. 'That was a stupid thing to say. I'm sorry.'

'Leave me be, Amelia. I'm not out to humiliate you. I just want my life back.'

'But …'

'Leave. Me. Alone.' Roland spat out the words. 'Just give me space. If you can do that, I will come back and help you set up Amelia's Haven. That's the only thing anyone has a right to take an interest in. But you and I are done.'

He shoved his hands in his pockets, turned around and walked off down the road in long, determined strides. A few drops of rain fell onto Amelia's freezing shoulders and then it turned into a torrent. She gave up any attempt to maintain her image and allowed the shivering to take over. There was a beep behind her and she turned to find the car had pulled up. The passenger window scrolled down. 'Get in the front. It's warmer here,' the Sheep said from inside.

She could feel the heat from where she stood and stumbled through the puddles to the passenger door. Her hands were too cold to work properly and she fumbled at the handle. The next moment, the door was propelled open from inside and she collapsed onto the seat, breathing hard. She didn't even try to hold back the tears that slid down her icy cheeks. Warm air blew at her and she slumped in her seat as the car moved forwards. She looked out of her window as they passed Roland, but he didn't turn. He walked tall and straight, his shoulders back and a smile on his face. He had clearly fallen completely out of love with her, and for all her psychic abilities she had not seen it coming.

29

JONAN

It was dark outside and rain drummed on the window of the shop. The last customer had left an hour ago and there were crystals littered over all the wrong surfaces. Jonan loved this part of the day, when silence had overtaken the chatter and the shop was calm and empty. He lit three candles and a stick of sage, feeling the peace deepen. Taking a deep breath, he hummed as he walked along the shelves, rearranging crystals, putting sage smudging sticks back in the basket and tidying up tarot decks.

The bell rang and the door clattered open. Jonan turned around, frowning. 'We're closed,' he said automatically. His eyes widened as he saw who was standing there. 'Roland! You're soaking wet.'

'I've been walking for hours. I don't suppose I could borrow some clothes?'

'Is everything okay?'

Roland shivered.

'You're cold. Of course you can borrow clothes. Come on, let's go upstairs. I'll light the fire.'

Starfolk Falling

Jonan locked the door and bounded up the stairs, leaving Roland to follow. He had dreamed of reconnecting with his brother, but they had drifted so far apart he had almost given up. But there was something different in the man's eyes tonight. He piled up wood in the fire, set it to burn, and then went through to his bedroom and pulled out some clothes. He and Roland were almost exactly the same size and shape. It was their colouring that most clearly distinguished them. Roland's hair was dark and his skin tanned quickly in the sun, while Jonan's blond hair and pale complexion just added to the otherworldly look he had always tried to mask.

'Here,' he handed Roland the pile of clothes. 'The bathroom is over there and there are towels in the cupboard. Have a shower, warm up and get into these. I'll put the kettle on.'

He whistled as he made the coffee and, on a whim, grabbed a bottle of whisky from the cupboard. The bathroom door opened as he put the drinks on the low table.

Roland came out, rubbing his hair with a towel. He looked younger damp and rumpled and Jonan's heart twinged. They had missed out on so much time.

'Whisky in your coffee?' Jonan said, raising an eyebrow.

Roland nodded and sat down in an armchair. He reached for the mug Jonan pushed towards him and cradled it between his hands.

'Is everything okay?' Jonan asked, his voice quiet.

'Look, I can't really tell you anything, okay. Can we just talk about something else?'

Jonan frowned. 'But …'

'Please?' Roland's face was pale despite the remnants of his summer tan. His eyes were bloodshot.

Jonan nodded. 'Of course.' He stared into the flames wondering what a safe topic of conversation would be. He couldn't ask about Amelia or the Haven, and those were the only things they had discussed in years.

'You're doing renovations?' Roland said, his voice flat.

'Yes.' Jonan watched Roland, wishing his brother would meet his gaze. 'We thought it was about time. Layla designed it.'

Roland looked up and for the first time his cheeks held a hint of colour. 'She did? Is that why you hired her?'

'Yes.' Jonan felt the lump in his chest ease at the light in Roland's eyes. 'She's been wonderful.'

'Is she still here?'

'No, I'm sorry. She leaves early to collect her daughter from school.'

Roland froze. 'A daughter?'

'Does that put you off?'

Roland's face went blank, and then he organised his features and ran a hand through his damp hair, smoothing it back into its normal order. 'I don't know what you're talking about. Layla seems perfectly nice, but I am not in the market for a relationship.'

'You know, it's okay to want more.' Jonan leaned back and put his feet up on the coffee table. 'I know you've been with Amelia for a long time, but it is okay to move on if things aren't working for you. Nobody would judge you.'

'Ha!' Roland rolled his eyes. 'Apart from half the country, you mean? How did you find it, being the person who publicly humiliated Amelia at the ball?'

Jonan shrugged. 'It wasn't my most comfortable moment, but you and I have what it takes to stand up to her.

Most people can't see through her manipulations. It's our responsibility to do the right thing.'

'Oh get off your soapbox.' Roland sighed. 'I had hoped for a bit of time-out here, for space from being harangued and told what to do. I guess I was wrong.' He stood up. 'Thanks for the clothes. I'll return them as soon as possible.'

'Roland, don't go.' Jonan got up and stepped towards the younger man, but Roland put his hands up. 'Please, don't. Don't pretend we have a relationship.'

Jonan flinched, but he stepped back. 'For the record, I hope we might have a relationship again someday, maybe soon. Know that you can talk to me any time, and you can trust me. I'm glad you're happy with Amelia. Please do send her my good wishes.'

'Not your love?' Roland's eyebrow shot up.

'I think that might be taken the wrong way.'

'You think? Do you have any idea how you have haunted me for my entire adult life? How was I ever supposed to compete with you?'

Jonan sat on the sofa and dropped his head into his hands. 'Roland, you don't have to compete. You're ten times the man I ever was.'

'Try telling Amelia that.' Roland pulled on his damp coat and opened the door. 'You reeled her in and then walked away and left me with nothing.'

Jonan looked up at Roland. 'Nothing?' His voice cracked. 'You've been with her for years.'

'Yeah, well. I'm a great lookalike.'

Jonan gaped. His stomach rolled and he swallowed back bile. What had he done all those years ago? And what was Amelia doing to his brother to make him look so beaten? Roland was a catch by anyone's estimation. He was staggeringly good looking and had the charisma to hold a room. He had always been surrounded by admirers and Jonan had assumed he stayed with Amelia because he was happy. What if that was not the case? Did she have some kind of hold over him? Or was he just too in love with her to leave? 'I don't know,' he said, trying to cover the hoarseness in his voice. 'You don't look that much like me.'

Roland laughed. 'Well at least you have a sense of humour. I've almost forgotten what that is. The inn is beautiful, but it's the most depressing place I've ever lived.'

'*Please* sit back down,' Jonan said. He let down all his guards and saw Roland's eyes widen. They had all grown so used to shielding their energy, it was almost shocking to experience it unfettered. It was freeing, but it filled Jonan with a homesickness so intense it took his breath away.

Roland swallowed and lowered slowly to the sofa. He closed his eyes.

With his heightened awareness, Jonan could see Roland was trying to centre himself, but was also letting down his own shields. As their energy connected, the sense of homesickness intensified.

When Roland opened his eyes, they were a deep purple. 'Do you ever miss it, brother?'

'It?' Jonan raised one eyebrow.

Roland flinched. 'That place that feels like home even though we have never been there in the flesh.'

Jonan could see he was fighting to keep his breathing steady.

'All the time. I have spent a lifetime mourning that place. I've only really settled here since Beth arrived. Does Amelia make you feel like that, Roland? I'm sorry I criticised you for being with her. If she makes you feel at home, I am utterly delighted for you.'

Roland swallowed. 'Amelia is certainly absorbing.'

Jonan slumped back onto the sofa. He could see Roland's aura, but it gave nothing away. His brother was shielding as much as he was revealing, and Jonan could feel the dread gathering in his middle. 'Has she hurt you?'

'Hurt me? Jonan, we are adults. We hurt each other all the time. This is normal.'

'No,' Jonan propelled himself to his feet and started pacing. 'No it's not. That isn't how it should be.'

'You like telling people how things should be don't you, brother. You and Amelia have that in common. Mother too. But life is different for me. I'm not a part of your precious Triad, first or second time around. I have my own path to walk and it is not your place to tell me which way it leads.'

Jonan's phone buzzed. He frowned and picked it up. There was a message from Layla.

> Abi is worried about Doriel. She dreamed Doriel was in prison and is convinced she's not safe. Is she with you?

Ice shot down Jonan's spine.

'Is everything okay?' Roland leaned forwards.

'I'm not sure. Layla's daughter, Abi, is worried about Doriel for some reason. And something doesn't feel right.'

> She went out for the first time but I'll find her. Tell Abi not to worry.

He sent the text to Layla, and then dialled Doriel's number. The phone rang out and went to her answer machine. 'Damn,' he said, standing up and starting to pace. He hung up and dialled again. She didn't answer. 'Hi Doriel,' he said into the phone. 'I just wanted to check in and make sure everything is okay. Please call me?' He hung up.

'Do we have any actual reason to worry?' Roland asked.

'No,' he said, running a hand through his hair. 'No, we don't.'

A loud bang crashed through the flat and then the door to the stairs slammed open.

'Doriel!' Roland crossed the room in three strides, pulling Doriel away from the top of the staircase, where she swayed, her face pale. He stood in front of her, crouched slightly at the knees to look her in the eye. 'What happened?' his voice was soft and hypnotic. 'What frightened you?'

She started, her eyes snapping into focus. 'Get off me!' she squealed, shoving him backwards. 'What are you doing here? Did she send you?'

'She?' Roland's voice was hard.

'Amelia, who else?' Doriel stuck her chin out and narrowed her eyes. She glared at him. 'I know she's pulling your strings, and now you're here, in my home, trying to extract information from me. But you know what frightened me, don't you? You know all about her plans and interferences. You know she's sent *him* after me.'

Roland turned his head, caught Jonan's eye, and then looked back to Doriel. He cleared his throat. 'Him?'

'You know who I'm talking about.' She moved closer so her face was only inches from his. 'After everything that happened, I can't believe you would agree to such a betrayal. What have I ever done to you?'

'Nothing.' His voice was hoarse, a mere whisper. 'And I'm not doing anything to you. I don't know who you've seen. I don't know who frightened you, or why. Tell me now and I will go after them.'

'Ha!' She shook her head, planting her hands on her hips. 'You seriously expect me to believe that? You are Amelia's puppy. You do whatever she tells you, whenever she tells you to do it. You knew all about my abduction. You know who she sent after me, and you know he's coming for me again.'

Roland paled. 'I don't know any such thing. Why do you think he's coming after you?'

'I saw him,' she said through gritted teeth. 'I know what's going on.'

'Well then, please enlighten me, because I haven't got a clue.'

Doriel stopped. She was breathing heavily and her hands were clenched into fists by her side. 'You really don't know?'

He shook his head.

She walked over to the sofa and slumped into one corner, pulling her legs up in front of her and dropping her forehead onto her knees.

'Doriel, what happened?' Jonan sat next to her. He reached out to touch her shoulder, but she flinched and he jerked backwards. 'Please tell me.'

She looked at him, her eyes bright even though her jaw was still tight.

'Now,' he said. 'No more excuses. Tell me what happened.'

30

BETH

Beth did a double take. The Brute was standing in the doorway to a coffee shop, a takeaway cup in his hand. His eyes were narrowed, closely following an unknown point in the distance.

Beth frowned, looking into the crowd. She went cold. Doriel was walking away from them towards Lunea.

Beth pulled out her phone and switched it into video mode. Pointing it into the crowds, she made sure she had both the Brute and Doriel in the picture before the woman disappeared through the throng of people. The Brute stepped out from the doorway, making after her.

'Hey,' Beth yelled, slipping her phone back into her pocket, and then ducking and diving through the crowds. She grabbed the man's sleeve and yanked. He stopped and turned around slowly.

He looked at Beth through narrowed eyes. 'You!' he said, his voice gravelly. 'What do *you* want?' His eyes flickered down to his wrist and he rubbed it.

Beth had a flash of memory: the crunch as Jonan's foot

bore down on the man's arm. She shuddered. 'I want to know why you are following her.'

'Which particular *her* are we talking about?' The Brute raised his eyebrows and grinned, but his eyes remained dull.

'You know who we're talking about.' Beth took a step closer, tilting her chin into the air. 'I will not let you hurt her again.'

The man bristled. 'I haven't hurt anyone.'

Beth stepped closer. She pushed out her energy to make herself seem bigger, but she was still dwarfed by the huge man. 'We were both there. I saw where you were keeping Doriel and Bill. I saw what state he was in under your care, and now he's dead. Did you know that?'

The Brute's hands bunched into fists at his side. 'You can't prove anything,' he hissed.

'How sure are you of that?'

'What do you mean?' He rolled his shoulders and cracked his knuckles as he loomed over her.

Beth swallowed. She looked from side to side. The pavements were heaving with people, but nobody was looking at her. She could see the blank faces and glazed eyes as people walked past, oblivious to everything around them. Then out of the corner of her eye, she spotted a man in a black uniform.

'Officer,' she shouted, and then turned her head for a moment and made eye contact with the policeman. 'Officer, this man is threatening me.'

The Brute's eyes widened. He held up his hands in front of him and shook his head as he stepped backwards. A shout came from behind him as he crashed into an elderly lady with a fabric shopping trolley. Crying out in pain, she hit the pavement hard.

The policeman dashed past Beth, speaking urgently into his walkie talkie. 'Are you alright, ma'am?' he said crouching down beside her.

'What do you think you're doing?' A large man squared up to the Brute, his face turning a deep shade of red. 'If you've hurt my mother, I'll …'

'Sir?' The policeman said, standing up. 'Sir, there is an ambulance on the way. Please could you sit with your mother?'

The man shook his fist at the Brute, and then turned away and crouched down to hold his mother's hand.

The policeman walked over to Beth. 'Is this the man who was harassing you?' He gestured at the Brute.

Beth nodded. 'I thought he was going to hit me or something.'

'Do you know this man?'

'We met before. He threatened my friend then, and this time he was following her.'

The Brute started, and then turned and walked off.

'Hey, come back!' The policeman followed him, breaking into a run. By the time he had caught him up they were too far away for Beth to hear what was said. The Brute's shoulders expanded as though he were rolling and flexing them as the policeman remonstrated with him, got out handcuffs and snapped them around his wrists. He spoke into his radio and moments later, a police car pulled up and the Brute was manhandled into the back. The policeman straightened his uniform, and then came back to Beth.

'Would you like to make a statement?'

Beth thought back over the exchange. She had the small bit of video, but nothing that implicated him in anything real. He hadn't touched her today, and last time they had made a statement they'd been dismissed. She needed to wait, gather evidence and then do this properly when she had something to prove. 'Thank you, Officer,' she said, shaking her head. 'But you've already resolved the situation. I just wanted to be left alone.'

The man nodded, and then turned and strode off.

31

AMELIA

Amelia picked up the phone and dialled. Roland's bombshell was still pounding through her blood, but one afternoon crying in her room was more than enough.

She felt a flutter of excitement as the phone rang and wondered whether the man would take her call. She had always been starstruck by the idea of him, but she was a celebrity now and was relying on that to open the door. He had a huge following of people who would be entirely susceptible to her stories, and Robson Fall was the perfect way to reach them.

She still remembered the first time she had seen Robson Fall. She had visited her mother and the old lady had shown her online videos of her favourite conspiracy theorist. The moment she saw him on the screen she was transfixed. He looked completely different to Jonan with a broader frame, thick dark hair and heavy stubble. But his clear, green eyes held all the intensity of Jonan's violet gaze and she had felt her heart race as she watched him.

'Mr Fall's office.' A curt, female voice interrupted the memory.

'Good evening,' Amelia said in a breathy voice. 'This is Amelia Faustus. Would Mr Fall be available for a chat?'

Silence.

Amelia smiled. She could feel the woman's surprise and excitement with more than a tinge of fear. It was snaking through the line and zeroing in on Amelia. She breathed it in, feeling herself light up, pushing back her earlier depletion.

'Erm, I'm sorry,' the woman stuttered. 'Did you say Amelia Faustus? *The* Amelia Faustus?'

'The very same.' Amelia's voice was smoother by the minute and she revelled in the sense of becoming herself again after her earlier defeat. The woman's fear and awe lit her up and she breathed deeply, feeling her chest expand and prickles of excitement cover her skin. 'I was hoping we might discuss possible opportunities to collaborate.'

'Yes, of course, Ms Faustus.' The woman was clutching at her professional demeanour, but the tang of conflicting emotions was ever stronger. 'Would you like to hold, or shall I ask Mr Fall to call you back?'

'I will hold.' Amelia sat down in the old-fashioned upright armchair and crossed her legs, allowing her thigh to slide through the slit in her tight skirt. There was nobody watching, but her beauty gave her a sense of power that she desperately needed right now and she smiled as her energy lifted further.

'Amelia Faustus.' The voice on the other end of the phone was so familiar that a shot of excitement spiked through her.

'Mr Fall, how nice to speak to you at last.'

'I was very sad to hear of the death of your mother. I understand she was a true follower.'

'It was a deep and wounding loss.' Amelia thought of Roland and used the emotion of his betrayal to make her breath catch. She willed her eyes to tear up, and allowed raw sadness to make her voice thick. She had barely thought of her mother since her death. The old bat had been a continual drain and she had been pleased to lose the load. 'In her memory, I was hoping we might be able to work together, Mr Fall. I know she would have wanted me to spread the word and I hope you understand the importance of my own little venture, offering people protection from the harsher forces in this world.'

'It's interesting that you called now. I was just thinking about you.'

'Oh really?' Amelia felt a fizz of excitement.

'Yes, you popped up in a media alert moments before the phone rang, and now here you are.'

'And I didn't even know I was in the media today. What it is to be in demand.'

He laughed. 'Well quite, if only we were as in demand as we liked to pretend. And yes, I would be delighted to explore a collaboration. Shall we do dinner and get to know each other properly?'

Amelia smiled. She could feel his excitement through the connection, could feel that he wanted her, and not just for her profile. This could be a more fruitful liaison than she had anticipated. 'Somewhere discreet, I think,' she purred and was pleased to hear the catch of his breath. 'Perhaps I could welcome you to the home of Amelia's Haven, the Monk's Inn?'

'I would be delighted.' His voice was husky.

Bingo.

'I will have my PA call you to arrange the details,' Amelia said, allowing her smile to flow into her voice. 'Ciao!'

She hung up.

Standing up, she popped the cork on a bottle of champagne and filled a flute to the brim. 'Cheers to me,' she said, holding up her glass. She drank it and filled it up again.

Her phone beeped. She picked it up and scrolled through the media alert. She put her glass down on the table and then reached for the chair, allowing herself to slump awkwardly into it. Her heart was hammering in her ears and the floor seemed to be shifting. She could hear laughing in her mind, but all she wanted to do was cry.

DISTRAUGHT AMELIA ABANDONED ON ROADSIDE BY LOVER

Amelia's head span. She dug her fingernails into the arms of the chair, but it just increased the rising panic in her chest. That must have been the alert Robson Fall saw. He had been laughing *at* her when she said she was in demand. The laughing in her mind intensified and echoed around the room. She squeezed her eyes tightly shut, pulled in deep breaths and let out long, slow exhales through her mouth. *Be gone.* She sent out the command.

This was what you always wanted, wasn't it, Amelia. The old man's voice was surprisingly sprightly in death. *To trap me here? Well you're stuck with me now.*

It was a long time since she'd helped a spirit cross. She'd spent the last few years encouraging them to stay, and somehow nothing worked now. She wasn't surprised when the laughter got louder. This building was supposed to amplify her abilities, not erode them, but she could feel her strength ebbing away.

She felt the shift in atmosphere as familiar footsteps came into the reception area on the other side of the hall. Roland. There was silence, and then the sound of Rose coming down the hall to meet him.

'She'll deal with it,' Amelia muttered to herself. 'There's no need for me to face *him*.'

She pressed her ear up against the door, listening to the angry exchange, feeling her heart beat furiously in her chest. 'Roland,' she whispered, but in her head, a different name repeated over and over.

Jonan.

32

ROLAND

Roland stopped at an ice-cream shop on the way back to the inn. He never ate ice cream and didn't much like it, but any delay was preferable to arriving at his so-called home.

The scene on the street was playing on a continual loop in his mind. He could see Amelia, rain soaked, tears streaming down her face while she begged him to take her back. He saw himself walking away, leaving her there with only her driver. Why hadn't he waited and done it in private? What had possessed him to take that leap in public when she had no support and no privacy to grieve? He shuddered at the memories and felt tears prick his eyes. She had been his world for years. Even though the love had long since passed, the grief was real and raw, layered in with the loss of his mother and Jonan.

'Excuse me,' a soft voice said on his right. He turned, disorientated for a moment. He had been so deep in thought, he had forgotten the damp street, the glare of the streetlamps and the smattering of people still out despite the fading light. He looked around and saw a young woman standing a few feet from him. She smiled and stepped closer. 'Are you Amelia's partner?' she said, shuffling closer.

'I ...' he tailed off, unsure of what to say.

'You were there in the bar, encouraging people to sign up for Amelia's Haven. It looked like you were working with her?'

Roland felt the pressure in his chest ease. Of course. She wasn't asking whether he was sleeping with Amelia, just whether they were working together. 'Yes, that's me. Is there something you'd like to know?'

'What would Amelia's Haven do to help me if I was infected by the Soul Snatchers? If I've paid my membership, would they protect me and cure the contagion? I really want to join, but I'm afraid of what might happen if I came into contact with the wrong people and the Haven found out.'

She looked at him, her big, blue eyes open and questioning.

He swallowed. They had never talked about this. Anyone associated with the Soul Snatchers had always been branded the enemy. The idea of people being victims in need of saving was completely alien to the project. 'The Haven will always protect its own,' Roland said, spreading his lips into a smile that felt awkward and fake. 'We are here to help. You will be safe with us.'

But would she? And would he? If he encountered this terrible enemy, would he even know it was there? Would he be able to tell if he was infected, or would he have to just wait to be ejected from the group he considered home?

'Thank you.' The woman reached out and took his hands in hers. She looked into his eyes and smiled. 'You have put my mind at rest.' She let go, turned and walked down the street.

Roland swallowed. He didn't move until she was completely out of sight. Taking a deep breath, he forced himself to put one foot in front of the other, trying to focus on the moment. He looked in the shop windows, examining the watches in the jewellers, looking at menus outside restaurants, and then stopping to admire the ancient architecture of the old prison archway. 'She is only human,' he kept repeating to himself. 'You've known her your whole life. You have nothing to be afraid of.' And yet, he knew in his heart that she was capable of a lot more harm than the average person. He had to remember how to access his own otherworldly power so he could stand up to her as Jonan did. His brother had always been more accomplished in that respect. It hadn't mattered before, but if he was going to be on the outside he would have to adjust.

Standing outside the inn, he steeled himself for what was to come. He clenched his hands into fists, took a deep breath and then pushed the door open. The inn was deadly silent. Then the sound of stilettos clicking over the tiled floors came closer. 'Hello, can I help?' Rose, Amelia's PA, came down the hall. She was smiling, but her face fell when she saw Roland.

'Ah, erm ...' she faltered, looking him up and down with a frown. She plastered a new grin across her face, but her eyes still looked troubled. 'Is there something I can do for you, Roland?'

Roland shook his head. 'No need. I'll just head upstairs.'

'Erm,' she said, stepping in front of the staircase 'I don't think that's a good idea. I can arrange to have your things delivered to your new place of residence.'

Roland gaped. 'She's throwing me out?'

'As I understand it, *you* cut ties with *her*. She wants to heal and can't do that with you in her home.'

'Okay, I will look for somewhere new tomorrow. For now, it's too late to relocate. Let me pass.'

She shook her head. 'You've been gone all afternoon. I trust you have been using that time wisely and have secured yourself new accommodation. Please write your new address on the notepad at reception. I will arrange to have your things delivered tomorrow. I'm sure you can manage for tonight.'

There were footsteps in the small room behind reception.

'How about I discuss this directly with Amelia,' Roland said, taking a step towards the door.

'You don't seem to understand.' Rose crossed her arms across her chest, pursing her lips. 'Amelia does not want to see you. She has left explicit instructions that you are to be kept away. She does not want you living here anymore, or having access to any of the information about Amelia's Haven. You have severed ties, Roland.'

He swallowed. 'So it would seem.'

'Please, Roland, don't make this harder than it needs to be. Just leave.'

He held his hands up. 'I would hate to make it hard for *you*, Rose,' he said, spitting the words out, wishing he could hurl his fury at the woman who deserved it. 'I don't currently have a place of residence. I will be in contact when I have something to tell you.'

They faced each other for a moment and then he turned, walked out through the door and slammed it as hard as he could behind him.

33

BETH

Betalia took a deep breath. This was really happening. She looked over at the Triad. Until this moment, they had always been a quartet, with Betalia's mother forming that strong, fourth pillar of light. Now, for the first time, the sisterhood was separating and none of them knew how they would reform.

Betalia watched the group energy as a gap grew between her mother and the others. The energetic cords that bound them were loosening, thinning and becoming more translucent. They would never break, but the connection was transforming before her eyes and it sent a chill down her spine.

Change may be coming to Earth, but it was spreading its fingers here too.

'It is time.' The Queen stood up. Her eyes glinted and Betalia saw a single tear slide down her cheek.

Jonan reached out a hand and Lunea took it, stepping delicately off the dais and onto the polished, golden floor. She walked, head held high, towards the enormous, heavy doors at the far end of the throne room.

The Triad followed.

Jonan reached out his hand again, and this time it was Betalia who took it.

He pulled her close as they walked. She knew that he too felt grief at this unnatural separation. On Earth, she would have no idea of their connection. They would live years of their lives never meeting. She liked to think that when they did meet she would recognise him, that she would believe everything he told her.

She had no idea whether or not this would turn out to be true.

They walked in silence through the long, crystal halls. Then Miranda intoned a note so pure Betalia shivered. It swelled, bolstered by the swirling light that grew brighter all around them.

Doriel joined, creating a chord that lulled Betalia into the beginnings of trance. The power grew as Amelia and Jonan added their sounds. Jonan's voice was deep, and she felt her aura vibrate, felt it touching his as she dropped further into trance.

Betalia's note came last.

She felt the thrill shiver through her energy as it cut the air, and she watched herself from outside her body, as her physical form grew ever more translucent.

First her feet vanished as she became less and less grounded. Her legs faded into nothingness as she glided, her long, indigo robe not quite sweeping the floor. Then her hands became fainter. She shimmered in the brightness from the windows as beams of light shone through her. The long, dark plait, woven with flowers, was the most solid thing about her and she focused on it, wanting to see the moment her body lay down and blinked out of existence.

Bodies were not important when you could manifest any shape you chose. It was fun to play with form, creating at will, but now Betalia had lost interest. Her body only existed for the moment it vanished, when she went through the portal and incarnated onto Earth without her memories.

The energy was all.

Starfolk Falling

Betalia was one with the Triad, one with her mother, and always one with Jonan. Separation fell away until she was barely aware of walking through the corridor. She felt only the light-bodies of the group, and the purity of the sound that enveloped her, lifting her higher.

Finally they reached their destination. The room was long and slender lined with tall, arched windows. The light was dazzling. They entered slowly, deliberately, lining up in front of the crystal slabs that lay in a row down the centre of the room.

The Queen walked a silent circuit. One by one, candles flickered into life, ignited by her gaze alone.

The Triad lay on the crystal slabs, and then Jonan took his place. Finally, Betalia lay on the last one.

The Queen lifted her arms above her head and closed her eyes. 'You leave together, my loved ones, in a moment of combined power and intention. Each of you will travel to the Earth time at which the stars align to support your journey. Go in light my loved ones. Fulfil your path and return home.

'Please state your intention,' The Queen's voice was haunted as it filled the room.

Betalia closed her eyes. I will go to Earth and embrace my path.

The thought filled her mind. It sank through the last vestiges of her physical form, and emanated out to the part of her that was watching. I will go to Earth. She thought again, and watched as her form blinked out.

She sank into blackness.

'Beth, Beth, wake up,' Jonan's voice nudged at the edges of her awareness.

'Go away. I'm sleeping,' she mumbled.

'I would if I could, but it's launch day.'

Beth sat up, wide awake now. 'What time is it?'

'Half-past seven. There's coffee and breakfast in the other room if you're hungry?'

Beth climbed out of bed and put on her dressing gown. 'I had another dream,' she said, walking through to the lounge. 'Wow, you really did make breakfast!'

Jonan grinned and held her chair out for her. There was a mug of coffee and a plate of egg on toast. Jonan sat opposite and took a gulp of coffee. 'What did you dream?'

'I dreamed about leaving our home.' Unbidden, Beth felt tears prick her eyes. 'It makes me feel homesick.'

Jonan nodded. 'We all get that.'

'Temperance,' Doriel's voice called through from her bedroom.

Beth raised her eyebrows at Jonan.

He shrugged. 'Ever since she got home yesterday, she has taken to her room and only spoken in tarot cards. I wish she'd come out and have a proper conversation so we could figure out what to do.'

'The Hermit,' her voice came through the door again.

'I know, I know,' he shouted back. 'But if you're going to be a hermit, surely you should stop listening to my private conversations?'

Beth laughed. 'I think I can figure out what the Hermit means, but what about Temperance?'

'Temperance is the angel of the tarot,' Jonan said, leaning back. 'It means you are being looked after.' A waft of lavender filled the room.

'Salu,' Beth whispered. 'Did I show you this?' She flicked through her phone and found the video of the Brute. She slid it across the table to Jonan. 'Watch that.'

Starfolk Falling

He clicked play and watched, his face darkening. 'Was this yesterday?'

Beth nodded.

'He's definitely following her. No wonder she was frightened.'

'The Seven of Swords,' Doriel's voice came through the wall, softer this time.

'I know, Doriel. Nobody's asking you to trust him, or Amelia for that matter. But you can trust *us*. Remember that Abi asked Layla to check on you? You have a team of people looking out for you and we need your help with the new shop. Please come out.'

'I can't. I'm reading tarot. I need to concentrate. You have Miranda. You don't need me.'

Jonan sighed. 'I'm going to call Amelia; find out why she's sending that man after Doriel. Will you go and start getting the shop ready for the opening? You've done such a great job at raising our profile. Hopefully we'll get lots of visitors.'

'On it.' Beth stood up. 'Good luck with Amelia.'

34

BETH

The door jingled as Layla came into the shop with two enormous containers filled with home-baked flapjacks, cupcakes and brownies. 'I thought we could offer these to the guests,' she said, fishing two large platters out of her bag and arranging the goodies. 'They're free from gluten, dairy and nuts.'

'You've thought of everything!' Beth said, pinching a brownie. Layla swiped at her hand, but she looked pleased.

'Abi and I spent hours cooking last night. Does it taste okay?'

'It's delicious,' Beth said, her mouth thick with cake. 'And the shop looks incredible. You've done an amazing job.' She looked around her, admiring the newly finished room. The cluttered shop had been replaced by a modern break-out space, with comfy chairs and clusters of products to try out. Upstairs had become an event space that doubled as a second floor for the shop.

The bells rang again and Miranda strode in. Layla

offered her the platter, but Miranda just shook her head. 'Where will I be working?'

'Upstairs. Shall I show you?' Beth reached towards the door.

'I know my way. Thank you.'

'Wow, she's not so much into the touchy feely, is she!' Layla said, gaping at the shut door. 'Is she really Roland and Jonan's mother? They're so ... different!'

Beth laughed. 'She's been alone for a long time. You'll get used to her.'

'How's Doriel?' Layla frowned. 'Is she coming to join us?'

Beth shook her head. 'She hasn't left her room since the encounter with the Brute. Abi might be able to lure her out though?'

Layla nodded. 'I'll bring her when school finishes. Should we open up?'

Jonan bounded into the room. 'Great to see you, Layla. Yes, let's open up. One question before we do. Have you seen Roland? I believe he relocated last night, but I have no idea where he's gone.'

Layla frowned. 'No, but I don't think he has any way to contact me apart from coming here.'

Jonan's eyebrows shot up. 'I thought you two were in touch?'

She shook her head. 'I'm sorry. Do you have another way to reach him?'

Jonan smiled but it didn't reach his eyes. 'I'll find a way.'

He opened the door with a flourish and grinned at the smattering of people outside.

A woman at the front of the group pulled up a placard. 'Down with the Soul Snatchers. Down with their followers,' she shouted, waving the board at Jonan. Someone else attached a large tablet to a selfie stick and cranked an Amelia interview up loud. 'You must be careful. Stay away from anyone different, anyone strange,' her voice blared down the street.

Jonan propped the door open, and then rearranged the crystals on a coffee table, pointedly ignoring the growing crowd outside the door.

Beth sat next to him. 'What did Amelia say? Did she admit to sending the Brute after Doriel?'

Jonan grimaced. 'She wouldn't speak to me. Rose answered the phone and asked if I had a forwarding address for Roland so they could send on his things. Apparently he's disappeared.'

Beth frowned. 'Disappeared? I thought he was with Amelia?'

'It seems that's no longer the case. We'll find him later. For now, let's pretend those protestors aren't bothering us.'

An hour later, not one person had stepped inside the shop.

Jonan was sitting behind the counter, doing paperwork and ignoring the growing ruckus outside.

Layla started walking over, and then her face crumpled and she veered off towards one of the displays.

'Layla?' Jonan said, putting his pen down. 'What's the matter?'

She sighed. 'It's all my fault. I was supposed to design a shop that would be approachable and not attract the wrong attention. I think we can all agree I've done a rotten job of that.'

'You give yourself too much credit.' Miranda walked into the room, dusting off her long skirt. 'This has

Amelia's signature all over it, but we all know that already.'

'You people always blame Amelia for everything.' The high-pitched voice came from the doorway. 'She is the one trying to save us all.'

Beth spun around. It was Laura, but the normal edgy and image-conscious woman looked as though she had rolled out of bed on a sick day. Her skin was sallow and dark circles haunted her eyes. She was dressed to camouflage and was glaring angrily at Beth.

'Laura! What are you doing here?'

'I warned you against getting caught up with these people. I hoped you might have walked away.'

White-hot anger shot through Beth. She closed her eyes as the ground swayed beneath her. Reaching out, she put her hand on a large, smoky quartz crystal ball that sat on the shelf to her left and felt herself steady. The flames of Amelia's energy were reaching for her, flickering ever closer whilst consuming Laura whole.

'Laura,' Beth said, her voice hoarse. 'I am one of these people. I'm not going to stay away. Think about all the time we lived together. Did you ever feel unsafe with me then?'

'Of course!' Laura's voice was almost a squeal. 'Why do you think I evicted you?'

Beth swallowed. 'Please, let me help you. You're not yourself.'

'I'm fine. I'm the best I've ever been.' Laura tilted up her chin, pressing her lips into a thin line.

Beth sighed. 'I know we didn't leave things well, but you're still my friend. I care.'

'Huh!' Laura took a step back, putting more space between them. 'I don't need you. Amelia is all the friend I will ever need.' She looked over her shoulder at the protesters and backed away towards them.

'Is this woman bothering you, Laura? Do you know her?' a voice from the crowd called.

'She is. And I would never associate with someone like this.' She backed into the crowd and was surrounded in a moment. 'Is anyone with me? Sign up for Amelia's Haven now. Let's stand with Amelia.'

The protestors cheered. Placards were waved in the air and someone whistled. The tablet on the selfie stick was panning the crowd, recording now.

Ice shot down Beth's spine. She moved closer to the door. 'Please, Laura. Amelia is not your friend. She doesn't care about you. She wants to control you. Please try to see.'

Laura kept the distance between them. 'I don't know why you care. I don't know you.'

'Enough,' Miranda said. Her voice was quiet, but it carried through the shop and out to the crowd in the street. They stilled, muttering and watchful.

Miranda went to the door and stepped outside. She stood still, the wind whipping her hair around her face. She looked up, slightly above the heads of the crowd and held out her arms, palms turned up to the sky. She didn't say a word.

Someone in the crowd gasped.

'Her eyes are purple!' a voice shouted.

Flashes went off, one after the other, as people took photographs. There were cheers of victory, and then groans of disappointment as they looked at the pictures.

'What is she?' The mutters increased and morphed as people shifted backwards and started moving away.

Jonan slipped out the door and took his own pictures of the crowd, the placards, and of Miranda.

Laura was the last to go. She stared at Beth, fury in every tense line of her body.

Finally, the street was silent.

Miranda nodded, walked back inside and went straight upstairs without a word.

Jonan followed her in, sat down and opened the gallery on his phone. There was nothing strange about Miranda. She was just a woman, standing in the wind in front of a shop looking up at the sky. The pictures of the crowd were something else. Their faces were angry, aggressive, leering. Their placards offered grim threats.

'We should keep those in case we ever need evidence,' Beth said, peering over his shoulder.

The bells on the door jingled. A woman in a long, red raincoat walked in and looked around. As she saw the welcoming room, the tension in her shoulders eased. 'This is a beautiful shop,' she said, walking over to a large, amethyst cathedral and touching it with the tips of her fingers. 'I wondered what was springing up when I saw the builders. I would have come earlier, but I didn't want to get caught up with that crowd.'

'I'm sorry you had to deal with them.' Beth offered her a cake from the platter and she took a flapjack with a smile. 'I'm sure they'll get bored of us soon.'

35

JONAN

An hour later, the shop was full to bursting with a workshop upstairs and a waiting list for the next. The cakes were dwindling fast and the kettle had been boiling almost constantly.

Beth was out and about with sign-up sheets for a steadily growing mailing list and a raft of different workshops. There was a buzz in the air and more than one person had told her what a relief it was to be amongst like-minded people, away from the glare of Amelia's followers.

Jonan stood behind the counter, surveying what they had created.

This morning he had thought the venture was doomed to failure, but it was dawning on him how many people Amelia was alienating and putting in danger. He would provide for these people whatever Amelia said or did.

The more he sank into the energy, the more he felt his own sense of purpose.

'Here,' Beth handed him a pile of sign-up sheets. 'Would you mind dealing with these for a bit? My phone has been beeping non-stop. I want to check the shop's new social media pages.'

Jonan took the sheets and leafed through them. There were so many names for their mailing list and workshops, but nobody asking for healing from Amelia's manipulations. 'I was hoping the healing sessions would take off,' he said. 'I'm surprised nobody's interested.'

Beth shrugged. 'Give it time. Amelia's followers aren't going to come for that, and I'm not sure she's branched further out yet. It'll happen when it's needed.'

Beth pulled out her phone and fired it up. She gasped as she scrolled through the notifications. 'So many.'

'Can I see? Are we creating a stir or a nightmare?' Jonan peered over her shoulder. There were people praising the shop, asking questions and saying they wished they could visit. But there were also trolls, reams and reams of them. The poison and insults crawled off the page towards him. He put up barriers, blocking the energy, but the words still hurt.

Beth put a hand on his arm. 'This was always going to happen if we managed to attract attention. Things are so polarised right now. Either we stay under the radar, or we take both the good and the bad.'

'Of course,' Jonan said, forcing a smile and swallowing down the lump in his throat. 'I wouldn't have expected any less from Amelia's followers. Let's hope this blows over, but we're also going to have to figure out how the people we want to help can find us without being harassed.'

Beth kissed him on the cheek, and then sat behind the desk and tapped furiously on her phone.

The bells on the door rang and Jonan turned, a professional smile back in place. Roland stood there, dark circles under his eyes, his face gaunt and a bottle of champagne in one hand. 'Roland!' Jonan jumped up and strode over to his brother, pulling him into a hug. 'I've been so worried. Where have you been?'

Roland pulled back and looked at Jonan, his forehead creased into a frown. 'What do you mean?'

'I spoke to Rose.'

Roland rolled his eyes. 'Of course you did. What did she have to say?'

She asked if I had a forwarding address for you, so she could send on your things. What happened?'

'Roland!' Layla came down the stairs and then bounded over to him and threw her arms around him. 'What possessed you to go missing like that? I insist you give me your phone number right now.'

Roland's mouth quirked into a smile. 'Happy to oblige. Is this a mutual exchange?'

Layla blushed. 'Wow, look at the time. I need to get Abi from school. Can you manage without me for a bit, Jonan?' She raised her eyebrows at him, deliberately avoiding looking at Roland. 'I can come back if you don't mind me bringing her?'

'Will you wait?' she said, meeting Roland's gaze head-on.

He nodded, all mirth gone. 'I'll help out here.' He smiled and turned to Jonan. 'It looks like you need it. This event is a huge success. I'm glad for you. I thought we could celebrate later?' He held up the bottle.

A knot eased in Jonan's chest. 'Thank you, brother. That means a lot. Here.' He handed Roland the pile of sign-up sheets. 'Would you mind handing these out and collecting the completed ones back? That way I can help the customers with their questions.'

'Right you are.' Roland took the pile of paper and moved into the crowd.

'He certainly knows how to charm people,' Beth said, coming out from behind the reception desk and sliding her hand into Jonan's. He seemed so obnoxious when we met him with Amelia. It's hard to believe this is the same man.'

Jonan sighed. 'Yes, well, we all know how much Amelia can mess with people. Roland is a good guy. He's hugely loyal and has a very strong sense of duty. It's just unfortunate that Amelia commanded so much of that loyalty.'

'Could he really have got away from her so fast?'

'No.' Jonan's forehead furrowed. His energy is all wrong, damped down. I think he's just used to functioning this way. Wow, that's depressing. I'm not sure he even knows there's anything wrong.'

Beth's phone let off a series of beeps. She hunched over it behind the reception desk. Jonan wandered around the shop, tidying up and helping customers, trying to ignore the constant series of beeps from behind him. Eventually, he circled back to the desk.

'Is everything going okay with that? What kind of impression are we making?'

Beth sighed.

Jonan quirked one eyebrow. 'That bad?'

'We're making a good impression on our customers, but Amelia is apparently offended by our opening and has launched a tirade against us online. She has done a live video talking about how dangerous we are and how people need to stay on their guard and protect themselves. She's basically sending her followers to stalk our customers.'

'You need to watch your backs.'

Jonan turned.

Roland handed him the sheaf of paper, and then shoved his hands in his pockets. 'It hurts me to say it, but Amelia is becoming increasingly unstable, and she really doesn't like you taking things into your own hands like this.'

'But Jonan's only relaunching his own business,' Beth said, folding her arms across her chest.

Roland shrugged. 'Don't ever underestimate Amelia's jealousy when it comes to Jonan. That drives her more of the time than you could possibly imagine. The man she has spent years pining for is setting his stall directly against hers. That hurts.'

Jonan closed his eyes. 'You know I never wanted to hurt her.'

Roland nodded. 'But that's irrelevant now, because she is hurt and you are on opposing sides.'

'And you?' Jonan's voice was soft.

Roland shook his head. 'I have no idea where I stand right now. But maybe we could get to know each other again and find out?'

Jonan let his breath out in a rush and pulled Roland into a hug. Roland stiffened and then relaxed and patted Jonan on the back.

'You're still open?'

Jonan pulled back and turned. Layla was in the doorway, Abi's hand clutched in hers. They both looked pale. 'Is everything okay?'

'Fine, thanks. Sorry it took us so long to get back. We had to go for an impromptu meeting at Abi's school, but I can help you close up if Doriel would be up for entertaining Abi for a bit?'

'Why don't you go straight up and find her, Abi?' Jonan said. 'I'm sure she'll be delighted to see you and you can tell her we're closing up now too.' He turned back to Layla as the little girl shot up the stairs. 'I can't believe how late it is. Today has been incredible, in spite of Amelia's attempts to derail us.'

Layla hung up her coat and rolled up her sleeves. 'You mean the protest, or has she done more?'

Beth's phone let off more beeps. Beth sighed. 'I don't think I can answer that question in polite company. Let's get the shop closed and I'll tell you everything.'

36

DORIEL

DORIEL SHUFFLED THE CARDS AGAIN AND LAID THEM OUT. There was a knock on the door. She sighed and put the Magician card on the table. 'Who is it?'

'It's Abi, Aunty Doriel, can I come in please?'

'Abi!' Doriel said, running a finger over the Magician. 'Of course, sweetheart, come right on in.' She swept up the cards and shuffled again.

'Aunty Doriel!' Abi left the door swinging on its hinges and ran over.

The air was knocked out of Doriel's chest when the little girl launched herself into her lap and wrapped her arms around her neck.

'I've missed you, Aunty Doriel. I hate school. They're mean to me. The teachers told Mummy I need to fit in, but I don't like those girls. I don't want to be like them.'

Doriel held Abi away so she could look at her properly. Abi's eyes were bloodshot and red rimmed. The back of her hand was inflamed as though she had been repeatedly scratching it. 'Has something happened, Abi?'

'Things are always happening. Will you read the cards for me Aunty Doriel?'

Doriel raised her eyebrows. 'The Tarot cards? What do you know about Tarot, honey?'

'My mummy reads them when I go to bed. She hardly ever tells me what they say though. Will you tell me?'

Doriel thought for a moment, and then shrugged. 'I'll read for you if you'd like me to. Here.' She handed Abi the cards. 'Do you know how to shuffle?'

Abi moved the cards around a bit, dropped half of them on the floor and scooped them up into a messy pile, which she handed back to Doriel.

Doriel shifted them into a neat pile without changing the order and then put down three cards, the Magician, the Moon and the Tower. She swallowed, gathered them up, shuffled herself and dealt again.

The Magician, the Moon and the Tower.

'Are they bad, Aunty Doriel?'

Doriel forced herself to smile. 'No, my love, none of the cards are bad. But they're saying you need to take care and be ready in case things change or get tricky. Could you do that, do you think?'

Abi bit her lip and scratched the red patch on the back of her hand. 'I don't understand, Aunty Doriel. What do I need to do?'

Doriel took her hands. 'Just be a bit careful. Do you hear those people outside?'

'The ones who are shouting?'

'Yes, those ones. I think they're a bit like the mean children at school. They're not being very nice at the moment, but if we make ourselves a bit less obvious they're more likely to leave us alone, like your teachers said.'

Abi pulled her hands out of Doriel's, tucked them behind her back and stepped away. 'You want me to give in, Aunty Doriel? You want me to pretend I'm someone different?'

Panic swept through Doriel, making her heart pound and her legs wobble. *She's only a child; she's not frightening. Come on woman, pull yourself together.* She repeated the words in her head like a mantra, but the sensations did not go away. 'I don't mean you should be someone different,' she said, wringing her hands, 'just don't give quite so much away. You don't want the school to start asking too many questions about home.'

'Are you suggesting there's something inappropriate about her home life?' Layla's voice was cold.

Doriel looked up, her eyes widening. 'Layla, I didn't hear you come in.'

'So I see. I feel sure that you wouldn't have given my daughter such terrible advice if you'd known I was listening. Come on, pumpkin, we're going home. Doriel, I suggest you take a bit of time out. Words have a lot of power; particularly *your* words. Abi idolises you and that comes with a lot of responsibility if you choose to spend time with her.'

'If I choose?' Doriel snapped, standing up and straightening, pushing her shoulders back and planting her hands on her hips. 'I didn't seek her out, she came to me and asked for a reading.'

'And it would never occur to you to say no? To say that if she wants a reading you should speak to me first? Do it when I'm there perhaps? You just did exactly what she asked and gave her life advice without thinking of mentioning it to me?'

'Yes, well maybe you should look after your own

daughter in future,' Doriel said through gritted teeth, her hands clenched into fists at her sides. 'I was doing you a favour.'

Layla winced.

'You don't want me here?' Abi's voice was small. She was close to tears. 'I thought we were friends.'

Doriel closed her eyes and reached out to grasp the edge of the bureau as the ground beneath her feet seemed to tilt.

'That wasn't what she meant at all, pumpkin,' Layla said. 'Doriel's just not feeling well. Come on, we're going home now. You can see Aunty Doriel another day. Goodbye, Doriel.' Layla's voice was almost normal, but Doriel could still hear the knife edge of anger. 'I suggest you take some time out until you're able to think clearly.'

The door slammed.

37

BETH

THE FLAT UPSTAIRS WAS CHAOS, STREWN WITH DISCARDED wrappers, boxes, and piles of new stock stacked in every possible space.

'I do hope you're planning to find somewhere else to use as a stockroom,' Miranda said, looking around the room with a disapproving glare, her hands planted firmly on her hips.

Jonan shrugged. 'Eventually, but for now the event space was more important. We can live with this for a while, at least.'

Beth rolled her eyes. 'Speak for yourself. I'm covered in bruises already.'

'Champagne, anyone?' Roland raised one eyebrow and held up the bottle he had brought with him. 'Do you have any glasses?'

'We have red wine glasses, will they do?' Jonan grinned.

Roland chuckled. 'Since Amelia's not here a mug would do, but red wine glasses would certainly be better.'

The door to Doriel's room opened. Layla carried Abi

Starfolk Falling

out into the living room and slammed the door behind her. She was flushed and her lips were compressed into a thin line. Putting Abi down, she closed her eyes for a moment and took a deep breath.

'Layla, is something wrong?' Beth stood up and walked over to Abi. She crouched down in front of her and took both the girl's hands in her own. They were clammy and shaking.

Abi yanked them away, glaring at Beth.

'Abi? Are you alright?' Beth stood up and stepped backwards, giving the girl space.

Abi nodded. 'I didn't like what Doriel said.'

'What did she say?' Jonan leaned forwards, frowning.

Layla shook her head. 'Go to the toilet, pumpkin. We're going home now.'

The little girl ran through to the bathroom.

'You need to figure out what's going on with Doriel,' Layla hissed, the anger in her voice clear even at low volume. 'She did a tarot reading for Abi without speaking to me first, and told her to stop drawing attention to herself or the school would look into our family circumstances. I can't believe she said that to a child. If she was concerned about my parenting, she should have spoken to me directly.'

'I know I should have, but please …' Doriel stood in her doorway, tears streaming down her face.

Layla held up a hand and shook her head. Abi crept out of the bathroom, looking around, her face fearful. 'Did I upset you, Aunty Doriel?'

'Not at all,' Doriel said, her voice surprisingly strong. 'I'm really fed up with my sister. She keeps taking my hairbrush without permission. I'm sorry if I took it out on you.'

Miranda's eyebrow rose, but she said nothing.

Abi shot Miranda a hard look. 'Come on, Mummy. I'm tired. Can we go home?'

'I will see you tomorrow,' Layla said, and it sounded for all the world like a threat. 'Roland, I'm sorry you had to see this. I hope you find somewhere new to live. I hope you might come in to see us again soon?' She didn't wait for an answer before slamming the door behind her.

They let out a collective breath as the two sets of footsteps retreated down the staircase.

'What the hell did you say to the kid, Doriel?' Jonan leaned back. Beth sat beside him, trying hard to shut out the raging anxiety that was pumping around the room. She imagined a bubble around herself. It lessened, and then it was gone. She looked over at Miranda, who had a smug smile on her face.

Doriel sighed and sat on a chair at the dining table. 'Pretty much what Layla told you I said, although I wasn't as explicit as all that. Something is going to happen to that girl and she's not protected enough. We have to do something.'

'Oh, I think you've done quite enough, sister,' Miranda said, raising one eyebrow. 'We both know that being an Oracle doesn't mean pushing our visions onto people when they haven't asked to be shown.'

'But Abi asked me.'

'Oh, come on now,' Miranda said, her voice a little softer. 'She's a child. She had no idea what she was asking. Her mother was perfectly right. You should not have read for her without permission, and without Layla present. But you know this, Doriel. What got into you?'

Doriel balled her fists and pushed them into her eye

sockets. 'I couldn't think.' Her voice was barely audible. 'I couldn't think. This place was so full of chaos and I couldn't find myself. I don't know who I am anymore. I'm certainly not the Mother of the Triad now. Something has changed and it's not going back. I can feel it.'

'You don't know that.' Getting up, Beth went over to stand behind Doriel's chair and massaged her shoulders. 'You'll get back to yourself, I know you will.'

'You never go backwards, love. Haven't you worked that out yet?' Doriel leaned into Beth's hands with a sigh. 'There is only ever forwards. There is only ever something new.'

Beth swallowed. 'You honestly think you're no longer the Mother? Does that mean the card will change?'

'No,' Jonan sighed. 'They're just illustrations, pretty pictures printed on normal card in the usual way. But if one of us shifts, anything else could change too. It's only ever happened once before and both Mother and Doriel changed.' Everyone turned to look at Miranda.

Miranda threw her arms up. 'Oh, don't look at me like that. Things will be as they will be. I'm here supporting my boys, aren't I? I'm out of seclusion and I've spent the day teaching group after group of noisy people. You can all draw your own conclusions from that, but I'm not going to talk about it now.'

'What are we going to do about Layla?' Beth said, looking from Doriel to Jonan.

'I'll talk to her,' Jonan cut in before Doriel could speak. 'I shouldn't have made an assumption about Doriel looking after Abi. That's on me.'

'I'll check on her tonight, too,' Roland said. 'She gave me her phone number.'

'You're not listening to me,' Doriel said, and her voice was little more than a whisper but it snaked through the air like a rope, pulling them all in. 'Something is going to happen. Something that will change everything. Abi is in danger.'

38

AMELIA

Amelia threw the tablet onto the chair and poured herself a drink. It was maddening. She had been trolling Jonan's shop all day, had sent her fans there to protest, even released a live video, but still the customers raved about how amazing it was. She had thought her profile would give her the power to shut it down before it got started, but instead she had given the opening the push it needed to go viral. They would be getting orders from all over the world by dinnertime.

She wished Roland was still by her side. He had always steadied her, moderated her excesses and kept her media ready. Without him, who knew how much trouble she would get herself into?

A slow smile spread across her face. There was plenty of mischief in her yet, even if her last stunt had backfired. They would never see her next move coming.

She heard the door, and then heard Rose click across the tiled floor to answer it, followed by murmurings. She looked around the room. What would her most advantageous pose be? She had cleared out the old man's furniture and the small room was now an elegant snug with a sleek, white modern sofa with lime green cushions, a thick white rug and a huge picture of Marilyn Monroe. She walked over to the smart fridge. *Call me.* A message from Roland filled the screen.

'Urgh, get out of my house,' she said, clicking the message closed. 'And get out of my head. You left me, remember?' She pulled up one of her own videos. She filled the screen now, spot lit, the camera panning in on her face, her long eyelashes fluttering, high cheekbones catching the light and the shadows. She muted the sound and left the images of herself flittering across the screen on repeat.

There was a knock on the door.

'It's Robson Fall, ma'am.' Rose's voice came through the solid wood.

'Thank you, Rose. Please send him in.'

The door opened and Robson Fall stood there, his arms reached out as though to hug her. He was smaller than she had expected, with dark, slicked-back hair. His face was pointier than it looked in the pictures, and she wondered how hard he worked to perfect his pose. She fixed a sickly smile on her face, but a shiver ran down her spine. She wasn't sure what she had ever seen in him.

His smile was self-satisfied. 'Amelia, my dear, it's such a pleasure to meet you at last.' He walked towards her and grasped her hands.

His skin was sweaty, and she pulled away. 'Mr Fall, how nice to meet you. My mother was such a fan of yours. I'm so sorry she couldn't be with us today.'

'Please, call me Rob,' he said, his eyes glinting with

something that sent ice across her skin. 'Yes, such a loss for you. I'm so sorry. How are you bearing up?'

'I'm adjusting, but it's a heavy burden.' She opened the fridge and pulled out a bottle of champagne. Popping off the cork, she filled two crystal glasses that were ready and waiting on the sideboard. She handed him one, forcing herself not to cringe as his fingers intentionally brushed hers. She stepped backwards. 'The staff have prepared a table for us in the ballroom, please do close the door behind you.'

She led the way into the ballroom, breathing a sigh of relief at the bustling atmosphere. She wasn't usually this jittery. Right now she was the queen of her castle. She had nothing to fear. So why was her stomach churning? She straightened, pushing her shoulders back, and walked over to the table in the middle of the ballroom. Rose pulled a chair out for her and she sat down, holding her hands out of the way as Rose spread a napkin over her signature white pencil skirt.

Rob was wide-eyed as he looked around the room. Rose pulled out a chair for him and he looked her up and down.

Amelia suppressed a shudder. A chill traced her back and she turned. *Back off.* She sent the words from her mind and heard laughing. Taking a gulp of champagne, she forced out a smile. 'Have you looked into the information I sent you about Amelia's Haven?'

Rob smiled. 'Such a fascinating project you have there. I'd love to hear more about this threat you have sensed.'

Rose came back in pushing a trolley. Amelia nodded and indicated her own place setting. Rose picked up one of the white plates which was adorned with a beautifully crafted salad arranged in the shape of an intricate flower, and set it in front of her.

'Truly exquisite,' Rob said, his fake smile cold and sickly.

Amelia tilted her head, broadening her smile further as Rose put the second plate in front of Robson Fall. 'So, you want to know more? Have you not read up on me or watched my videos? All the information you could possibly want is already in the public domain.'

'Ah, but there must be juicy details that aren't online. Tell me more about this spirit. What do you think it was? How do you envisage these Soul Snatchers? Do you think they're ghosts? Aliens?'

The chill across Amelia's back spread, numbing her brain and sending ice through her teeth. 'The Soul Snatchers are very good at hiding where they come from. They pretend to be one thing when they are really something else. I believe they are more insidious than simple ghosts.'

Rob took an enormous bite of bread and chewed with his mouth open. 'Interesting. Maybe we should do a study. I have an excellent paranormal investigator. I could set him up in an affected area so we could get some solid information on this. And while we're on the topic, I have a contract. Just so terms are entirely clear.' He slapped an envelope on the table.

Amelia picked it up and slid out a few sheets of paper.

'Oh,' he laughed, 'no need to read all of that now. Very standard wording, there's nothing to worry yourself about. You just sign it and we can get onto the interesting stuff.'

Amelia looked up at him and raised her eyebrows. 'I *never* sign anything without reading every detail myself first.

Surely you wouldn't expect anything else from a professional, Mr Fall?'

He coughed. 'Quite right. And please, call me Rob.'

She read in silence, unmoving, feeling him squirm as she went over every detail. She held her fury tightly under control. The man must think she was stupid. He was trying to take Amelia's Haven right out from under her, but he would not have the chance to add it to his own sprawling empire. He would find out how difficult it was to manipulate her, and he would regret the heavy weight of this mistake.

She put the paper on the table, looked up and crossed her arms across her chest, knowing it accentuated her cleavage. 'Why would you want to hire a paranormal investigator, *Rob*? Do you doubt my word?'

He swallowed. 'Well, no, of course not. But …'

'I assure you my senses are particularly honed and far more accurate than any piece of equipment your investigators may have. I believe you have not yet realised quite *who* you are dealing with.' Amelia pushed her chair back and it scraped over the floor with a screech that jarred through her body.'

Amelia, a voice sounded in her mind. *Did you think I had gone?*

'Who are you?' she demanded, spinning round.

Bill, the name sounded and then repeated, over and over.

Rob giggled nervously. 'Who am I? You can't be talking to me, surely?'

Amelia swallowed.

He was looking at her, eyes narrowed, his lips pressed together as though to hide the way they were turning up at the edges. He knew he was regaining the upper hand; she could feel it deep in her bones. She would not let him win.

He can see you for what you are, the voice whispered into her mind.

Amelia gritted her teeth, and then sat down again. She would not be beaten by the ghost of a measly old man and that washed-out, scheming fraud sitting in front of her. Why had she wasted so much time on that one? She would blame her mother. The old bat had been responsible for so much. One more thing wouldn't break those long-dead shoulders. She took a deep breath and let it out slowly, feeling her body calm into exhaustion. She needed to get her energy up somehow and she knew exactly how to do that.

She reached beyond the irritating presence, out into the depths of the inn to find the Monks. The sludgy energy inched closer, bit by bit, responding to her call. Robson Fall was watching her now, the triumphant grin starting to droop as he felt the drain. She could sense the prickling start to his fear as the Monks drifted into the room. His gaze darted around and she knew he was seeing shapes move from the corner of his eye, but nothing more.

'Is something wrong, Mr Fall?' she drawled, trying not to laugh as his skin paled. She called the Monks in closer. His breathing was rough now. She could feel her own power and energy soar as his crashed and burned.

Feeling into her own growing strength, she sent out cords towards him, marvelling at the vine-like way they grew across the floor and began to wind up his legs from his feet.

He shifted, looking down, his forehead furrowing. He moved his feet and then looked back up at her, unsure.

The vines continued to grow, strangling his senses even

though his body could move. The colour was draining from his face, and he kept looking over one shoulder, and then the other, pushing his chair back and leaning forward, hands on the table as he searched the room for the threat he felt so clearly.

'Are you okay, Mr Fall?' Amelia asked, her voice sickly sweet. She smiled as she watched the cords loop around his neck over and over.

'Yes,' he croaked and then cleared his throat. He pushed his chair back even further, increasing the distance between them, and stood up. Holding onto the table, he steadied himself against the wobbling of his legs and shook his head. 'I have to get out of here.'

'Of course.' She put a hand on his arm, gripping just a little too tightly and walked him to the door, feeling the drag as he failed to keep up. 'Don't you worry. We'll do this again just as soon as you're feeling better.'

He lurched through the door, not answering. Looking back once, halfway up the hill, he stumbled and then disappeared around the corner.

Amelia went back inside the inn, laughing to herself.

'Has he gone already?' Rose stood in the reception area, a basket of wood clutched in her arms, a box of matches caught between two fingers.

'Let's just say he was indisposed,' Amelia said with a chuckle. 'I don't think this is going to pan out how I anticipated. Please have my lawyers call me first thing in the morning. We will need a rock-solid contract.'

39

JONAN

'Sit with me,' Jonan said, tilting his head towards the sofa as he shuffled the cards.

Doriel watched him, lips pursed. 'Why? You want me to sit there so you can tell me I'm losing the plot. But I'm not and you're wrong.'

'Okay, fine. I'm wrong. But that wasn't why I was asking you to sit with me. I'd just like to chat. You're my Earth Guide, Doriel. You always have been and it's always been about me. Maybe now is a good moment to turn things around. It's about time I returned the favour.'

'You're Beth's Earth Guide,' Doriel said, 'not mine.' She sat down anyway.

'Beth is happy to share my intuitive services.' Jonan winked.

Doriel rolled her eyes. 'Okay, what did you have in mind?'

'I thought we could play a little Tarot.' Jonan grinned. 'I will lay some cards about what is happening right now and we can each say what they mean.'

'You want to teach me Tarot?' Doriel raised her eyebrows. 'I know you're good, Jonan, but do you seriously think you can out-read an Oracle?'

'Ah, but you're not the Oracle anymore, are you?'

'I'll always be an Oracle and you know it just as well as I do. Miranda will always be your mother, and I will always be your second mother, no matter which Arcana card I start to embody. I will never be less than I am now, Jonan. Only more.'

'Ahhh,' Jonan said with a laugh. 'There's the Doriel I know and love. You have no idea how good it is to have you back, even for a moment.'

Doriel rolled her eyes again, but she looked pleased. 'Are you going to do something with those cards?'

Jonan chuckled, and then cut the deck and laid out three cards, The Magician, The Tower and Judgement. Jonan whistled. 'All Major Arcana.'

Doriel pulled her legs up and crossed them on the sofa. 'So, what's your reading?' She had a smile tugging at the edge of her lips.

'You already know what it means, don't you?' Jonan said with a sigh.

Doriel shrugged. 'Well, I *think* I do, but I may be wrong, or I may have missed something. I would honestly like to hear what you think.'

'I think we haven't seen Judgment in a while.'

Doriel flushed slightly and Jonan waited for her to say something, but she just watched him in silence.

Jonan leaned back on the sofa and crossed his arms over his chest. 'I can't be the only one to have noticed the similarity between the Magician and Abi.'

Doriel gave the barest hint of a smile.

'Do you see what this disaster is that you're predicting?'

The smile vanished. Doriel shifted in her seat. 'No, only that with her manifesting potential we need to be very careful about what we create. And that she will get caught up in this murderous storm Amelia is creating. What's it like out there? Is she getting to people?'

Jonan sighed. 'The edginess has amped up to a ridiculous degree. Everyone is ready to snap at the least provocation, and Beth is constantly lost in a stream of online arguments. I'm not sure how to handle it. She's getting us amazing exposure and we're getting orders and contact from people all over the world, but the strain on her is huge. I can feel the energy of it on her and it makes my skin crawl.'

Doriel closed her eyes. 'She's bright, though. She's carrying a lot, but she's not sinking, not like last time. Not like me.'

'Are you sinking?'

'Maybe not. Maybe I'm just changing. Who knows.'

The doorbell rang.

'It's Abi,' Doriel said, jumping up and running to the stairs. She left the door swinging on its hinges as she raced down to open the shop door.

Jonan could hear voices and crying, and then footsteps on the stairs. 'Is everything okay?' he said as they came into the living room.

Doriel was carrying Abi, whose face was streaked with tears. Her face was buried in Doriel's neck and her little body was shaking with sobs.

Fear shot through Jonan. 'What's happened?' He reached out and put a hand on Layla's arm.

She was pale, but calm. 'Abi is being bullied. The children said her clothes marked her out as a Soul Snatcher. They have been taunting and threatening her.'

'What about the school? Are they being supportive?' Jonan ushered Layla to the sofa. Abi was already curled around Doriel in an armchair, calmer now. Doriel was singing softly to her and stroking her hair.

'Huh, supportive?' Layla pushed a lock of bright pink hair out of her eyes. 'They said they'd warned me there would be trouble if Abi didn't tone herself down. What can they possibly be thinking? Abi is a good girl. She never causes trouble, she's never mean, she does all her work to the best of her ability, and they're telling *her* to tone herself down?'

'Is she okay?' Beth walked in from the bedroom. She was pale, her scraped-back hair tugged out in tufts.

Abi sat up and looked Beth straight in the eye. 'They're horrible children. I did nothing bad.'

'Oh, I know you didn't, sweetie. Everyone's acting so strangely right now, aren't they? I've spent all day dealing with bullies too. Is there something I can do to help you get yours to stop?'

'You need to tell the school, please, Beth? They're not listening to my mummy. They just tell her she needs to sort this out before someone gets hurt. That person is me, isn't it, Beth? They think someone's going to hurt me, and they're not going to stop it happening.' A single tear slid down her cheek.

'Who is your favourite teacher, Abi?' Doriel said, stroking her head. 'There must be one, surely?'

Abi sat up a little straighter and her lips turned up in a smile. 'I like Miss Graham. She's kind. She likes the stories I write.'

'Could you speak to Miss Graham?' Jonan looked at Layla.

Layla bit her lip. 'Maybe if I went in first thing. I don't know. They don't normally give out meetings with random teachers like that. And they're already wary of us. Urgh, I'm so tired of doing everything alone.'

'Would you like me to come with you, just for a bit of moral support?' Beth sat down next to her and took her hand. 'You don't have to be alone. You have us now.'

Layla's eyes widened and then a tear slid down her cheek. 'You'd do that?'

'Of course! Give me your address. I'll come over in the morning and we can walk there together.' Beth held out a piece of paper and a pen.

'Thank you,' Layla said. She wrote on the paper, handed it back to Beth and slung her bag over her shoulder.

'Do we have to go home, mummy?' Abi wrapped her arms tightly around Doriel. 'I want to stay here.'

'Don't worry, sweetie, you can come back tomorrow,' Doriel said giving her a tight hug, and then unlacing Abi's arms from behind her back. 'I need some help with the crystals and none of that lot are anywhere near as good at sorting them as you.'

Abi climbed out of her lap and bounced over to Layla, her tears forgotten. 'Can I come back tomorrow, Mummy?'

Layla smiled. 'Yes, of course, sweetie. That will give us both something nice to look forward to after school. Say goodnight now, and we'll see everyone tomorrow.'

Ice shot down Jonan's spine, but he just smiled and waved.

40

BETH

'Come on in.' Layla ushered Beth into her hall the next morning. 'Abi's just looking for her shoes.'

Abi was quiet on the way to school, dragging her feet along the pavement and hanging back, clutching Layla's hand and stretching her arm out behind her.

'Come on, darling,' Layla said, turning and pulling her into a hug. 'It's going to be okay, but we need to get there.'

Abi hung her head but nodded.

At the school everything seemed achingly normal. Children kicked balls around, played on the climbing frame and tried to catch each other. Parents stood in small groups, bleary eyed as they talked.

'Can I help you?' A woman in a suit said, looking Beth up and down.

'It's okay, she's with me,' Layla said, standing up straighter and holding the woman's gaze. Layla was dressed for work, her sleek, pink hair carefully styled and her black trench coat, pencil skirt and knee-high boots a contrast to the woman's conservative suit.

The woman pursed her lips and narrowed her eyes but said nothing.

'Goodbye, sweetie.' Layla kissed Abi on the top of her head and watched until she disappeared through the door. Letting out a breath, she seemed to deflate. A single tear ran down her cheek.

'Are you ready?' Beth said, her voice low.

Layla brushed the tear away. 'Let's do this.' She strode over to the main door, pressed the buzzer and held the door open for Beth.

'I'd like to speak to Miss Graham please,' she said to the receptionist.

'I'm sorry, why?' The woman narrowed her eyes at Layla, fixing her gaze on the sleek, pink bob.

'She is one of Abi's teachers.'

'I am well aware of that, but if you have a problem, it would be most appropriate to speak to Abi's class teacher, or the Head. Which would you prefer?'

'I have already spoken to both, but my daughter has a bond with Miss Graham, and I would like to speak to her directly, please.'

'I'm sorry, but that can't be arranged. Who are *you*?' The woman turned her stare on Beth.

'I'm here with Layla.'

Layla squared her shoulders and stepped closer to the reception desk. 'I am concerned about Abi's reports of bullying.'

'Abi's social issues have been dealt with. It is not the school's fault if a child is incapable of bonding with its peers.'

Beth narrowed her eyes and focused on the woman's energy. It was muddy and stilted.

'Is this a normal approach to caring for children?' Layla snapped, gripping the edge of the desk so her knuckles went white. 'I was under the impression bullying was frowned upon.' The woman blanched. Her gaze flickered to the anti-bullying poster on the wall behind Beth, and Beth turned to look at it pointedly.

'Is there a time we could meet Miss Graham?' Layla said through gritted teeth.

'Huh!' the woman said, picking up a pile of papers and shuffling them. 'I couldn't possibly say. I will speak to Miss Graham and get back to you when I can. In the meantime, please *do* remind your daughter she has a responsibility to fit in. We are an Amelia's Haven-protected institution, and if there is any hint that Abigail has been unduly impacted by anything suspect, she will be suspended indefinitely.'

Beth gaped.

'I just want to speak to Miss Graham,' Layla said, stepping back from the desk. 'I will wait for you to contact me with a time. Beth, shall we go?'

Beth followed her out the door. 'You were amazing in there.'

'You think?' Layla frowned. 'She looked furious with me.'

'This way, please,' the woman at the gate called. 'We're locking up now.'

'Of course she was furious. She's riddled with Amelia's interference. It was shot through her energy.'

'Oh God,' Layla dug the heel of her hand into her forehead. 'These people have control over my child and they're taking out their prejudice on her.'

Beth put her arm around Layla. 'We're here for you,

Layla, and you are all that she needs. She's lucky to have you on her side.'

'Huh, I wish you were right.' Layla dug into her bag and pulled out her phone. 'Listen, I have a meeting to get to. See you at the shop later?'

Beth smiled. 'See you then.' The sun was out but the air was bitingly cold. Beth wrapped her scarf tighter around her neck as she walked down the hill towards town.

The shop was quiet when she got back. Miranda was sitting behind the desk, reading a book on crystals.

'Miranda, I wasn't expecting to see you here today,' Beth said as she hung up her coat. 'To what do we owe this honour?'

'It seemed like a good day to pop in,' Miranda said vaguely. 'Jonan is putting the kettle on if you want to get your order in.'

'Thanks,' Beth said, ducking up the stairs. Jonan was in the kitchen, singing to himself and tidying up as the kettle boiled.

'Were you expecting to see your mum today?' Beth asked, grabbing a biscuit and leaning against the work surface.

'No, she just turned up. I suspect we'll be glad of that by the end of the day, we just don't know why yet.'

Beth raised her eyebrows. 'An advantage of being surrounded by psychics?'

'Exactly.' Jonan handed her a mug of coffee.

The phone rang.

'I'll get it.' Beth walked through to the living room. A shiver ran down her spine as she reached for the receiver.

'Beth, thank God! It's Layla. I'm sorry to ask, but I need your help. The school just called. There's some kind of emergency and they want me to go in now. But I'm sitting on a train heading in the wrong direction and it's not due to stop anywhere for another hour. Would you go in my place?'

'Of course. Will you tell the school I'm coming?'

'I'll call them now. Thank you so much.' The line went dead.

Beth slammed the phone down. 'Jonan, something's wrong with Abi. We need to go to her school. Will you drive?'

41

BETH

'What's happened?' Jonan came out of the kitchen, grabbed his jacket from over the back of the chair and picked up his car keys from the bowl on the sideboard. 'Is she okay?'

Beth opened the door to the stairs and followed Jonan down. 'Layla just said it was an emergency.'

'So, we know why I'm here?' Miranda raised one eyebrow, the glint in her eyes showing a hint of smugness.

'We do, Mother. Thank you for taking over.'

Miranda sighed. 'Of course. You attend to whatever crisis is calling.'

'Thanks, Miranda,' Beth called as the door shut behind them.

The car was parked in its usual spot on one of the narrow side roads. 'Where is the school?' Jonan asked. 'Is it far?'

'Only a few minutes, but I don't know how long we have, or whether we'll need to go on …' Beth paused, 'somewhere afterwards.'

Starfolk Falling

Jonan held her gaze for a moment, and then clicked the key fob and the lights flashed. They climbed in and Beth directed Jonan to the school.

The playground was silent and empty. They walked around the perimeter and buzzed to be let in. 'It's Beth Meyer. I'm here for Abi Pinkerton.'

'Finally,' the voice on the other end of the intercom said and the machine buzzed.

Beth exchanged looks with Jonan and they jogged around the side of the school and in through reception, their sense of dread growing.

'What's happened?' Beth asked the woman at reception without introducing herself. 'Is Abi okay?'

The receptionist buzzed them through and ushered them into a small, airy office on the opposite side of the common area.

'Thank you for coming.' A woman in a suit with long hair pulled back into a low ponytail walked in, shut the door firmly behind her and shook their hands. Beth recognised her from the gate that morning. 'I am so pleased to get a chance to talk to you properly. Will you sit down?'

'Could you please tell us what's going on? Is Abi alright?'

'Miss Meyer, there has been an incident at the school, and we can no longer accept Abigail's presence here. I'm afraid she is expelled with immediate effect.'

'What?' Jonan said, his voice loud in the small room. 'Does Layla know?'

'I thought it better to give the news in person.'

There was a knock on the door.

'Please come back later,' the woman said, her voice sharp.

'I'm sorry, but there's been an accident.'

The headteacher frowned and then stood up. 'Wait here,' she said and disappeared through the door.

There was muttering outside the door, but Beth couldn't hear what they were saying. She pulled her phone out of her bag and dialled Layla. It went straight to voicemail. Beth sighed. 'She was on a train. She's probably in a tunnel, or something. Can you hear what they're saying?'

'No, but the energy isn't good. They're worried. Have you noticed that?' Jonan pointed to a plaque on the headteacher's desk. It proclaimed that this was an Amelia's Haven school. 'I bet I can guess why Abi's been expelled.'

The muttering outside the door stopped and footsteps sounded, moving further away. There was shuffling outside the door, and then someone coughed and gave a nervous giggle. The handle turned.

The receptionist poked her head around. 'Abi has had an accident. Please could you come?'

There was a roaring in Beth's mind. What had they done to Abi? She was running before she had even decided what to do. She froze in the playground. A small body lay on the grass at the foot of the climbing frame, surrounded by a distant circle of people. Everything was too quiet. The headteacher was ushering curious children away, her whispers not carrying across the playground. Nobody was with Abi. Nobody at all.

'Abi!' Beth screamed as she ran. She could hear muttering from the teachers and the crowd of children watching, but none of it mattered. Nothing mattered apart from the tiny figure lying at the bottom of the climbing frame.

42

BETH

'I can't believe they wouldn't let me stay with her.' Beth slammed the door behind her, letting her frustration out on Jonan's car. 'Abi clearly didn't want that teacher to go with her in the ambulance.'

'There she is.' Jonan locked the car and nodded towards the entrance to the A&E department. Abi looked tiny in the big wheelchair, huddling as far from the teacher as possible. 'Go in with her before you lose her. They might not let you in later. I'll find you.'

The paramedic was crouched on the ground talking to Abi when Beth ran up. The teacher was hanging back, keeping her distance from the little girl, but when she saw Beth she moved forwards, crowding Abi and the paramedic.

'Step back please,' the paramedic said, putting herself between Abi and the teacher. 'Give the girl room to breathe.'

'Please can Beth come with me?' Abi's voice was small, but her hand was steady when she reached for Beth. 'She's my mummy's friend. Mummy trusts her. Please? I don't want to be on my own.'

'Don't be silly, Abi. I will be with you,' the teacher said, a fake smile plastered across her face.

The paramedic turned to Beth. 'Are you available to accompany her?'

'But,' the teacher cut in.

The paramedic raised her eyebrows. 'You didn't hold her hand or say a word to her on the journey here. You kept as far away as possible and faced forward to avoid looking at her. I suggest you head back to school to take care of the children you do feel some compassion for.'

'You can't do that!' The teacher's voice was high pitched, but she edged further away from Abi. 'I was being sensible. This girl has been infiltrated by the Soul Snatchers. I have to make sure I am not infected. I have a duty not to pass on anything unsavoury to the other children.'

'Don't talk to me about duty, and don't bring that nonsense in here.' The paramedic turned her back on her. 'You take Beth with you, Abi. This nice lady will look after you now.'

Beth took hold of Abi's hand and crouched down while the paramedic talked to the nurse. 'Was it exciting travelling in the ambulance?'

Abi swallowed. 'It would have been better if you'd been there, but the lady was nice.'

'Come on, sweetie,' the nurse said. 'I'm going to take you in now.'

Beth stood up but kept hold of Abi's hand as they went inside. She looked back just before she went through the door. The teacher was glaring at her, but she didn't follow.

The hospital was chaotic. They were taken through a corridor and into a large ward with rows of beds on either side, each surrounded by a curtain rail. Most of the curtains were closed, but there were five empty beds on one side waiting to be filled. The woman took Abi to one and helped her up onto the bed. 'Would you mind coming to the desk to fill in the paperwork please?' She looked at Beth, her eyebrows raised.

'I'm sorry. Her mother is on the way. I'm just keeping Abi company until she arrives.'

The woman pressed her lips together but said nothing as she drew the curtains. They heard her footsteps retreating.

'What happened, Abi? Did you fall from the climbing frame?' Beth sat on the side of the bed and took Abi's hand in her own.

A tear slid down Abi's face. 'They were mean to me. They were chasing me, telling me I was a Soul Snatcher. I tried to get away, but they wouldn't leave me alone. They were getting too close, so I climbed up the climbing frame, but they followed and I was trapped at the top. I couldn't get away.' Her breath hitched. 'One of the girls reached up and grabbed my ankle. She pulled, Beth. She pulled and I fell off. I hit my head on one of the bars as I fell and I was so dizzy. My head aches so much.'

Beth swallowed. 'Don't worry, we won't let them do anything like that again.'

The curtains were drawn back. 'Anything like what? What happened?'

'Mummy!' Abi leapt off the bed, and then grabbed onto the metal frame and swayed, clasping her head with one hand.

'Oh my goodness, what happened to you, pumpkin?' Layla put down her bag, and a car booster cushion, and gathered Abi up in her arms. Carrying her back to the bed, she sat down and cradled the girl on her lap. 'Who did this to you, beautiful?'

She looked up at Beth. 'Thank you so much for looking after her.'

Abi was sobbing now, showing no inclination to answer.

'What happened?' Layla looked up at Beth. 'I haven't been able to get through to the school.'

Beth swallowed. 'They've expelled her. They were asking us to take her home when the accident happened.'

'They expelled her? Why?'

Beth shook her head. 'The woman was called away before she could explain. All I know is that there was an incident and they talked about being an Amelia's Haven school.'

Layla paled. 'Is *that* what this is all about?'

'I'm making assumptions, but I think so. There was an Amelia's Haven plaque on the headteacher's desk and the teacher who went with her in the ambulance said she had to stay away from Abi to avoid being infected.'

Layla looked ashen. She held Abi to her body and rocked the little girl while she sobbed. Layla took a deep breath and let it out slowly. Tears were streaming down her face now, but she was steady, her eyes blazing. 'How am I going to find her a school if they've expelled her for being a Soul Snatcher? Nobody wants that on their record. I'll have to home-school her. I won't let anybody hurt her again.'

'I'm sorry, I—'

'I know you are, but it doesn't really help. I have to focus on Abi. Please, give us some space.'

Starfolk Falling

'But—'

Layla shook her head. 'I'm serious. Nobody threatened Abi until I took the job at Lunea. I need to think.'

'I understand.'

'You told me she was dangerous, but I thought you were exaggerating. I was wrong. Being around you has put my child in danger.'

A single tear slid down Beth's cheek. Layla was scared and angry, but she wasn't wrong. Turning, she walked slowly out to the reception desk. Jonan was there, talking to Roland.

Roland looked up as she approached, and then jogged over to meet her before she reached Jonan. 'Are they okay? Did you find out what happened?'

Beth nodded. She sank onto a thinly padded seat by the wall. She wondered how she could possibly put her afternoon into words, and then it all came out in a torrent, the fear when they were told Abi had an accident, the horror at the way the school treated her, the chaotic journey to the hospital, and then the heartbreak of hearing Abi's story. She was sobbing by the end.

Jonan sat down next to her and pulled her to him. 'Don't worry. Layla just needs a chance to calm down. She'll come around.'

'I don't know,' Beth said, hunting in her bag for a packet of tissues. 'She shouldn't. She's right. This happened because of us.'

'Where is Layla? I need to find her.' Roland's voice was soft, nothing like the man she had first met at the Monk's Inn.

'She's in there.' Beth pointed at the curtain. 'But I wouldn't expect her to be glad to see you.'

Roland smiled. 'At least she'll know I'm here for her. You go home. I promise I'll call if anything changes.' He smiled at the nurse behind the desk, and then walked over to Abi's cubicle without asking permission. He didn't come out.

43

ROLAND

Layla was sitting on the bed with Abi cradled in her arms. She sang as she rocked backwards and forwards, her eyes closed, pink hair tucked behind her ears and tears dried onto her pale cheeks. The girl was asleep now, her eyelids fluttering as she breathed.

'Layla?' Roland's voice was barely a whisper, but Layla jolted, sitting bolt upright, her eyes shooting open.

'Mummy?' Abi stared at her, awake now.

'It's okay, pumpkin, it's only Roland.' Layla's voice was thick with exhaustion, or was it tears?

Abi's eyes fluttered closed again. 'Did she send you in?'

'No. She told me you wanted to be left alone. I came anyway because I thought you might like some support.'

Layla's shoulders slumped. 'I put Abi in danger by getting involved with Lunea. This is all my fault.'

Roland sat on the bed next to her and took her hand in his. 'Oh Layla, it's not your fault, and it's not Beth's fault either. The kids who pulled her off the climbing frame are to blame, as are the teachers who didn't stop them. This is a horrible situation, but it isn't your fault.'

She pulled her hand out of Roland's. 'They thought she was a Soul Snatcher. They're playing into your little story.'

Roland sighed. 'It's not my story. I supported Amelia because I loved her. We have now gone our separate ways.'

'And what do you think about the Soul Snatchers now?'

He shrugged. 'I honestly don't know. It's easier to think clearly now Amelia is further away, but I can't see my way to understanding what's going on yet.'

Layla sighed. 'That's because it's all a pack of lies designed to turn people against anyone different, anyone like Abi or me.'

'No, that's not true,' Roland said, sitting up straighter. 'Amelia can be very dramatic and she likes to exaggerate things, but I don't think she'd lie to me.'

Layla shuffled to the side, to be as far away from him as she could manage. 'I think you should leave.'

'Don't do that to me as well,' Roland said, not budging. 'I have complete faith in you. You and Abi are not contaminated by the Soul Snatchers. I would know.'

'How would you know?' She looked at him, her deep brown eyes clear now, the colour returned to her cheeks. 'How would you know whether we were completely ourselves? Either you are sure about the Soul Snatchers, or you're not.'

He swallowed. He had no answer. Amelia's claims had seemed more and more unlikely the further away he got from her. He had stopped looking at people with suspicion, had stopped wondering whether they were in their right mind. He felt more relaxed now than he had in a long time, even though he had lost his home and the woman he thought he loved. One thing he was sure of: he wanted to spend more time with Layla and Abi.

The curtain was drawn back sharply. 'How's she doing then?' A nurse checked Abi's vitals and sat on the opposite side of the bed to Roland. He stood up and stepped back to give them some space.

'She's sleeping. She seems calmer.'

'Have you eaten yet?'

Layla sighed. 'No, but I'll be fine. I don't want to leave her.'

'You won't be leaving her. You'll be going to the cafe, having dinner and a drink, and taking a breather. Sleeping on a put-up bed in a hospital ward is no picnic. There is noise all night and it's unlikely either of you will get much rest. You'll need your stamina, so go with this nice man and give yourself a break.'

Layla's arms tightened around Abi for a moment, and then she lowered her gently onto the bed and tucked her in. 'You'll come and get me straight away if she wakes?'

'Of course,' the nurse said, ushering her out of the cubicle and pointing down the corridor. 'It's just through those doors. No distance at all.'

Roland put an arm around Layla's waist. 'Come on. Let's get some food. I'm starving.'

Layla walked in a daze as he ushered her out through the doors, past the lifts and into the cafe on the other side. 'What would you like?' he asked.

She stared at the menu, her eyes glazed.

'Is there *anything* you fancy?'

She shrugged. 'I don't care. I'll have the same as you.' She dropped the menu and found a table in the back corner of the room. Slumping into the chair next to the window, she stared out, her face still blank.

He ordered them each a baked potato with beans and cheese, a big salad and a piece of apple pie, as well as two cups of hot chocolate and bottles of water. He took the first tray over to the table and she didn't move as he put it down and went for the second. When he returned, she was still staring out the window.

'Come on, Layla, eat up, and then we can get you back to Abi.'

That stirred her. She jolted as though waking from a dream and took in the food and drink in front of her. 'Oh wow, thank you. What do I owe you?'

He shook his head. 'You just tuck in. Remember what that nurse said?'

She nodded and picked at the potato. 'Abi said she knew this would happen, because Doriel told her. I was angry at Doriel for scaring Abi, but she was right and I didn't do anything about it.'

Roland reached out and took her hand in his. 'But you did. You went to the school with Beth. You tried to talk to them. Life just moved faster than you did.'

'I should have moved faster.' Layla pulled her hand away. 'I should have done more. I should have known this was coming.'

'That's an awful lot of shoulds. None of us know everything that's coming our way, even the psychics. It doesn't matter how switched on they are when they're reading for other people, they miss all kinds of things in their own lives.'

'They? I thought you were one of them?'

Roland shrugged. 'I may be family, but I was passed over when it came to the gifts.'

Layla narrowed her eyes and titled her head to the side. 'That's not true. You have weird energy around you and it's hemming you in. I think you'll surprise yourself, and everyone else, when you break free of that and find out what's hidden underneath. You certainly haven't missed out on the gifts. You just haven't unearthed them yet.'

Roland raised one eyebrow. 'It seems you haven't missed out on them either.'

Layla shrugged. 'Fat lot of use they are to me when I failed to protect my own daughter.'

Roland put down his knife and fork, and took a mouthful of hot chocolate. 'Look, for what it's worth, I also think Doriel was inappropriate. She should have spoken quietly to you, not directly to Abi. Her judgment is completely off right now and she knows it in theory, but she's not controlling it well yet. I think you were right to tell her to back off. The fact that she was also right doesn't change any of that.'

Layla sighed and picked up her knife and fork. 'I couldn't save her from this, but I can at least eat and be on form for her, right?'

'Right.' Roland smiled as she tucked into her baked potato. Layla was a mystery, so open one minute and unpredictable the next. He hadn't realised she was psychic, but maybe he hadn't wanted to. Could she have been right? And if she was, how could he cut through the weird energy that could only have come from Amelia?

44

ROLAND

He wasn't supposed to come back to the hospital until visiting hours, but insomnia had given him enough chance to practise waiting at home and he was done with it. A book lay unopened on the seat next to him, along with the barely touched sandwich he had brought for breakfast. He had come believing it would be better to know that Layla and Abi were nearby, but now it was taking all his strength to remain in the car.

When he had slept, he had been plagued by dreams of Abi falling again, and again, and again. He could still see the image of her lying broken on the ground. Sometimes he was pleased to have been spared the gifts the rest of his family prized so highly. Would he have been able to tell whether a dream like that was fear or prophesy? He wasn't convinced he would, and the idea of having the responsibility of pre-knowledge sent chills down his spine.

He jolted as his phone rang, his heart racing and bile rising up his throat. He picked up the handset, but his heart sank. It was Amelia. He leaned his head back against the headrest hoping she would hang up, but the phone kept ringing. He counted the rings up to ten, waiting for the answer machine to take over. Moments later, the phone rang again. The fourth time through, he gave in and swiped the screen.

'Amelia, what a surprise.' He wondered if she could hear the sarcasm in his voice.

'Roland, how lovely to speak to you. I believe you were looking for me.'

'That's why you called me four times? Because you thought *I* wanted to speak to *you*? How very self-sacrificing of you.' He laughed and felt her irritation like a probe through the phone. He could feel his insides start to deaden and heard Layla's words in his head. *You have weird energy around you and it's hemming you in. I think you'll surprise yourself, and everyone else, when you break free of that and find out what's hidden underneath.* He could feel Amelia's energy snaking out through the phone and twining around him, locking him into place. His legs had always turned to jelly when he looked at her. He had thought that was desire, but now he was starting to wonder.

'Is everything okay, Roland?' Amelia's voice was hard but curious. He would not give her the satisfaction of knowing how much she was getting to him.

'Thanks for calling, but I have resolved things without you. If there's nothing else?'

'Why? You want to sit in the carpark on your own for longer?'

'Stop stalking me, Amelia. I'm serious. If you wanted to know what I was up to, you shouldn't have kicked me out.'

'What are you going to do?'

'I have a lot of information on you, Amelia. You have

already thrown my loyalty out of the window. Don't push my restraint too.'

Amelia swallowed. 'Look, there's no need to cut off contact. Why don't you join me for a drink?'

'Why?'

'What do you mean *why*?'

Roland sighed. 'You've made yourself perfectly clear. You don't want me around. Why are you dialling back on that now? What do you want from me?'

'Roland!' Amelia's voice was high pitched. 'You were always on my side. You saw through all their manipulation.'

Roland gave a hard laugh. 'Or I fell for yours.'

'Don't say that. If I've lost you, I've lost everything.'

'Look,' Roland said, opening the car door and climbing out. 'I don't have time for this. I'm sorry you're feeling lonely, but I'm not your man anymore.' He hung up. He stood stock-still for a moment, waiting to see if the phone would ring again, but Amelia hated rejection. She wasn't likely to court it twice.

He looked at his watch. Visiting hours weren't until one o'clock, and it was only nine in the morning. It was ridiculous that he had come this early, but he hadn't been able to stop himself.

The phone rang.

'Amelia,' he muttered under his breath. He swiped the screen. 'What is it now?'

'Oh, erm, I'm sorry. Is it a bad time?' Layla's voice was thick with exhaustion.

'Not at all. Are you okay? How's Abi?'

'Abi's fine. They're discharging us. Is there any chance you could pick us up?'

Joy shot through Roland. 'Of course. I'm actually just round the corner. I can come now if you're ready.'

'Thank you.' Layla let out a sob. 'I just want to get out of here.'

'Get your coat on. I'm in the carpark now. I'll come and find you.'

The hospital was a winding maze of sterile corridors, but he had taken extra care to remember the way and arrived at the ward with only three wrong turns.

There was one tired-looking nurse at the desk when he arrived.

'I'm here to collect Abi and Layla,' he smiled, hoping to cut through her obvious irritation.

She looked at him, a frown creasing her forehead, and then she nodded. 'Take a seat please.' She disappeared in the direction of Abi's cubicle.

'Roland.'

Roland looked up. Abi's curtains were drawn back now, and Layla stood in the gap, her face pale, dark circles under her eyes. Abi stepped out from behind her, clinging to her mother's arm. She had bruising on one side of her face, and she was protecting one arm. She said nothing. Roland stood up and strode over to them crouching down in front of Abi. 'Are you okay? Have they looked after you properly?'

She nodded without a word and clutched her mum's arm tighter.

Roland reached out and took Layla's hand in his. Her skin was cold in spite of the warmth. He squeezed it, gently. 'You're freezing. You must be exhausted. Come on, give me your things. I'll take you home.'

Layla handed him her bag and the car booster cushion, and picked Abi up. She carried the girl all the way out to the car without complaint and then put her in the back of the car on the booster seat and strapped her in. Opening the passenger door, she slumped in the front seat, her shoulders rounded, and leaned her pale face against the cold window. Roland slid into the seat next to her and turned the key.

'Where are we going?' he asked, as her eyelids fluttered and almost closed.

'Sorry, what?' she said, jerking awake.

'Your address?'

'Oh,' she said, leaning back in relief and rolled off a street name he was vaguely familiar with.

It was the tail-end of rush hour and it took them a full hour to get back. Roland could see Abi in his rear-view mirror. She leaned her head on the back of the seat, her eyelids fluttering between open and closed, but she jumped at every loud noise, her gaze darting between the different windows.

'Are you okay, Abi?' Roland asked.

Layla jerked upright. 'I was asleep. Has something happened?'

'Everything's fine and we're nearly home.'

He pulled up outside her house. Both Layla and Abi had fallen back to sleep already so he sat in the car for a few minutes. Layla's frown had smoothed, but she jolted periodically in her sleep, haunted by some unsettling dream. He put his hand on her arm and she jerked awake.

'We're here. You're home,' he said, his voice soft. 'Could we carry Abi in without waking her? I'd be happy to try.'

'No,' Layla snapped.

Roland raised one eyebrow. 'Okay, we can wake her up or just sit here for a while.'

'I will carry her.'

Roland nodded. 'Great idea. I'll bring your bag.' Something flashed across Layla's eyes and he nodded.

Layla swallowed. He could see the conflict of emotion in her eyes and nodded again.

'I should probably head over to Lunea and let Jonan know you're not coming in today. I'll cover for you if he needs help. You take as much time as you need with Abi.'

She relaxed now and he felt his own heart slow back to normal, mirroring hers. His body seemed so attuned to hers it was unnerving. He had never experienced this connection with Amelia and was starting to wonder what else he had been missing for all those years.

45

AMELIA

'Welcome to the breakfast news.' The newsreader stared directly into the camera, his brows pulled together, forehead creased. 'Today we are waking up to news of a new attack in St Albans by the Soul Snatchers. Yesterday an infected girl terrorised her classmates at Monkstreet Primary School. Before authorities could arrive she was whisked away by her co-conspirators. It is unclear whether any other children were contaminated. We have Amelia Faustus here with us today to talk about the increase in attacks and how we can all protect ourselves from this insidious threat.' He leaned back and turned to the left. 'Amelia, welcome. Do you have any insight into what happened yesterday?'

'Thank you, Francis.' Amelia beamed under the warming glow of the camera focus. 'I am delighted to be here. I was so sad to hear about the incident at the school yesterday, but luckily Monkstreet Primary School is a member of Amelia's Haven and was well prepared to spot and deal with such an infiltration. The children were quick to leap to the defence of their classmates and put an end to the risk posed by the perpetrator. This just shows the importance of making sure your children are under the care of an organisation that has been vetted and trained by Amelia's Haven.'

The newsreader leaned one elbow on the desk and frowned. 'You talk about the perpetrator, but my understanding is that she was a six-year-old child. Can you confirm this?'

'I believe so, yes.'

'And isn't it questionable to call a six-year-old child a perpetrator, when she is in fact the victim of the Soul Snatchers herself?'

Amelia drew in her eyebrows in an expression of sympathy. 'It is very sad and I send my full condolences to the family.'

The man leaned back and raised his eyebrows. 'Your condolences? Has she died?'

Amelia crossed her arms over her chest. 'No, but, Francis, you must understand, there is currently no cure for infection by the Soul Snatchers. Once someone has been taken, they are irredeemable. That is a grief that many families will have to face, but we are doing everything we can to minimise the risk.'

'Can you confirm whether or not the infected child was, in fact, a member of Amelia's Haven?'

Amelia gave a sickly smile and looked directly into the camera. 'She was not. I can confirm that her mother is an employee at Lunea in St Albans, the shop which used to be called the Third Eye and is run by suspected Soul Snatchers. They are targeting Amelia's Haven, trying to prevent people from seeking the protections they need and deserve. This business needs to be stopped.'

46

BETH

'Urgh!' Beth took a swig of coffee and switched off the TV. Amelia is unbelievable. Those kids weren't heroes, they were hateful and vicious. And the teachers were even worse because they should have known better.'

Jonan took hold of her hand. 'She's sunk to a new low, targeting a six-year-old. I wonder what Roland thinks of this?'

The door opened. 'You wonder what Roland thinks of what?' Roland stood in the doorway, his face pale, dark circles under his eyes.

Jonan raised one eyebrow. 'Where did you come from?'

'Doriel let me in. Have you got any more of that coffee? I didn't get much sleep last night.'

'I can see that.' Jonan got up and went through to the kitchen. 'Is Abi okay? What happened?'

Roland sighed and sat down on the armchair. 'Physically, she's fine. I picked them up from the hospital first thing and dropped them home. Mentally, I'm not so sure.

They looked so frightened and twitchy. I'm worried about them.'

Jonan paused in the doorway, a cup of coffee in one hand. He met Beth's gaze.

'Roland, do you know if either of them have had direct contact with Amelia?' Beth said, watching Roland's energy for any sense of discomfort.

Roland frowned. 'Not as far as I know. Why?'

Jonan handed him his coffee, and then sat down next to Beth. 'When Amelia got to Beth in the theatre, that's exactly how she was.' Jonan laced his fingers through Beth's and then turned to look at her. 'It nearly broke my heart to see it.'

Beth swallowed. She hadn't really taken in how much it had impacted Jonan to see her fear, but the glisten of his eyes in the pale morning light told her that he still wasn't over it. 'I'm okay now, Jonan. Your heart doesn't need to break anymore.'

He swallowed. 'Not for you, but for Layla maybe.'

'You think this is Amelia's fault?' Roland raised one eyebrow. Beth scanned his energy again. She still wasn't convinced by his turnaround, but there was no sign of anything underhand in his aura.

'She was just on television talking about Abi as "the perpetrator", and commending the school children for containing her. I have no idea where she got that story, but I was there, and I can tell you that wasn't how it played out.'

Roland blanched, and then his face darkened. 'That woman is the bane of my existence. I will talk to her. If she had any involvement I *will* find out.'

Jonan raised a single eyebrow in a mirror image of Roland's earlier expression. 'It's really over, then?'

'It's been over for longer than I was prepared to admit.' Roland slouched in his chair, closing his eyes for a moment. 'Amelia was my adult life. I still don't know who I am without her.'

'Do you think Layla might help you find out?' Beth asked, her voice quiet.

'Huh,' he laughed, but the sound was brittle. 'She wouldn't even let me carry her bag into the hall this morning.'

'Give her time, Roland. She may need help to get away from Amelia's influence.'

He shrugged. 'I don't know how to help her. All those gifts you have? I don't have any of them. I seem to have been side-lined when the best bits of the family gene pool were distributed. I can't help her.'

Beth frowned. 'Of course you can. I can see it. But you may need to be helped first.'

'What do you mean?'

'Your energy is thick with Amelia's interference. I think it's pretty clear how she got you to stay with her all that time.'

'You think Amelia has hidden my gifts?' He laughed, and then his expression sobered. 'Layla said something similar, but I wasn't sure what she meant. Can you help me?'

Jonan looked at him, his face unreadable. 'Of course. You were with her a long time though, and her energy will be deeply embedded. You'll need to be patient with yourself.'

Beth looked at her watch. 'We need to open the shop. Doriel won't want to stay down there once customers arrive.'

'Is that why Doriel isn't back to normal? Has Amelia done something to her too?' Roland frowned.

Jonan raised one eyebrow. 'Did you really not know any of this, brother?'

Roland sighed. 'I tried to talk Amelia out of that stupid abduction charade, but I believed her when she said Doriel was relaxing in a spa. I honestly thought no harm was intended. She's so focused on her performance she doesn't know where to draw the line. This whole thing was just about giving people a way to stay safe from the Soul Snatchers. I know you don't like Amelia any more, but the Haven is a good thing, surely?'

'Roland,' Jonan said, his eyes wary. 'What did Amelia tell you about the original attack? Did she tell you what happened?'

He shrugged. 'Just what she told everyone else. Amelia is an open book.'

'Are you sure about that?' Doriel's voice came from the door. 'Do you remember Jonan's visit to the manor? He saw how Amelia was behaving. That certainly was not the image she projects in front of the camera.'

He let out a slow exhale. 'Well, no. But surely her own fears and insecurities are her own business? She doesn't owe the world a view into her personal fears.'

'She does if she's trying to snare people with them,' Doriel said. She glared at Roland, lips pressed together. 'You say no harm was intended with the abduction, but a man died. How do you square that with your strong sense of duty? Or has that gone? You were the victim all those years ago, but this time you have been a perpetrator.'

He swallowed. 'I was devastated by Bill's death. I still am. It was a stupid stunt that went catastrophically wrong and I will always have that on my conscience. But why would you see me as a perpetrator?'

Doriel rolled her eyes. 'Roland, there are no Soul Snatchers. Surely you know this. Amelia's mysterious visitor was Salu. I know you struggle to access your gifts, but surely you can still hear him?'

Roland paled. 'Salu? It can't have been. Amelia wouldn't have …' He swallowed, flushed and looked at the floor. He took a deep breath, let it out slowly and then looked up and held Doriel's direct gaze. 'I lost my gifts a long time ago. I haven't heard Salu since I was a child.'

Jonan narrowed his eyes. 'How old were you when your gifts faded?'

'It was just after you left.'

'When you started spending more time with Amelia?'

Roland shook his head. 'You can't blame everything on her.'

Beth looked at her watch. 'I'd better go and open up. You stay here and keep talking.' She pulled on her shoes and went down the staircase, listening to the silence, and then the murmur as their voices started up again.

47

JONAN

Roland was quiet as they walked towards the inn. Jonan watched him, noting the dejected slump of his shoulders and the tension in his jaw. His energy was flat and lifeless, and confronting Amelia in this state wasn't going to improve his state of mind. Jonan remembered every brush with Amelia's manipulation, and each one still sent chills down his spine. But Roland seemed to have been absorbed by it until he didn't know where his energy ended and hers began. Jonan knew he would always blame himself for leaving his brother with her.

Roland pushed the door to the inn, but it was locked. He frowned and then rang the bell. They heard the clacking of heels and then Rose opened the door.

She sighed. 'What do you want? Did you think I *needed* to have my day made harder?'

Most people wouldn't have noticed the increased sag of Roland's shoulders, or the fact that he forced his face into a smile. But even after years of separation, Jonan knew his brother well enough to see the man's hurt. He had built his life here and now everything he knew had come crashing down.

'Don't worry, Rose, we're here to see Amelia, not you. Point me in the right direction and you can ignore me. I don't need to ruin *your* day at all.'

Rose laughed, but the sound was harsh. 'You think Amelia would see *you*? I suggest you leave.'

Roland put a hand on the doorknob. 'Look, Rose, this is getting ridiculous. You have to let me in.'

'Wait,' Jonan said under his breath.

Roland stilled and turned to his brother, one eyebrow raised.

Jonan nodded towards the door.

Amelia was standing in reception with a slick-haired man beside her.

Jonan pitched his voice low so that only Roland would hear. 'Isn't that …'

Roland nodded. 'Robson Fall. She didn't waste any time.'

Amelia was pale and thick makeup failed to hide her exhaustion. Gritting her teeth, she put her wine glass on the reception desk. 'Meet me in the ballroom, darling,' she said, gesturing to the door. 'I need to send these two packing.'

She walked over. 'Thank you, Rose,' she said, taking the door handle and crowding the woman out the way. 'Please do go and see that Mr Fall is comfortable.'

Rose compressed her lips but did as she was asked.

'What are you doing here?' Amelia stepped out through the door and pulled it closed behind her. 'I thought I'd made it clear neither of you were welcome.'

'When you attack an innocent girl to get back at me,

your wishes are of no consequence,' Roland said, his voice quiet but cutting.

'You're so sure you have the moral high ground, but you're the one that left me broken on the side of the road.'

'I regret that,' Roland said, holding her gaze. 'But punishing a child to get back at me is beneath you.'

'Beneath me?' Amelia gave a high-pitched laugh. 'I think that's for me to decide, don't you? Anyway, I had no idea you even knew the girl. This is not about you.'

Roland flushed and took a step backwards. 'You didn't know? Then why?'

Amelia shrugged. 'Monkstreet Primary School is a member of Amelia's Haven. They asked to me to do it.'

'To cover their backs?' Jonan raised one eyebrow.

Amelia rolled her eyes. 'You can't get to me with that single eyebrow raise anymore, Jonan. It was cute when you were seventeen, but your glow has worn off.'

'You reckon?' Roland's voice was bitter.

Jonan sighed. 'We just want you to leave the child alone.'

The door creaked behind her and Robson Fall stepped through, his eyes narrowing at Jonan and Roland. 'Is everything okay?' He put a hand on Amelia's waist.

She stiffened for a moment, and then her face went blank and she slid her arm around his back. 'Of course. Jonan and Roland are just leaving.'

'Robson Fall is the last person you should be hanging around with,' Roland said, his hands clenched into fists at his side. 'You're close enough to the edge. This guy will push you over.'

'Hahaha, you're so funny, Rolo.' Amelia glared at him. 'It's such a shame you can't stay. As for the child, she's old news. The world will have moved on to the next story by tomorrow. What happens to her is between the school and her parents. It's nothing to do with me.' She slammed the door in their faces with considerable force.

The key turned in the lock.

Roland swallowed. He leaned on the wall of the building, clasping his hands together, but they still shook slightly.

'Are you okay?' Jonan put a hand on his shoulder.

'I will be. Will she ever stop getting to me?'

Jonan sighed. 'Maybe, maybe not, but I'm pretty sure it's all up from here. Can I ask you something?'

'Will I regret saying yes?'

Jonan laughed. 'I always assumed you were a knowing participant in Amelia's manipulations. But now I'm wondering. Did you genuinely believe in the Soul Snatchers?'

Roland straightened and turned to face him. 'I still do. What makes you think they're not real?'

'I know what happened that night. I was there. Amelia twisted it all.'

'Are you sure?'

'Absolutely. The real danger is the anger and hate she is stirring up.'

Roland sighed and started walking up the hill.

Jonan kept pace, monitoring his energy. It became clearer and clearer the further they were from Amelia.

'She's more dangerous than you realise,' Roland said. 'She might have made this up but she's now buying into her own stories. She's completely sunk in fear and that building isn't helping. Now she's linked with Robson Fall. She used to laugh at him when her mother was a fan, but now the old lady has gone, she's rewriting history. She was unbelievably matter of fact when her mother died. I knew they weren't close, but I was shocked at how little she cared. Now she's created a new set of memories to justify and promote this connection with Fall. Her dead mother's devotion to him is her only route to his millions of followers and she knows it. So she pretends to grieve and tells him he heals her sadness. He clearly thinks he has power over her because of it, but I think we both know he's underestimating her. I really have no idea how far she will go with this.'

'What do you know about Robson Fall?' Jonan asked as they walked past the Abbey. A crow cawed and a blast of wind made him shiver. He zipped up his jacket and shoved his hands in his pockets.

'That's the first time I've met him and he gives me the creeps. People either love him or hate him. Whichever group you talk to, they're convinced the other side is blind to the truth. It's unnerving to see how much he polarises people.'

'So he's a proven expert at what Amelia is trying to do?'

Roland shivered. 'I don't know how I didn't see it before. I feel like a mug.'

'Don't. We've all been there. Come on, let's get in the warm.' They walked up past the clocktower. 'After you,' Jonan said, gesturing towards the door of Lunea.

48

BETH

The shop was empty. Beth wished someone would come in and distract her. Ever since Jonan and Roland left to confront Amelia, Beth's mind had been replaying bad memories on repeat in crystal-clear technicolour. She was almost over the fact that Jonan and Amelia had once been lovers. Most of the time it didn't bother her, but she knew it gave Amelia a route into his mind and heart that made him particularly vulnerable to her manipulations. She had seen it before the charity dinner at the Monk's Inn. Amelia had tried so hard to use Jonan's fears to sever his connection to Beth. She had arrived at the right moment, and still wondered what would have happened if she hadn't.

The bells on the door jingled. Beth looked up to see a woman and her daughter. They were both dressed in loose black clothes, in the typical uniform of people who had been impacted by Amelia. Beth sighed and plastered a smile on her face, mentally strengthening her protections. Then she did a double take. It was Layla and Abi. Layla's hair was now dark brown, with no hint of her usual pink. Both were pale with dark circles under their eyes. Beth swallowed. 'Layla? Abi? Are you okay? I thought you weren't coming in today. Roland said you needed to rest.'

'Yes, well. I have some news.' Layla avoided Beth's gaze. 'I have come to hand in my notice.'

Beth felt the flood of adrenaline before she registered what it was. Her heart rate increased, her mind fogged over and her legs went weak. *It's not mine. Let it go*, she told herself, imagining roots growing from her feet into the ground below her.

Layla met Beth's gaze, tilting up her chin in defiance. 'My job put Abi in danger. She has been expelled from school because of the vile actions of other children. I won't put her through something like that again. We're moving away. I listed my house with the estate agents this morning and for now we will move back in with my parents. We will find a new school for Abi, somewhere more open-minded, and a long way away from Amelia. I will get a job somewhere unremarkable, somewhere she won't think to look. We will disappear and have a life again. Now the shop has been relaunched, you don't need me here anyway.' Layla had one hand on the desk now and was tapping furiously. Abi was clinging onto her coat.

Beth reached out and put a hand on the large amethyst next to her. 'That is your choice, of course, but please, wait and say goodbye to Jonan and Roland first. They'll be back soon, and I know they'd be devastated if they missed you.'

Layla pressed her lips together and ran a hand over her hair. 'I don't think so. I'd rather Roland didn't see me like this. Let him remember me how I used to be.'

'For goodness sakes, Layla, you don't look so different.

You've dyed your hair, that's all. Roland is so worried about you. Please, give him closure.'

Layla glared at Beth, her teeth gritted, but she said nothing. A moment later her shoulders slumped. 'Fine, I'll wait for one hour, but if they're not back by then it will be too late.'

49

ROLAND

Roland was almost touching the handle when the door to Lunea swung open. A woman slammed into him and he staggered back, winded, with only the vaguest impression of the woman's scraped-back brown hair and black clothes. She pulled a child after her.

'Layla, what happened to you?' Jonan's voice snapped Roland to attention.

'You've arrived. Finally. I had given up on waiting for you. I was leaving.' Layla looked from one to the other of them, her eyes hard, jaw jutting forwards.

Roland winced as she glared at him. She had changed so much in the few hours since he had seen her last. How had his bright, sparkly Layla dimmed so much? He swallowed. 'Where are you going?' Dread settled in his stomach. Something wasn't right.

'I'm leaving.' Her voice was high-pitched. She pulled Abi in closer. The girl was far too pale. She swayed.

'Abi,' Roland barked, closing the distance between them, and steadying her as he crouched down on the floor.

'Layla, she's going to fall over. Let's get her inside. She can lie down while you tell me what's going on.'

Layla shook her head, but she bent down and picked Abi up. 'We have to go. Now. My car is round the corner. Abi can rest in there. We're going to stay with my parents in Bournemouth.'

Roland stood up. 'Please, don't. Not now. She was in hospital with concussion last night. It can't be safe to take her on a long journey. What will you do if something happens when you're on the motorway? She needs to be resting at home.'

'Don't tell me how to look after my own daughter,' Layla said through gritted teeth.

'When will you be home?' He didn't want to hear the catch in his voice, didn't want to guilt-trip her when she was so vulnerable, but the last of his own strength was evaporating. Layla was his only tether as the rest of the world shifted around him. He didn't know what he would do if that cord was cut.

Layla's eyes clouded and her forehead furrowed. 'Roland, look at me. I'm broken. I have nothing to offer you now.'

'You don't need to offer me anything. I'll look after you until you're ready.'

She shook her head. 'I can't. I'm sorry. Since I joined Lunea everything has gone wrong and that woman is at the centre of it all. As long as we're near you, we will be in her sights. I'm going to disappear and, I'm really sorry, but you can't stop me. Goodbye, Roland.'

'Goodbye,' Abi whispered. A tear fell from her sleepy eyes and tracked down her pale cheek to Layla's shoulder.

Layla swallowed a sob, turned and walked away.

Starfolk Falling

Roland watched her until she was out of sight. His feet were so heavy he couldn't make himself move another step. His breathing was too shallow, but he felt as though a deep breath would break him. He wanted to sit down, to curl up on the side of the pavement and let the grief take him. For a moment, he saw an image of Amelia staring at him in shock and betrayal, barefoot on the pavement in the rain. He had done this to her, and now the tables had turned.

Jonan took his arm. 'Come on, brother, let's get you inside and warmed up.'

Roland allowed Jonan to lead him in and up the stairs. The shop was buzzing, but he couldn't make out any distinct sounds beyond the pounding in his head. It was all disconnected, as though he were in a goldfish bowl, separated from the rest of the world by the sound of his own breathing.

The stairs were exhausting. They sapped the very last bit of his strength and he collapsed onto the sofa. Jonan covered him with a blanket and he stretched out, wrapping the scratchy woollen fabric around him as he shivered.

Jonan lit the fire and then went into the kitchen and came back out with a steaming mug of coffee. He held it out. 'Here, sit up and drink this.'

Roland pulled himself up to sitting and then took the coffee. It burned his mouth but at least the hot liquid going down his throat broke through the numbness. 'Will she infect everything in my life?'

Jonan raised one eyebrow. 'Amelia?'

Roland nodded.

'She'll try. The question is, will you let her?'

Roland sighed. 'She's stronger than me, brother. You

have all your skills. I have nothing apart from a stupidly strong sense of duty. I am no match for Amelia.'

Jonan sat on the arm of the sofa. 'You have more than a sense of duty. You have the strongest sense of right and wrong I've ever encountered. You are unstoppable when you choose to protect someone and stand by them, and you are passionate in a way that lights up the room.'

Roland laughed. 'I haven't been that way in a long time.'

'No? Well, Amelia has dimmed your light by surrounding you with shadow, but you are the light. You can burn the fog away if you choose.'

'You make it sound so easy,' Roland said with a yawn.

'Just because it's not easy doesn't mean he's wrong,' Doriel said from the doorway to her bedroom. 'We've ended up in the same hole, you and I, and we've got to make a choice. We can either let Amelia and her mob win, or we can step into our power. I love Amelia; you love Amelia.'

Roland raised one eyebrow.

'Okay, you loved Amelia. But we can't let her desire for the spotlight push us off our own stages. We came here for a reason.'

'You did. I have no destiny.'

'Of course you have a destiny. You knew it once; you just have to remember.'

'But …' An image flashed into Roland's mind. He was standing in the sea at sunset, fully clothed and dripping wet. Layla was standing in front of him, holding his hands. As a seagull wheeled overhead, he cupped her cheek and then bent to kiss her.

Roland closed his eyes and swallowed, his hand gripping the arm of the sofa.

Starfolk Falling

'You remember?' Doriel whispered.

Roland opened his eyes. He swallowed. 'How could I have forgotten,' his voice cracked. 'How could I have forgotten her? And how did you make it come back?'

'You didn't forget her,' Doriel said, sitting down next to him and wrapping his hand with her own. 'You knew her as soon as you saw her. You ran to her and her daughter when they were in trouble and cared for them as though they were your own, even though you'd barely met in this life. You did not forget. And I did not make you remember. That was all you.'

Roland swallowed again. 'But it's pointless. That destiny I thought I saw all those years ago was just a boyish dream. It has to have been. Layla chose to walk away from me. It is my duty to respect that.'

'Of course it is!' Doriel nodded. But she left because she's scared of catching Amelia's attention, not yours. Make it safe for her to come back to you when she's ready. Deal with Amelia, and your problems all drop away.'

50

BETH

Beth sighed as she rearranged the bookcase of tarot cards. She loved it when it was quiet in here. The crystals made the room so peaceful.

Jonan slipped his arm around her waist and kissed her cheek. 'Do you mind if I get out for a bit? I promised I'd help Roland settle into his new place.'

'Yeah, you go. I'll be fine here.'

'Are you sure?'

'Just go! I'll call if I need you.'

The single customer bought a meditation CD and a few tumble stones, and then the shop was empty. Beth was tempted to lock the door, although she wasn't sure why. Somehow the peace and silence seemed too precious. She took down *The Starfolk Tarot* and looked at the face on the spine. That face had called to her when she first bought this deck. Back then, she had no idea why. Now she knew this image was of her Starfolk mother and she felt a stab of sadness all over again.

I am here. The voice sounded in her mind. She felt a

moment of joy, and then apprehension settled in her stomach.

I am also here. Salu's velvety voice played through her mind.

Why? Why are you telling me this? she thought back. *Should I be afraid to be alone?*

The door rattled as it slammed against the doorstop. The bell jarred, sending adrenaline shooting through Beth. She reached out, placing her hand on the large amethyst to calm herself, and then turned.

Laura stood in the doorway. Her hair was slicked back from her face. She was dressed completely in fitted black clothes and was wearing the thickest makeup Beth had ever seen. But it did little to hide the dark circles under her eyes or the pallor of her skin.

Beth swallowed. 'Laura, how lovely to see you. Can I get you a cuppa?'

Laura looked over her shoulder and a moment later the Brute came through the door and shut it forcefully behind him, making the bells rattle.

Beth lurched backwards. 'What are *you* doing here?'

'He's with me,' Laura said, tilting her chin up and glaring down her nose at Beth. 'And I wouldn't drink anything you gave me. You would probably drug me.'

Beth's adrenaline spiked, but she forced herself to appear calm. 'You know he works for Amelia, right?'

Laura stood up straighter and a smile spread across her face. 'We both do.'

'You work for Amelia?'

Laura nodded. 'She trusts me.'

Beth gripped the side of the desk. 'Well, I'm sure you

didn't come in here to buy anything, so how can I help you?'

'You can't help me. It's too late,' Laura said, walking closer. The Brute followed. She turned and looked out the door. Beth saw more people drifting towards the shop. She grabbed the key and moved towards the entrance, but the Brute stepped out and blocked her way, bunching his hands into fists at his sides.

'Are you threatening me?' Beth kept her voice low. She cast her gaze about, looking for her phone, but it wasn't there.

'Do I need to threaten you?' Laura's voice was cold and blank. 'Or are you going to co-operate?'

'Co-operate with what?'

'With me,' a familiar voice said from the direction of the door.

Beth turned. Amelia looked completely different. Her glossy hair was pulled back into a thick, high ponytail, and she had replaced her tight skirts with a pair of sleek, white joggers and a zip-up hoodie. Her make-up looked completely natural from this distance, but it was too perfect, too dewy and healthy to be real. She looked like the girl you would invite home for a film and a pizza.

'Leave,' Beth said. She pushed past the Brute and yanked the door open. 'I'm closing the shop now.'

Amelia laughed, and it actually sounded friendly. 'Oh, don't worry, darling. This will be easy if you just do as you're told.'

'How's that worked out for you before?' Beth pasted a fake grin on her face, hoping it was convincing.

'I'm sure we've all learned from past experiences.' Amelia sauntered further into the room, picking up a beautiful quartz carving of a dolphin and tossing it from one hand to the other. 'Aren't you going to call Jonan? Or Doriel maybe?'

'There's only me.'

Amelia smirked and wandered into the centre of the room.

'You knew I was alone today, didn't you?' Beth said, following her and crossing her arms over her chest. *Mother, Salu, are you still there?* Beth felt a rush of light surround her and the anxiety fell away.

Amelia's face darkened. 'Get out!' she said from between gritted teeth. 'This is my space now.'

'Oh, I don't think so.' Beth squared her shoulders. 'Did you think I would be as helpless as before?'

Amelia's gaze flickered around the room, and then she smirked again. 'Well actually, I think you might be.'

The room was filling with people. Amelia's followers spread, forming a circle around Beth and Amelia. A vision flashed into Beth's mind of her linked with Jonan and Miranda, Amelia isolated between them.

'The tables have turned now, haven't they, little mouse?' Amelia's grin was wide and she let out a belly laugh that took Beth by surprise. 'I've caught you in my trap. Won't Jonan be distraught when you're gone?' Amelia threw her arms up in the air. 'Have your way, my children!' she shouted, and brought her arms down in a movement that seemed ritualistic.

'Even me?' the Brute said, cracking his knuckles.

Amelia laughed again. 'Oh, especially you.'

51

BETH

The Brute advanced on Beth, bringing his fists up in front of his face. 'We have history to deal with. You had me arrested. Did you think I would let that go?'

Beth swallowed.

Amelia chuckled softly. Beth spun around and lurched backwards, but crashed into a woman standing off to the side. She was completely hemmed in. Amelia was on one side, the Brute and Laura were on the other, and far too many other people were crowded in-between. 'Have you learned nothing?' Amelia said, stepping closer. 'I have the police in my pocket. That's why my followers will never be charged, no matter what they do to you.'

Beth frowned and turned to the Brute. 'But you said …'

'That I was arrested? I was released without charge half an hour later. It only took a phone call from Amelia. This time will be no different. And your little old man friend has given us great practise in hushing up bad news.'

'Oh for goodness sake, keep your mouth shut.' Amelia's

voice was icy. 'Your job does not involve talking or thinking. Just follow orders.'

'Yes ma'am.' The Brute flushed almost purple, and then he reached out, grabbed Beth's hair and yanked.

Beth screamed, lost her balance and fell. She felt some of her hair rip out, and then jerked against his fist as he wound the long strands tighter around his knuckles.

'Let go of me,' she shouted over the growing roar of voices and the crash of falling crystals and books.

'Never, little mouse.' The Brute breathed hot, damp air down her neck as he whispered directly into her ear. 'I have you now and you're not getting away.'

A large quartz point skidded across the floor towards her. She thought it was going to hit her in the face and braced for impact, but the air around her filled with lavender and the crystal ground to an abrupt stop right in front of her. She grabbed it, and then swung her arm and hit the Brute in the head with the blunt end.

'Urgh,' he groaned, falling backwards, her hair still wrapped around his hand. She lurched after him, cursing her stupidity. But she still had the quartz.

Laura stepped on her other hand and Beth screamed.

Amelia crouched down next to Beth. She stifled a groan. She would not let Amelia see how much she was hurting. 'A feisty one, aren't you?' she said, grinning at Beth. 'Not many women would take on someone four times their size. Or do you think it's five? hmmm.' She laughed, and then stood up and walked off.

The Brute sat up and yanked Beth's head towards him. He reached over, grabbed the quartz point and smashed it on the floor next to her.

When you want help, you only have to ask. The words floated through her mind, accompanied by the scent of lavender.

'Now!' she said through gritted teeth. 'I want help now.' Then she punched the Brute in the stomach. Her fist met a wall of muscle. He didn't flinch, just wrapped her hair tighter around his fist and pulled her closer so she could feel the heat and stench of his breath in her face.

'Don't ever do that again,' he breathed.

She choked as the smell of rot swamped her senses. 'Let go of me.'

'What did you say?' he said, even closer this time.

'She said, let her go.'

Beth shrieked as the Brute leapt to his feet, jerking her with him. A figure stood in front of them, shimmering. He was heavily muscled with long, golden hair that fell over his shoulders and parted at his pointed ears. For a moment, he seemed solid, and then the image shifted and he became translucent in the dimming daylight.

Letting go of her hair, the Brute shoved her into a bookcase of crystals. It rocked for a moment, and then steadied.

'What. Are. You?' he demanded. He puffed himself up, but his voice shook and he edged backwards.

The figure tilted his head and looked at the man. 'I am Salu. If you lay one finger on Beth again, I will haunt you for the rest of your life.'

The Brute stumbled backwards into a crystal display, sending it crashing onto the crowd of people by the door. There were screams and shouts as it fell, and then nothing.

'Well, well, well.' Amelia's voice filled the silence. 'The original Soul Snatcher himself.'

There were screams from the crowd and Amelia smiled, basking in their fear.

'They were right,' Beth whispered. 'You really were talking about Salu. I did wonder if you had somehow convinced yourself you were telling the truth, but you just made this whole thing up.'

Amelia's eyebrows shot up. 'Do you hear her?' she said to the crowd, spreading her arms wide. 'The Soul Snatcher stands before us, out in the open, and she claims I am making it up! Is she lying or deluded, do you think?'

There was a roar of voices and the bodies crowded forwards, all lunging towards Beth. Images of the theatre flickered through her mind. It felt so similar, but this time the threat came from Amelia's followers, and they were definitely able to hurt her. *How can I get out?* She projected the thought. The scent of lavender surrounded her again and an arm reached down through the crush of bodies. She took hold of the hand, marvelling at how solid it felt in spite of its translucence. A moment later she was on her feet. People lurched backwards, staring at her and Salu in horror. He just laughed and leaned in closer, wrapping an arm around her shoulders.

The air around them shimmered and the light crept outwards. Beth felt relief spread through her, and a new sense of safety. Those who were caught in the glow became confused, looking around at each other in surprise.

'Step back!' Amelia shouted. 'Remember everything I told you. Remember how beguiling these beings are? They draw you in and make you feel safe and peaceful. Don't let them ensnare you. Don't let them trick you with their games. Stay out of their light and you will be safe. Let me protect you.'

'And is Amelia's Haven protecting you, sister?' The voice was so velvety soft that Beth's breath caught.

Lunea.

'Mother?' Beth whispered.

Salu squeezed her hand.

'I would hate to think of you ensnared in anyone's games, sister. Is your Haven truly giving you what you need?'

'Listen to them!' Amelia shouted, spreading her arms wide. 'They are trying to draw you all into their illusions. You are stronger than this. You know how to see the truth. I have faith in you, my darlings. Together we can be safe and strong, but we have to see off this threat. Are you with me?'

'Yes!' the voices shouted in unison.

52

AMELIA

'I HAVE WARNED YOU ABOUT THIS SHOP.' AMELIA SPREAD HER arms wide, feeling the attention bathe her in its warmth. She spun around so her followers could see her. 'And now the Soul Snatchers themselves have taken corporeal form right in front of you. They want to draw you in. I am your only protection. Hold strong.'

'You're wrong.' Salu was gone from Beth's side and appeared next to Amelia. He had expanded and dwarfed her, his head almost touching the ceiling. 'We are not here for any of you. The state of your souls long since stopped mattering to me. I am here for Beth only. I will not let you touch her.'

Amelia gritted her teeth and turned to Lunea. The Queen still made the breath catch in her throat. She had all the light of the world they had come from and it made Amelia's heart ache to remember what she had lost when she incarnated here. Had she moved too far from her path to go back? If she had, it was already too late. She shook off the thoughts.

'He's right,' Lunea said. 'You made your intentions very clear and we will not interfere where we are not wanted. We are here for Beth.'

There was a hammering at the door. Amelia turned. Jonan and Roland were outside, Jonan's palms stretched across the glass, his mouth open in a furious gasp. Roland was glaring at her. When she turned back, Salu and Lunea had gone.

'Don't let them in.' Amelia's voice was sharp. Her followers surged towards the door just as the glass shattered.

There were screams as shards of glass flew into the crowd. Jonan and Roland leapt back, covering their faces with their arms. Then there was silence. Jonan brushed the glass from his coat and stepped through the empty wooden door-frame, Roland behind him.

'What are you doing, Amelia?' Jonan's face was white with fury. His fists were clenched, but his voice was calm and even. 'Why are you in my shop?'

'Your shop was open. Is there any reason I shouldn't be in here?'

'It is now closed. Everyone leave.' Jonan opened the now-useless door, and held it wide, gesturing at the space.

Nobody moved.

'You want me to leave?' the Sheep said, flexing his muscles and bunching his fists. 'Come and make me.'

Jonan walked towards him, and he seemed to increase in size the closer he got. 'Are you sure that's what you want?' His voice was low, but it carried through the now-silent room.

The Sheep laughed. 'Are you trying to frighten me?'

Jonan barrelled into him head-first.

Amelia shrieked, jumping back as they lurched towards

her, only narrowly getting out of the way in time. 'What are you doing?' she yelled and pummelled the Sheep on the back.

He lurched up, fists raised, and then froze when he saw who was hitting him. 'I was doing it for you,' he said, eyes wide.

'Don't be ridiculous, you're three times his size. You can't take him on.'

'I told you,' Roland said from the door. They all turned to look at him. 'There's no way Amelia would let anyone hurt *you*.'

Jonan picked himself up from the floor, gingerly feeling his jaw. 'Well, that's debatable.'

Amelia slapped him. 'What were you thinking, you idiot?'

Jonan darted away. 'Seriously, Amelia, stay away from me,' he said, leaning one hand on the wall and bowing his head.

Beth stepped past them all and went to Jonan, putting her arm around him and murmuring into his ear. Amelia felt her insides clench. Would the woman never back off?

'Then I echo her words.' Beth's voice cut through her thoughts. 'What were you thinking?'

'I was helping you.' Jonan gave a humourless laugh.

'Don't worry, Beth,' Roland said. 'The day Amelia stands by and lets the Sheep beat Jonan up, I think the world might implode.'

Fury pounded through Amelia. Rolo was supposed to be on her side! She clenched her fists so tightly that her long fingernails dug into her palms.

Beth frowned and tilted her head. 'The Sheep? You

mean him?' She pointed at the man who was brushing down his black clothes. 'Is that what you call him?'

The Sheep bristled, bunching his hands into fists at his side. 'My name is Steve.'

Laura slid her hand into his. 'Of course Amelia knows your name. He's just trying to turn you against her. You have been her most faithful follower for two years.'

The Sheep frowned at Amelia. '*Do* you know my name?'

She swallowed. 'Of course,' she said, with a forced smile. 'Your name is Steve. As Laura said, you've worked for me for two years.'

'And *of course* you knew that before they told you?' Roland raised one eyebrow.

'And you!' Laura said, turning on Roland. 'You are supposed to be on our side. You signed me up to Amelia's Haven and offered me this job. And here you stand, with *them?* You should be ashamed of yourself. What happened to you?'

'He was polluted by the Soul Snatchers,' Amelia whispered into Laura's ear, sending the sound out through the stifling air in the shop and allowing it to settle as a pool of dread in the chest of every person there. 'He was my biggest support and a founder of Amelia's Haven. And now he's been infected! Do not trust him anymore.'

'Don't be ridiculous,' Roland said from between gritted teeth. 'You made sure we were not on the same side when you kicked me out and attacked a small girl. Did you really think you could do whatever you wanted to me, and I would still crawl back like a whipped puppy?'

'You see?' Amelia said, throwing her arms into the air. 'He admits he's not on our side. Does anyone here really believe I would attack a small girl?'

'No!' someone shouted from deep in the crowd. 'Amelia would never do that. But they would!' The crowd surged forwards. Roland stepped back, tripped on a vase and fell as the crowd surrounded him.

'Stop!' Jonan shouted. 'Get away from him.' He pushed his way into the crowd to get to Roland.

'Jonan!' Beth said and made to follow him, but the Sheep grabbed her and pulled her back.

'Let go of me!' Beth hit out at him.

Amelia smirked.

Jonan turned, his face darkening. 'Get away from her!' he shouted. Reaching down he yanked Roland up and together they fought their way out and made for Beth.

The Brute let go of Beth and squared up to the two men.

'Wait …' Amelia said, desperate to stall them. 'Surely we don't need to be at loggerheads anymore? Join me, Jonan. Head up Amelia's Haven with me. Together we would be unstoppable.'

'Are you kidding me?' Jonan's voice cracked. 'After everything you've done, peddling your lies and putting other people at risk, after all *that* you think I would join you? Stay away from me.'

'So that's it,' Amelia whispered to herself. 'He really has chosen.'

She turned around. Roland was brushing himself off, rolling his shoulders out and muttering to himself. She walked over, turning down the light that usually drew followers to her like moths to a flame. 'She's right,' she said, quietly enough that only he could hear. 'You were supposed to be on my side.'

Roland sighed and sagged back against the payment

desk. Amelia hadn't noticed before how pale he looked, or how dark the circles were under his eyes. What had happened to him?'

'I was on your side, Amelia.' His voice cracked, but he carried on. 'I fought for you for so long. I would have stood by you forever, but it wasn't really me you wanted, was it?'

'Of course it was,' she said, but even she could tell how unconvincing she sounded.

'You keep saying it. Maybe you'll believe it one day. When are you going to stop pushing all of us off our own life paths, just so you feel better about abandoning yours?'

'I thought *you* didn't have a life path? I thought you were the odd one out of the group?'

Roland folded his arms across his chest. 'It seems I had other memories once upon a time. I wonder why those disappeared. Do you have any idea?'

Dread pooled in the pit of Amelia's stomach. He had remembered.

'Isn't it a funny coincidence that the woman I was waiting for, the one I mysteriously forgot, is the same woman whose daughter was targeted by Amelia's Haven? I really would think it was an amazing coincidence … if I believed in coincidence.'

'I don't know what you think you're accusing me of.' Amelia stuck her chin out. 'I did nothing other than give you a home and you betrayed me.'

'Isn't it a good thing I did?' Roland raised one eyebrow. 'You would never have caught Robson Fall's attention with me on your arm.'

'This is ridiculous.' Amelia raised her voice and everyone fell silent as all eyes turned to her. She strode into the centre of the room, sending out energy that she knew would hold them transfixed.

'Every word they say incriminates them. I call on you, my followers, to exact justice on these Soul Snatchers. I promise that you will not face retribution, instead you will be celebrated as heroes.'

'Heroes,' called a voice from the crowd.

'Retribution,' shouted another.

The door to the upstairs flat flew open and Doriel and Miranda stumbled into the room, dragged out by three men.

'Got them, Amelia,' the first man said.

'Excellent.' She smiled.

'Doriel,' Beth's voice rang out through the sudden silence, and then the crowd started pushing forwards.

Doriel and Miranda were herded into the middle of the room along with Beth, Jonan and Roland.

'That's it, my lovelies. You have them now,' Amelia yelled over the noise.

The crowd pushed forwards further until they had them trapped in a tight circle.

'What are you doing?' Jonan asked, putting himself between Amelia and the others. 'How do you see this ending?'

'Ending?' Amelia said with a throaty laugh. 'I'm only just beginning.'

53

BETH

'You thought you were so powerful; you and your little band of detectives,' Amelia said, and Beth could feel the grey cords of energy coiling around her feet, beginning to rise up her legs.

'No!' Beth said and kicked out, but there was nothing to hit out against. The cords just stretched and then pinged back into place.

Amelia laughed. 'You underestimate me over and over again. And this isn't going to change. As long as you are here, taking my place in the Triad, and my place with Jonan, we will be adversaries. Is that really what you want from life? You could walk away now, start somewhere new and I promise we would never meet again.'

Beth swallowed. She could feel Jonan's gaze boring into her back. This was as much for his benefit as hers, she knew. Amelia wanted two things: power and Jonan.

'I will never walk away,' she said, lifting her chin defiantly. 'I haven't taken your place; I've stepped into my own.

You created this split through your own actions. You can't blame me for that.'

'Not my actions alone.'

'No.' Jonan's voice was rough. 'And I will always feel responsible for my part in this, but I won't carry yours any longer.'

Amelia shook her head. 'Enough. You set your traps and expect me to just walk into them. But we are here, in your shop, right now, because you pose a threat to everyone in Amelia's Haven and we will not stand for it. Will we?'

'No!' A few voices called from the crowd.

They started pushing forwards again. Someone poked Beth in the ribs, and someone else grabbed her hair and tugged. She heard a shout from Roland behind her and then a thud followed by a crunch. Roland groaned and sagged backwards into Beth.

'Jonan, help me!' Beth yelled as she grabbed hold of Roland and dragged him upright. She needed to get out, to get him away from these people and into the fresh air, but there was no route to the door.

Remember you can ask for help. The words played into her mind.

Yes, please, help us get out of here. She sent out the words with every ounce of intention she had.

Jonan's head whipped around, his forehead furrowing and his head tilting as he watched her.

'Don't you dare,' Amelia hissed under her breath.

Now, please help. Beth sent the thought again. A light started building around her and she imagined it spreading out to cover the whole group. *Salu?*

Here, sister. The words floated into her mind.

More, she thought, and the light grew brighter.

'Get back,' Amelia shouted, glaring at Beth. 'Don't let her light touch you. Someone, bolt the door.'

'Erm, Amelia, it's smashed,' Laura said.

'Damn,' Amelia said under her breath. She sent out her smoky cords, pushing them towards the light, trying to nudge it back.

There was a gasp from the crowd and Beth felt a feather-light touch on her arm.

We are here, daughter. Beth turned and swallowed. Lunea stood beside her smiling.

'Come on,' Jonan said, and then cleared his throat. 'Let's get him out.' He crouched down, scooped Roland up in his arms, and strode through the path of light that opened up in front of him step by step.

He was nearly out the door when a figure hurled itself across the room and barrelled into him. Beth screamed as Jonan lurched to the side, roaring as Roland was knocked out of his arms towards the stone doorstep. The air turned purple around him as he fell and, at the last moment, he woke up and rolled to the side, narrowly missing hitting his head on the concrete step outside the door.

'Sheep!' Amelia's voice was everywhere and nowhere. Beth could have sworn that her mouth didn't move, but the sound shivered down her spine and across the skin of her arms.

Steve stopped, reaching out his arms and sinking into his knees. He swayed from side to side in front of Jonan. 'Think you can get past me, do you?'

Jonan staggered to his feet, his face pale, mouth set in grim determination. 'You've got what you wanted,' he said, his voice full of fury. 'You've destroyed my shop, ruined all the hard work we've put into this place, and scared off our customers. What more do you want?'

'Hmm.' Steve looked around him. 'It doesn't look destroyed to me. A bit battered, maybe. I think we could do better.'

Jonan bunched his fists up by his sides and advanced on the man.

The light around them flared and Doriel and Miranda stumbled to the front of the shop and out the door.

'Please, Steve, just let him pass before this gets any uglier,' Beth said, with no attempt to hide the tremor in her voice. 'Just let us go.'

Steve stepped back and gestured to the door. 'Yes, why not. Run away, little man.'

Jonan advanced on Steve slowly, allowing the tension to build between them as he seemed to grow in size, expanding as he gradually let go of the control he usually held over his energy.

'Jonan,' Miranda's voice cut through the tension. 'Don't allow her to do this to you. Don't do something you can't walk away from later.'

Jonan's gaze flickered over to the door where Miranda stood, pale and defiant, her clothes ripped in several places. Then his gaze met Beth's. Without his barriers, the pain in his eyes floored her, but slowly, he brought his shields back in and let his hands unclench. His jaw was tight as he walked past the Brute, only stopping for a moment to meet his gaze. 'You don't know what she's doing to you. She's using and manipulating you. You don't have to live in her cage any longer if you don't want to. Remember that. The choice is always yours.'

Walking over to Beth, he took her hand, nodded and led

her out through the door. Outside, Beth put an arm around Roland's waist and Miranda held him up on the other side. Doriel leaned into Jonan. Together they watched through the windows as Amelia's supporters destroyed what was left of the shop.

54

BETH

It was another two hours before the last straggler left the shop. They stood outside throughout, holding vigil.

When the shop was empty, Jonan walked slowly up to the door and stepped through. He stood there, unmoving, as they came through after him into complete carnage. Everything was gone. Crystals were smashed, tarot cards were emptied from their boxes and spread around the shop, and the till was hanging open, empty. Even the shelving units and reception desk were broken.

Beth threaded an arm around his waist. 'Come on, this can wait until tomorrow. There's nothing left to steal anyway.

Jonan nodded and led the way to the staircase. Holding the door open for the others, he locked it behind them, shutting out the chaos of the destroyed shop. 'At least they've left. I thought for a while she was going to bring the whole building down.' In the flat, Miranda crouched down to light a fire, and the others slumped on the sofa and chairs.

Roland sighed. 'She wants to show you how wrong you were to abandon her, but she doesn't want to destroy you. She wants you to run back to her, begging for forgiveness.'

'And nobody is ever going to be safe until he does that, are they?' Beth said, her voice flat. 'I'm the one she hates. As long as I'm here, you are all in danger.'

'Don't even think it,' Jonan said, gripping her hand too tight.

'Jonan.' She loosened his fingers and turned so that she faced him. Reaching up, she stroked his cheek and then cupped his face in both of her hands. 'It's time we were real about what we're facing.'

'No!' Jonan pulled away, jumped to his feet and started pacing.

Roland sighed. 'She lives more in her own mind every day. She's so convinced by her power that she can't imagine things might not turn out her way.'

'Maybe she's right,' Doriel said, rubbing her forehead. 'The destroyed shop downstairs certainly backs up her confidence. We did a lot of damage all those years ago. If we'd been less horrified by the idea of Amelia and Jonan, and more ready to look for a resolution, we might have avoided this mess. And Bill would still be alive.'

'But you weren't and you didn't,' Beth said, looking from one woman to the other. 'And now *we* have to find a way to take things forward. Going over and over the past isn't going to help. Amelia has changed. Jonan has changed and now I'm here too. Whatever happened then is done. We need to deal with the choices everyone is making now.'

'You're right,' Doriel said, her voice soft. 'But fixing this isn't the *Triad's* responsibility anymore. Our job is to heal and find a new adventure. Going over the past *is* what we need to do. We must connect and fix what is broken in our lives and our hearts. I meant what I said. The path is yours now. We have other journeys to take, journeys that may surprise you and that may not feel relevant to where you stand.'

Beth swallowed. 'You won't help us?'

Miranda smiled. 'We'll help where we can, but Doriel is right. It's time for you to take the reins and drive this one forwards. We are not the Triad any longer, but we are old friends and we have some mending to do.'

'Does Layla fit into this anywhere?' Roland said, sitting up and leaning his elbows on his thighs.

'You tell me.' Doriel tilted her head, and watched Roland.

'I'm going to find her. Jonan, will you teach me to help her when I get there?'

Jonan stopped pacing. 'Of course. But, Roland, what are you offering her? Why would she come back? Have you let go of Amelia?'

'A long time ago, but I thought I owed her. I have let go of that now too.'

Beth sighed. 'I'm sorry Roland. I want to support you in this, but Layla left for a reason and nothing has changed. If anything, Amelia has become more dangerous. Do you really want to persuade her to bring Abi back to this?'

Roland swallowed and closed his eyes for a moment. When he opened them, they glinted with tears. 'I need her.'

'Can't you go to Bournemouth with her instead?'

He dropped his head into his hands. 'Maybe. But she said it wasn't safe to be around me.'

'Then make it safe for her and Abi to be with you, here or in Bournemouth. She has the right, and the duty, to protect her daughter.'

'But she's not herself. Amelia has got into her head.'

Dread settled into the pit of Beth's stomach as she realised what she had to do. When she spoke, her voice was soft. 'Maybe we can solve two problems at once. I'll go to Bournemouth and stay with her. If she wants help, I'll give it. After all, I've been through what she's experiencing.'

Jonan frowned. 'For how long?'

Beth got up and walked over to him. She took his hands in her own and kissed them. 'For as long as it takes to make sure you are safe. I won't let anything happen to you, Jonan.'

'No,' he whispered, his voice cracking. 'No, you can't. We've been here before. If you leave, she will defeat us.'

'That's not true,' Beth said, pulling him into a hug. But he stood straight, unyielding. 'This isn't the past, Jonan. This is our chance to change the cycle, to make things different.'

'That's what we were trying to do. But if you walk away, you're falling right back into those old traps, and Amelia knows it. If you go, you'll be giving her exactly what she wants.'

'Yes,' Beth said, dropping her hands and stepping backwards. 'I'll be giving her what she wants so that you can fix whatever is really broken. At the moment she's too angry to reconcile. She is so busy hating me that she's not willing to come to terms with the past. I am her excuse for staying as she is. I won't be that anymore. And I'm not leaving you. I'll just go away for a bit to help Layla and Abi. In the meantime, you can make things up with Amelia and come to some kind of truce. Hopefully you can even persuade her to drop this Soul Snatcher punishment routine. Jonan, we can't go on like this.'

'And when will you go?'

'Tomorrow.'

Jonan swallowed, and then turned and strode out of the room, slamming the bedroom door behind him.

Beth stared after him for a moment, her chest constricting, and then she let out a sob. 'Jonan,' she whispered.

Doriel came over and pulled her into a hug, holding her tight while she shook. 'He'll come around, love. You're right. Only Jonan can go back to the root of this sorry mess. But I do believe you can weather it if you don't push each other away. In the meantime…' She stepped back, holding Beth at arm's length, scrutinising her face. 'In the meantime, I will give you something for Abi from her Aunty Doriel.' She walked over to the sideboard and rummaged in a drawer, pulling out a greetings card and some crystals.

Roland heaved himself up from the sofa. 'Will you give Layla a letter from me?'

Beth gave him a shaky smile. 'Of course.'

He nodded and sighed. 'I will bring it over tomorrow. Please don't leave before then. I hope you don't mind, I'm going to head home. I still have unpacking to do before bed.'

Beth watched as he trudged to the stairs, letting the door slam behind him.

'He'll be okay. This will all work out.' Miranda smiled as she reached for her coat.

'Is that foresight?' Beth asked.

Miranda chuckled. 'You can call it a hunch.' She walked

over to Beth and put her hands on her shoulders. 'You've made a good call today, Beth. I'm proud of you.'

Then she was gone.

Beth went down to the shop and stood in the middle of the shattered room, allowing the tears to come. Just this morning, life had been so different. She had Jonan, a job she loved and wonderful friends. Now everything was falling apart. A car drove down the narrow road outside the shop and for a moment, the headlights lit up something on the floor. She crouched down and picked it up. It was a tiny rose quartz heart, completely undamaged. Slipping it into her pocket, she went up to the flat, locking the door to the shop behind her.

Upstairs, Doriel was gone and Jonan was standing in front of the fire, his back to the room. Beth walked up behind him and threaded her arms around his waist, leaning her cheek against his back.

'Have they gone?' Jonan's voice was rough.

'Yes.'

Jonan loosened her arms, turned around and stepped away. 'I can't believe you're leaving.'

She shook her head. 'I'm not leaving forever, Jonan. But together we're making things worse. Let me help Layla. You focus on fixing things with Amelia. Make it safe for me to bring Layla and Abi home. I *will* come back to you.'

Jonan traced her jaw with one finger. 'Is that a promise?'

She smiled. 'I've waited lifetimes to be with you too, you know. I'm not ready to let you go.'

Don't forget us. Salu shimmered into the room, Lunea close behind him.

Jonan sighed. 'The original Soul Snatchers.'

Beth stepped back but kept a tight hold of his hand.

'Amelia is in a dark place,' Lunea said. 'A lot hinges on the next stage. Don't forget we are here to help you. This is bigger than you remember, even you, Jonan.'

'Can we succeed?' Beth asked.

'That depends on your choices. Amelia has the power to turn each one of you towards fear. Whether or not you allow her is up to you.'

Jonan shook his head. 'I'm not sure I have the strength to do this.'

'I have faith in you.' Lunea put a hand on his arm. 'Amelia is fire and ice. She inhabits the extremes and pulls everyone with her. To resist, you must hold to your balance and strength. Keep moving forwards with the faith that you are going in the right direction. Give yourselves time to heal whenever she wounds you, rather than running from the pain she chooses for you. You are strong enough; just hold to your path.'

'And Layla?' Beth could hear the hope in her own voice.

Lunea smiled. 'You must leave that to Roland. You will clear the way and then we shall see.'

The figures flickered and then faded.

'So that's it.' Beth let out a slow breath. 'If we want a life together, the only way is through.'

'Do you want a life with me?' Jonan said, cupping her cheek.

'I've never wanted anything more. Here.' She held out her hand. 'I found this downstairs. In spite of all that carnage, this heart is still whole. Keep this, and know that one way or another I will come back for you.'

Jonan kissed her, and for a moment she forgot everything. There was only the man she loved, warm and solid in her arms. When he pulled back just enough to look at her, the pain in his eyes knifed through her and she gasped. His eyes were the deepest purple she had ever seen, and his ears grew into points that almost looked solid. He nodded, and stepped back, keeping hold of one hand. 'Then, my love, through we shall go.'

LETTER FROM THE AUTHOR

Dear Reader

Thank you for taking this next step on the Starfolk journey with me. Your support means everything. I hope you're looking forward to the final book in the trilogy, Starfolk Rising, which will be released in March 2024.

If you've enjoyed Starfolk Falling, please do consider leaving a review. Even a few words help make a book more visible. Leaving reviews is one of the best ways to support your favourite authors and help them write new stories.

If you would like to read Starfolk Illusions, the prequel story to The Starfolk Arcana, please do sign up to my newsletter and I will send it to you for free. So if you're wondering what *really* happened the night Amelia claims to have seen a Soul Snatcher, this is your moment. You will also find out about my new releases and receive any extra content I put out, such as deleted scenes.

Lots of love and happy reading,
Martha

ACKNOWLEDGMENTS

As ever, thank you to Kathryn Cottam who is always at my virtual side while I write, bringing her structural wisdom, enthusiasm and all-round support. Kathryn, you are a star and I love you.

Thank you to Eleanor Leese, my copy editor, and to Ravven for my gorgeous cover. You are both a joy to work with.

To my early readers, Murray, Judith, Miriam and Janet, thank you for being there for every book. And to Trish Terrell, your unending support and enthusiasm means so much to me.

Finally, thank you to my family, for always being there no matter what. I love you all.

ABOUT THE AUTHOR

Author of The Starfolk Trilogy and Wild Shadow, Martha is a dreamer and a lover of stories. She likes nothing better than spending her days getting to know the characters in her head.

She is a tarot card reader and reiki master, and loves to chat reading, writing and all things mystical on social media, as well as posting pictures of her fellow pack-member, Bertie the Cavalier.

Martha is a fiddle player who fell in love with traditional music, particularly Irish, and is also teaching herself to play the Irish Bouzouki. She played her way through her English degree at York and remembers that time as much for the music as the books.

You can keep up with Martha's news, book releases and extra content on her website. Picture by Gene Genie Photography.

facebook.com/MarthaDunlopStories
x.com/MarthaDunlop
instagram.com/marthadunlop
tiktok.com/@marthadunlopwrites

OUT IN MARCH 2024

*A love that spans lifetimes. A deadly vendetta.
Two fates destined to collide.*

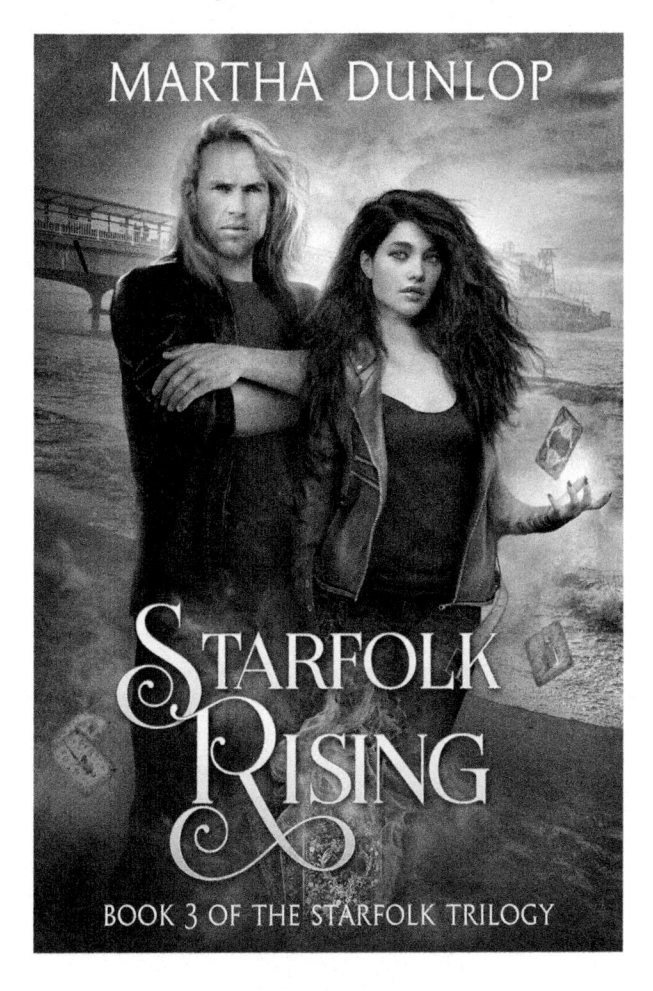

MARTHA DUNLOP
STARFOLK RISING

BOOK 3 OF THE STARFOLK TRILOGY

www.marthadunlop.com

*Only Dylan can see the tiger.
Is it real? His muse? Or something else entirely?*

MARTHA DUNLOP

WILD SHADOW

Only Dylan can see the tiger.
Is it real? His muse? Or something else entirely?

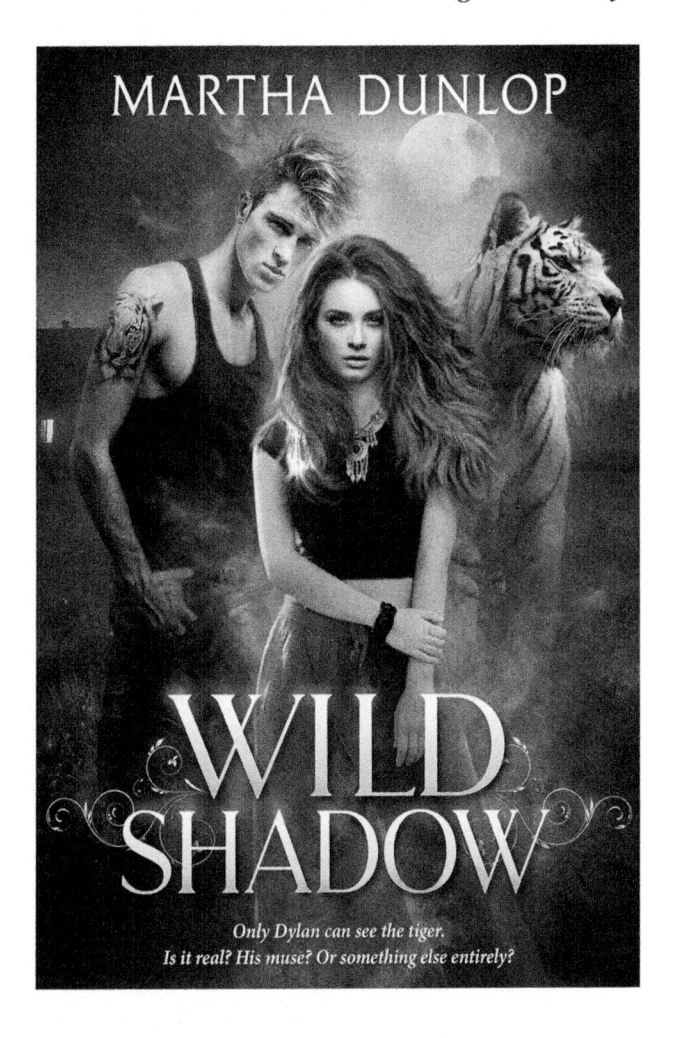

www.marthadunlop.com

*They've spent lifetimes being pulled apart.
This time, they're ready to fight.*

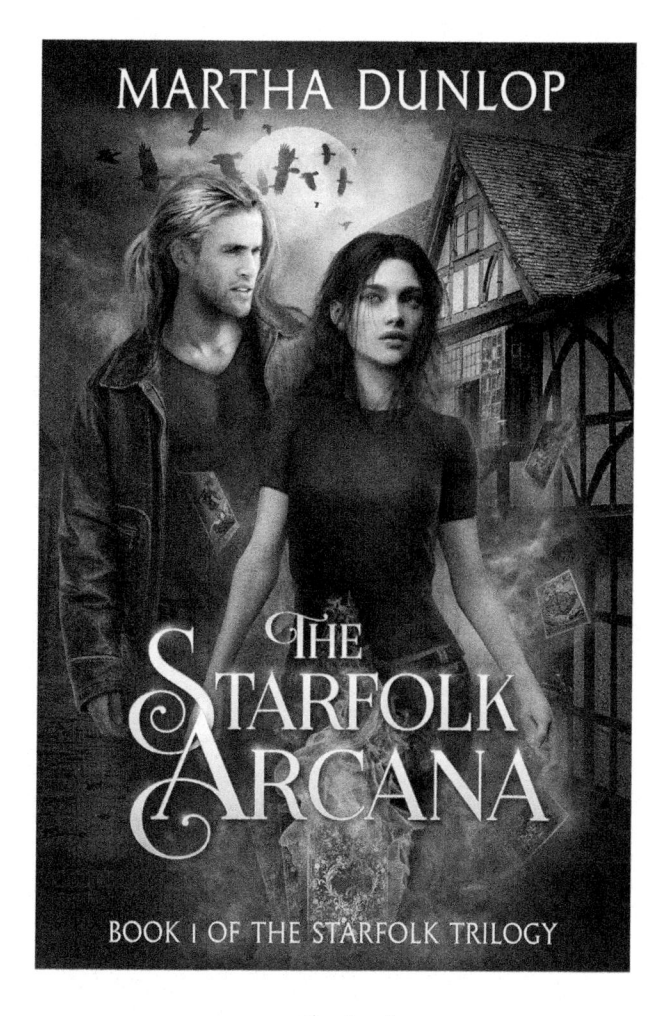

MARTHA DUNLOP

THE STARFOLK ARCANA

BOOK 1 OF THE STARFOLK TRILOGY

www.marthadunlop.com

Printed in Dunstable, United Kingdom